"Oh, indeed. I am fiercely jealous of your attachment to the man. You realize that you must agree to give me exactly the same number of minutes as you give to him."

"Minutes?"

"Minutes, down to the last half a one! If you go to the theatre with him, then you must spend the same amount of time with me the next night. And so it shall go forward, 'an eye for an eye, a tooth for a tooth.' "

"That refers to revenge."

"In this case, battle. Like two knights, doing battle to win the affections of the princess. Princess Pamela, whose name means 'all-honey.' "

She gaped at him, again feeling the pull of flattery to find that he knew the meaning of her name, from the Greek.

He smiled at her amazement, caressing her cheek with the tip of her own hair as he said, "Honey—your name, the color of your hair, your eyes, and the essence of your personality. You see, Pamela-Honey, I am a formidable opponent."

"I see," she whispered, wondering somewhat wildly if he thought of Captain Penford—or herself—as his adversary?

"I believe it is customary for a lady to give her knight a token before he rides off to battle."

"I am not your lady."

"Not yet." He smiled again, released her hair, and leaned forward to press his mouth to hers . . .

KT-153-627

ELEGANT LOVE STILL FLOURISHES —
Wrap yourself in a Zebra Regency Romance.

A MATCHMAKER'S MATCH   (3783, $3.50/$4.50)
by Nina Porter

To save herself from a loveless marriage, Lady Psyche Veringham pretends to be a bluestocking. Resigned to spinsterhood at twenty-three, Psyche sets her keen mind to snaring a husband for her young charge, Amanda. She sets her cap for long-time bachelor, Justin St. James. This man of the world has had his fill of frothy-headed debutantes and turns the tables on Psyche. Can a bluestocking and a man about town find true love?

FIRES IN THE SNOW   (3809, $3.99/$4.99)
by Janis Laden

Because of an unhappy occurrence, Diana Ruskin knew that a secure marriage was not in her future. She was content to assist her physician father and follow in his footsteps . . . until now. After meeting Adam, Duke of Marchmaine, Diana's precise world is shattered. She would simply have to avoid the temptation of his gentle touch and stunning physique — and by doing so break her own heart!

FIRST SEASON   (3810, $3.50/$4.50)
by Anne Baldwin

When country heiress Laetitia Biddle arrives in London for the Season, she harbors dreams of triumph and applause. Instead, she becomes the laughingstock of drawing rooms and ballrooms, alike. This headstrong miss blames the rakish Lord Wakeford for her miserable debut, and she vows to rise above her many faux pas. Vowing to become an Original, Letty proves that she's more than a match for this eligible, seasoned Lord.

AN UNCOMMON INTRIGUE   (3701, $3.99/$4.99)
by Georgina Devon

Miss Mary Elizabeth Sinclair was rather startled when the British Home Office employed her as a spy. Posing as "Tasha," an exotic fortune-teller, she expected to encounter unforeseen dangers. However, nothing could have prepared her for Lord Eric Stewart, her dashing and infuriating partner. Giving her heart to this haughty rogue would be the most reckless hazard of all.

A MADDENING MINX   (3702, $3.50/$4.50)
by Mary Kingsley

After a curricle accident, Miss Sarah Chadwick is literally thrust into the arms of Philip Thornton. While other women shy away from Thornton's eyepatch and aloof exterior, Sarah finds herself drawn to discover why this man is physically and emotionally scarred.

Available wherever paperbacks are sold, or order direct from the Publisher. Send cover price plus 50¢ per copy for mailing and handling to Penguin USA, P.O. Box 999, c/o Dept. 17109, Bergenfield, NJ 07621. Residents of New York and Tennessee must include sales tax. DO NOT SEND CASH.

A Scandalous Proposal

Teresa DesJardien

ZEBRA BOOKS
KENSINGTON PUBLISHING CORP.

ZEBRA BOOKS are published by

Kensington Publishing Corp.
475 Park Avenue South
New York, NY 10016

Copyright © 1994 by Teresa DesJardien

All rights reserved. No part of this book may be reproduced in any form or by any means without the prior written consent of the Publisher, excepting brief quotes used in reviews.

If you purchased this book without a cover you should be aware that this book is stolen property. It was reported as "unsold and destroyed" to the Publisher and neither the Author nor the Publisher has received any payment for this "stripped book."

Zebra and the Z logo Reg. U.S. Pat & TM Off.

First Printing: March, 1994

Printed in the United States of America

My eternal thanks to Karen Harbaugh, Mary Chase Comstock, and Pamela Bradburn, three of the most gracious and demmed fine Regency novel critiquing ladies in the Pacific Northwest, and

To Karen Carton, who, despite having had to know me for all my life and most of hers, has become more than a reader, editorial assistant, and even a sister: thanks for also being a friend.

Author's Note:

To those who might be interested, this novel begins on the date of March 30, 1815, for no greater or deeper reason than the fact that it does.

Chapter 1

"Would you do me the honor of agreeing to become my wife?" Lord Marchmont asked in the middle of the waltz.

Lady Pamela Thorpe, only daughter of the Earl of Premington, threw back her head, setting the ostrich feathers in her hair to dancing, and laughed.

He smiled at the delightful sound even as he bent his head, leaning forward to assure her, "My dear, I am entirely serious."

"It would serve you right if I accepted such a proposal," Lady Pamela told him, shaking her head as she smiled up at him.

"I assure you, 'twould please me greatly."

"You rapscallion!" She laughed again, tapping his shoulder with her fan as they swayed together.

"You think I am teasing," he went on. His visage was still pleasantly graced with a slight smile, but his tone had become solemn. "I am not."

Finally Lady Pamela looked up at him with a dawning seriousness in her eyes, almost losing her step as she saw the apparently matching seriousness in his own. "My lord?" she murmured, her eyes steady on his although she felt a flush creeping up her face. "I must own I never thought to hear such words from you."

This time it was he who laughed. He explained, "I am glad you do not say 'la, sir, how unexpected,' or any of the other dozen practiced answers ladies are taught to give. It is why I desire you, you know, this forthrightness of yours, this inability to be conventional. Of course you never thought to hear an actual proposal from the lips of the Marchmont Rake! No female ever has before this day, and that is a very well known fact. I own I never thought to hear it myself. But what do you say to it, my lady? Will you have me?"

"Of course I shall not," she answered at once, her eyes wide.

"No? Whyever not?"

"Whyever not?" she echoed, stunned by the question as much as the proposal. "Well, I . . . that is to say . . . this has come as a bit of a shock—"

"No, it is too late to fall back upon the old adages of 'you have spoken too soon' or 'you have caught me quite unawares'—all that pap. You must see, Lady Pamela, as true as all those old, tired words may be, and as much as we could both recite them chapter and verse, utterly wasting our time while still arriving at no decision, I ask that we do not succumb to the temptation to give them voice. What then, since I see I have left you speechless? Let us look instead at my qualifications: I am passing fair to look upon, as are

8

you. I have more than enough blunt to keep a wife in fashion, although your dowry will without doubt advance our existence to a shade beyond that I currently enjoy as a bachelor. You look to make an attachment before the end of the Season, and I am suitably free to make such an attachment, not to mention the fact that I am madly in love with you. So, what say you? Is that not all that a lady could wish?''

She stared at him, at his calm demeanor, only belatedly realizing that she had ceased to dance and that they were standing, staring at one another, in the middle of the dance floor.

''Escort me away from here at once,'' she demanded in a flustered whisper. She flipped open her fan and began fanning her face furiously as she took his proffered arm.

He led her to an alcove, looking over his shoulder before turning rapidly back to her. ''Your mama approaches. Quickly, love, give me your affirmation, that we may give her the happy news upon her arrival.''

''My answer was no, is no, and shall remain no,'' she said breathlessly, still fanning quickly, although she was truly using it more as a shield against his encroaching height than to actually stir a breeze.

''No? But why not?'' he cried, his eyes round with surprise, just as her mama called out, ''Pamela!''

They turned as one to greet the rather large Lady Premington, her rather daunting bosom, draped as it was in mauve silk and amethysts, preceding her by perhaps as much as half a second.

Marchmont's features remained calm as the lady

stepped up to them, though now there was a tightness around his mouth. "Lady Premington," Marchmont greeted the matron with a bow of his head.

"Marchmont," she replied crisply, her sharp, dark eyes boring into his own rich green ones. "Why have you drawn my daughter from the dance floor?" she asked bluntly.

"She requested it, my lady."

"Did she indeed," Lady Premington stated; it was no question. She turned to her daughter, instantly dismissive of the gentleman, and demanded, "Well?"

"I did, Mama."

"And why did you do so?"

"Because he had proposed to me, Mama, and I was momentarily flustered," she answered truthfully.

Lady Premington's dark eyes glittered for a moment in the candlelight, filled with a kind of smug satisfaction. She clasped her hands together and sighed, "An incomparable! I said you should be one, and one you shall be. Two weeks in London and already you have received your first proposal! Good show, that, Marchmont," she said, allowing for a moment the fact that the Baron existed, or perhaps it was to her daughter she offered the comment. "Come along, Pamela. The evening is young, and we have other hearts to steal, other proposals to win."

"Indeed you do not, my lady," Lord Marchmont spoke up at once, laying his hand on Pamela's arm. "The lady's hand has already been requested."

"And denied," Pamela said, just as her mother said, "Oh, posh!"

"Posh, my lady?" Marchmont echoed in astonished accents.

"Posh indeed."

"Oh, Mama, pray do not be so direct," Pamela scolded, her flushed cheeks darkening. Heads had begun to turn at the confrontation occurring in the alcove. She lowered her voice and said to the Baron, "Thank you very kindly for your . . . considerate proposal, Lord Marchmont, but I find I am unable to return your regard. Pray, do not be offended, and let us make every effort to remain friends."

"Friends?" Marchmont said, rather in a fashion he might have said "rodents?" He stared, open-mouthed for a moment, then cried, "Do you mean to tell me the rather remarkable fact that I am in love with you means nothing to you?"

"My lord, I scarce know you. Perhaps if I loved you in return—"

"My daughter, an *Earl's* daughter, to marry a ne'er-do-well Baron?" Lady Premington cried, her voice as loud as ever. "A rake! An *avowed* rake, who is rumored to have a heart of stone? Not to say anything to the fact that your grandfather was in trade? No, sir"—she waved a dismissive hand—"such an arrangement will never come to be."

"One of your own grandfathers was no doubt once in trade, my lady—" Marchmont said, but not with any sign of irritation. If anything, he looked faintly amused. However, he was not given the opportunity to finish his statement.

"And you are not rich. Your pockets are practically to let."

"My pockets are not to let!" he cried, and now there was indignation in his voice, which had risen to match hers.

"The tattlemongers have it that your lack of flash is directly tied to your purse, sir. I daresay they are close enough to the truth as makes no never mind. No, my daughter is quite right to turn your offer aside. Nothing against your family, mind you, but you have to own, my lord, you are quite beyond the pale for an Earl's daughter. Good evening. Do try the *pate de fois gras*—it will quite make you believe you are in Paris," she added with an idle, polite inclination of her head toward the buffet.

So saying, Lady Premington moved between the two of them, separating them quite efficiently with her own girth as she took up her daughter's arm. Pamela gave Lord Marchmont a slightly embarrassed glance, and murmured, "You see from whence comes my forthrightness which you claim to so admire."

As her mother proceeded to draw her from the alcove, she looked over her shoulder and cried, "I *do* thank you for your request, knowing no other lady has been so honored. Good evening, my lord."

"Good gad!" Marchmont cried as he stood and stared after the only lady he had ever claimed to love.

Chapter 2

"They say he is too often in his cups these days."

"He was ever in his cups, although now he appears as a love-sick puppy, they say."

"I own, he is rather charming with that pained and suffering look about him. He has a face that is well-suited to melancholy."

"And given to wearing dark colors, almost as though he were in mourning. They say he has no dash, but *I* say dash is how one wears one's clothing, and not the other way around."

Pamela listened to the comments that flew around her, not participating—except to listen. Her eyes were lowered to the folded hands in her lap, and it was a supreme effort not to squirm in discomfort.

Everyone knew. Everyone knew that Marchmont had offered for her—how could they have missed that disgracefully public display?—and it had been the juiciest *on dit* for the past week. No one thought anything of speaking of it in front of her, for the subject had come up in her very own mama's home, and besides, hadn't she refused the gentleman? Surely that meant her affections were not engaged. That being so, then how better to find out more and thereby enhance the tarradiddles than by going directly to the horse's mouth?

"I hear he went down on both knees," Miss Skerry said at her side. It was more a question than a comment, but Pamela was not about to respond to it.

She had no need to; her mother spoke for her. "He did not. He proposed while they were waltzing."

"Oh, waltzing!" Miss Skerry cried, then giggled, then exchanged a low-voiced whisper with the girl, Lady Jane, on her other side.

"Mama," Pamela said in a quiet, warning voice.

She was ignored as her mother went on. "You may have heard that he pulled her into an alcove, but I mean to assure you I saw it at once, as would any good mother. They were not alone above half a minute, and that time was taken up by Marchmont's protestations of affection."

"Mama!" Pamela said a little more forcefully. She was not terribly hopeful that her mother would cease to speak, however. Her mother had been an Earl's daughter before she was an Earl's wife, and had developed the unfortunate habit of speaking her mind, having been indulged in the matter her entire life. For a certainty, none of the ladies gathered at this tea party thought anything at all of Lady Premington's outspoken nature; it was, in fact, that which made her one of society's most sought-after hostesses, for

14

she knew and spoke of every scandal that passed through London. Hers was a house where every sensation could be heard and dissected. Her doors were wide open to her large body of friends from the rather shocking early hour of noon until dinnertime, every day they were in residence, even holidays. Of course, they were seldom *not* in residence, as Lady Premington found the country to be extremely wearying, and often stayed year-round in the city, even in the uncomfortably warm days past the Season.

Pamela's qualms were fulfilled: her mother did not restrain herself.

"I vow, for a moment I actually considered the matter. I mean to say, the man has the greenest eyes, and the most attractive hair—dark as sea waves at night, do you not think, if you will pardon me for waxing poetic—and I thought me: truly, Pamela could do worse than marry such a truly fine representative of his gender! But, of course, that was a fleeting thought only, for my daughter shall marry a superior, upstanding gentleman, correct in his behavior as well as his appearance. Is that not so, Pamela?"

Pamela looked up, further embarrassed to find that now she was to be included in this debacle of a debate. "I should hope so," she managed to say, trusting her expression was not as sour as her tone.

"We even have a certain someone in mind—"

"Mama!" Pamela cried, coming to her feet. She spoke to the group in short, clipped words, "I am assured that Lord Marchmont was simply exercising his renowned and considerable wit. I vow *I* never truly thought it was an earnest proposal, and neither

15

should any of you. I daresay Lord Marchmont is currently chuckling over the thought even as we speak. After all, he has himself declared he has no need or inclination to wed. Now, will you all please excuse me? I fear I have developed a megrim. Mama, will you be so good as to accompany me to my room, so that you may administer a headache powder to me?''

"The maid may see to that—"

"Mama!" Pamela said through gritted teeth, her eyes offering no quarter.

At last Lady Premington gave in to her daughter's determination, offering a quick word of excuse before she followed Pamela from the room.

They came to the stairs, passing the wall that had been twice repapered, once when Pamela was three, and then again when she was six, due to the ''art'' she had created there with her watercolor cakes to ''enhance'' her mama's choice of decorative paper. They climbed to the top of the stairs, which had been carpeted after Pamela had mimicked the way the maids applied beeswax to protect the wooden table tops, thereby almost killing the butler, Lawlton, one afternoon as he attempted, unknowingly, to mount the waxed stairs. They went down the hall, stepping over the area where several boards had been replaced after Pamela had been discovered just starting a little campfire for herself at the age of nine. They went to her room, which had known two complete sets of draperies—a fact she blamed in part on a particular pet cat who was much given over to climbing, and partly on her enthusiasm at ''rescuing'' said cat from its favorite perch atop the curtain rod.

All that was in the past now, however. Pamela was eighteen years of age, and had not colored on a wall in well over ten years. Now she was capable of behaving correctly. She was a proper young lady . . . well, at least in most regards. She did not consider it a fault that she had learned from being Lady Premington's daughter all these years (and thereby well-tutored in the area of forcefulness of nature) how to speak firmly when necessary, even as she did now. "Mama, you are no longer to discuss with *anyone* the matter of where my affections lie. You will never, *ever* speak of the gentleman I hope will one day—"

"Better be soon," her mother interjected.

" will one day request my hand. To speak of him is to drive him in the opposite direction, make no mistake of that, Mama."

"But he is only a captain in the army—"

"And second son to the Marquess of Waller. And, uncomfortable as it is to harbor such thoughts, we both know his elder brother is not long for this world and that one day Captain Penford shall be the Marquess. No, Mama, he is the one for me, and you are not to interfere, by deed or speech. If you do, by even so little as one word, I shall cry and moan and bewail to Papa that I am dying to see the countryside until he has no choice but to take us off to Kent at once."

"That is blackmail." Her mother scowled, but there was a grudging respect in her voice as well.

"It is, and a practice to which I seldom stoop, but in this one matter I must have your compliance, Mama. Please! It is very important to me."

Her mother stopped, taking up her hand, now

smiling. "Of course it is. Captain Penford is all that may be called desirable. He is handsome, in a rugged, strong-chinned manner, and although I could wish that his mustache was of a tidier size and was less red—"

"He has a hint of red in his hair," Pamela said, with a light of appreciation growing in her eyes.

"Fortunately it is more blond than red. Wavy, too, which is pleasant. He carries himself as a soldier, and in his uniform he does cut a fine figure. With his blue eyes, it is hardly to be wondered at that you should find the fellow to be of merit. And the title that ought to be his one day—well! One cannot wish much more for one's daughter than that she should become a Marchioness!"

As Pamela nodded over this piece of logic, her mother frowned. "Still, to have him now, when he is but a captain, and once free of the army a mere 'mister'—that would never do." She lifted a hand, making a little play-acting movement as she quoted, "Mister Roger and Lady Pamela Penford.' It does not wear well on the ear, now does it?"

At her daughter's quickly compressed lips, she went on, "Perhaps he will be rewarded for his service in the army and come into a title of his own, all the sooner, eh? Do you think he could manage to rescue someone dear to the Regent? One of the Royal Princes, perhaps? Ah well, I suppose that is mere daydreaming," she said as she saw the added exasperated shake of her daughter's head. "It makes no never mind. If this is the man of your dreams, and all wisdom seems to indicate he shall inherit the title from Waller, then of course I shall do all in my power to see that you are brought together."

"You will do that most effectively by doing nothing yourself and allowing *me* to plan how I shall bring Captain Penford to fall madly in love with me."

"You will," her mother said, smiling even more widely. "Of course you will. After all, you *are* my daughter, and we Premington females always get what we want."

"Well, you certainly always have," Pamela conceded with a grin as her mother patted her cheek.

"Exactly so, my dear, exactly so."

Chapter 3

Pamela did not take to her bed—never having had a case of the megrims in fact—but instead went to her sitting room and sat at her escritoire. There she wrote in her journal, which had been neglected for three days.

Very unpleasant morning spent with callers. Much gossipmongering concerning Marchmont's proposal. Most uncomfortable. Made pretense that it was matter of humor only. Was it? No, I think not. No.

One part of me wishes he had never made his offer, yet another part must allow that it is most flattering to have an offer only two weeks into my debut, and from such a handsome gentleman. Although, to be correct, it is said he is no true gentleman. It is said he is a rake and a spendthrift, caring more for his comforts and his pleasures than he cares for any other thing. He has always been most pleasant to me, as noted in prior passages, but I own I was most startled to hear him speak to me of love. After two weeks and three dances? No, it is clear: there was no love there, but quite possibly infatuation on his part. I could wish that infatuation had not led to the public display of a proposal, although Mama thinks it is all that is fine, that it enhances my reputation. "Incomparable" indeed! I am hardly anything out of the ordinary.

She frowned down at her writing, seeing aspects of vanity and—more disturbing yet—her criticisms of Marchmont, which were very like the gossip she was now the victim of herself.

She almost tore the page from her journal, but did not. She never had, not in the seven years she had been keeping one. It was sometimes amusing, and sometimes painful or embarrassing, to look back on one's thoughts from a more mature vantage point, but it was also always revealing. Even unfortunate memories could serve their purpose, if only to remind her how to behave like a lady and not the hoyden she had been as a child.

There was a rap at her door. She closed the journal, not bothering to close or lock the escritoire, for everyone knew she kept a journal. Her brother, Owen, had stolen it once, and produced it at the breakfast table the next day, declaring it the most boring and stifling reading he had ever done. He had received the sting of his father's cane across his hand for his actions, and ever since then there had been no need to hide the journal. Owen would, no doubt, say that was more the result of the paltry stuffiness of her writing than from the blow. Fortunately that event had occurred before Pamela had put some of her more scandalous thoughts, such as occurred to a young lady whose body was changing, to paper. If her brother had suspected such contemplations, he would never have been able to resist taking the journal, despite the threat of another punishment. But, by leaving her journal in plain sight, and sometimes reading aloud to her parents the blameless passages wherein she recorded what occurred at this party or that affair, the journal had lost any hint of sensation and therefore never interested her brother again.

"Enter," she called, settling her quill next to the journal.

It was the subject of her very thoughts who entered, his very light brown hair as her own, with its many highlights of silken gold.

"Owen," she said in some surprise, for her brother seldom came to her room, not now that she, five years his junior, had been declared old enough to be among company.

"Good morning, Pammy."

She scowled, just as she always did when he called her that atrocious nickname, just as he had no doubt intended she should.

"Has it been so long since you have tortured me that you find a need to do so earlier in the day than usual?" she asked tartly, but her scowl dissipated as he crossed to her side, leaving the door open behind him. Owen was her only sibling, and so had become a companion despite the difference of gender and the matter of five years. There was no one in the household who would deny that Lady Pamela loved her older brother, although neither would they deny he was enough of a scamp sometimes to earn even his once wayward sister's censure.

"It was not I but someone else who set me on this mission so bright and early," Owen said, dragging a stool over by hooking his foot on one of the legs to pull it near her seat at the escritoire. He sat upon the stool, and grinned up at her from his lower seat.

She knew that impish grin—something was afoot.

"What is it?" she asked suspiciously.

"Not what, but who. Marchmont requests a moment of your time."

"Marchmont! Never say he is below stairs with the other callers? What will he say? Oh, Owen, why is he here?" Pamela cried.

"Hush, Pammy! How you do go on. No, he is not with Mama's callers. In point of fact, he has arrived via the servants' entrance—"

"The servants' entrance! What can the man be thinking of?"

"He's thinking of having a quiet, unnoted word with you," Owen pointed out.

"It will never serve. Send him away."

"But, Pammy, he only wishes to speak with you. I shall be right here. There can be no harm in that."

She compressed her lips for a moment, then spoke firmly: "I know you are well-pleased to be counted among his circle, disreputable as that claim most surely is, Brother, but you must not think because you wish to dance to the tune the man plays you, *I*

23

must do so as well. No, send him away, I say—'' She had no more than said the words when a shape filled the doorway.

''Too late, I fear,'' Marchmont said to them both.

Owen stood, casting a quick and faintly apologetic glance at his sister before gesturing the Baron forward. Pamela's hand flew to her throat in a defensive gesture, and she was instantly grateful that the door to her bedchamber was closed. It was ghastly enough that he had come like this to her sitting room, but she could not have borne it if those clever eyes had seen her private sanctum, a place even most of her female friends had not been invited to view. The various collections in her room would have made him smile in a knowing fashion, she was sure.

Even as she knew brief relief that she had been spared at least that indignity, she could not help but stare up at the man standing in the doorway of her sitting room. He was dressed in dark charcoal gray, a color that made his dark hair seem all the darker and his green eyes all the greener in contrast. His shirt was simple, his waistcoat a solid gray silk. He held his right hand to his breast as he made her a bow, and she saw ruby lights twinkle in the rather bulky ring he wore on the ring finger of that hand. Its size and brilliant flashes of color seemed somewhat out of tune with his otherwise sober ensemble.

Marchmont came into the room, nodding at Owen. ''Powell,'' he said politely to the light-haired man, but with that in his voice that made the single word a dismissal.

Owen shuffled his feet, casting glances between

the man and Pamela, until finally he turned back to his sister, announcing, ''I believe you both have need of a private discussion. However, I shall be in the hallway, and the door shall remain open. You have but to raise your voice only a little, Pamela, and I shall come at once.'' So saying, he turned on his heel and strode from the room, making a point of pushing the door open to its fullest extent.

Pamela stared after him, refusing to meet the Baron's eyes.

She was forced to it, however, when he took a seat on the stool that Owen had just vacated, immediately before her skirts. There was nowhere else to look *but* at him, or else display the most shocking and reticent manners, and Pamela was not usually a reticent girl. She raised her eyes to his, finding those shockingly green orbs staring quietly back at her. Really, they were quite the color of a new leaf. She had not known it was possible for eyes to be so very green; they were almost unsettling in their intensity of color. Perhaps that was why her gaze slid away again, down to the hand that lay frozen in her lap.

His hand came over hers, enveloping and obscuring it, causing her to look up yet again, even as she tried to suppress a gasp at the unexpected, warm touch.

''I waited a whole week to see you, to ask you.''

''Ask me?'' she echoed faintly.

''You never did tell me why not,'' he said quietly. As always there was a faint smile in his eyes, if not around his mouth.

She blushed, unable to pretend she misunderstood. "Mama explained," she said in a near whisper. Her other hand remained at her throat, for now she had no idea where it might lie. If it dropped to cover his, it would speak an invitation she did not intend; if it dropped to her side, it would be a rebuff she did not wish to offer, for his actions to date might be termed more awkward than offensive.

"Your mama told me why *she* wished me refused, but you never told me why *you* were willing to refuse my offer."

"But I must follow my mama's dictates," she said.

"Tush! Such nonsense from a sensible girl such as you, Lady Pamela. No, you need not. *I* never have." He smiled at her.

"You are a man." She felt a sudden impulse, firmly repressed, to smile back, such was the draw of that charming smile.

"Which gives me some freedoms you do not have, true. But, Lady Pamela, you have but to say 'yes' or 'no' to me. Your mama cannot make you say either, for you are no marionette. It is, and always is, up to you what you will say or not say."

"I could be disowned," she said logically. "If I go against my parents' wishes, they could cast me out on the street, and what would become of me then?"

"They could, but I doubt they would. For what crime? For marrying a peer? No, do not blush; I know my position in society is not so fine as some would have it, but 'tis well enough. There would be no shame in having me. And, even so, should your doting parents harden their hearts and cast you out, you will have me, to catch you up in my arms, make you

26

my bride, and bring you all the respectability you could desire. So, love, you see there truly is no impediment, not from parents. So then, I have to ask, whatever stops you from making us both so very happy? Is it that you should be but a Baroness?''

She shook her head a little, overwhelmed by his presence here, alone with her, and with—admittedly—the logic of his arguments.

''Is it that you do not care for my company?''

She shook her head again, speaking to clarify the motion. ''That is to say, I like you quite well, my lord, for all that I scarce know you.''

His hand squeezed over the top of hers, making her all the more aware that they were alone together. The touch of his hand on hers, the foreign scents of some kind of cigarillo smoke and a cologne that accompanied his person, the way he stared into her eyes unblinkingly, with all his attention apparently centered only on her—all made the moment feel strangely ethereal. The silence that had fallen between them was oddly comfortable, only adding to the strangeness of the moment, for they were virtual strangers. Suddenly more words rushed from her mouth, words blurted so that the silence might be broken.

''I might ask you, however, what is it about *me* that so attracts you?'' She colored then, and cried, ''Oh, dear, I hope you realize I am not fishing for compliments, but—''

''I know you are not,'' He sat back a little, though he did not release her hand. ''That is one of the things I admire so about you: you do not need constant reminders of your fine looks. Perhaps that is because

God graced you with more than your fair share, but nonetheless it is charmingly refreshing to hold a conversation with a lady who already understands she is all that is attractive. But, truth to tell, it is mostly the things you say that fascinate me so. Every time you open your mouth, you say all that is proper, and yet it is also fresh somehow. You make me see the world anew, by dint of a simple sentence. You make me laugh, and I am overly fond of laughing. It is how I became a rake, as I am well aware I am called; as I call myself, and rightly so. I am a creature given over to gaiety, and I cannot think of a finer person to share my days—and nights—with than someone who is of such like mind as are you."

"I do not think of myself as gay," she fluttered, ignoring his reference to the night, for she could hardly comment upon it, not even to scold.

"You think of yourself as a proper young lady, I know. But, Pamela—"

She made a small noise that noted he had dropped her title without permission.

"—anyone may be proper. Yet how many of us may be happy? I swear I could make you happy, if you would but accept me."

He was smiling again now, an encouraging smile, and she felt again that pull to respond to it; but she dared not. She started to shake her head.

"Pamela," he said, his other hand reaching for and taking the hand at her throat and pulling it down next to where he held the other in her lap. "I desire you. You say you could have a care for me. We could be the rare couple that actually enjoys each other. Make it so, my girl, by one small word. Make it so.''

She met those green eyes, and felt a tickle of tears at the back of her own, for his words were so eager. It was really most flattering, and yet, too, so very uncomfortable. Strange creature! He could make comfortable silences followed at once by uncomfortable words; he was a chameleon, an enigma. Where had such intensity come from? What had she ever done to earn such devotion? A curious devotion, one that seemed to have erupted far too suddenly. Yes, there was something wrong about it. The words were right, but the timing was wrong, or a little off, or perhaps skewed by desires that had nothing to do with true affection. . . . After all, did she not know what real love was? Was not the admiration she felt toward Captain Penford a fine and good thing? Were not those feelings such that could surely lead to something more, something even grander than mere admiration? Was not love supposed to be something that ennobled the spirit rather than making it feel all topsy-turvy? Yes, this . . . this emotion—she could not name it love—that Marchmont professed was not right. And she had to put an end to it.

Blinking back the unexpected and unwelcome tears, she cried out the only thing she knew he would understand and accept as her final denial. ''But, my lord, I love another!''

His hands went still where they wrapped around hers, and his shoulders went stiff. His face lost its animation, and the green eyes became chips of polar ice. ''Who?'' he asked through tight lips.

29

"It matters not—"

"Who!" he cried.

"Captain Roger Penford," she said weakly, just managing to pull her hands from his tight grip, for the pressure there had begun to hurt her hands.

His hands pulled away, hovering in the air between them. "I am sorry," he apologized at once, taking up her hands again and massaging the backs of them with his thumbs. He went on, "And he loves you?"

"I do not know."

"But you have hopes?"

"Must we speak of this?"

"He has been in London but a week. How well could you know him? You do know he returns to his regiment as soon as his wound is healed?" he demanded, and some life came back into his features.

"I know."

"Has he proposed?"

"No."

His head cocked a little to one side at the tone of her voice. "Has he hinted at an affection?"

"No. My lord, please, can you not merely accept that my affections lie—"

"I see. Oh, yes, I see the matter most clearly now! Captain Penford may not even be aware of your affections, eh? That is it, is it not? You have set your cap in his direction, and the poor sot does not even know it! How often have you spoken? Have you danced? No, not with his wounded foot, of course not. And I would swear you certainly have not kissed!"

"My lord!" she scolded, allowing a frown to settle between her brows.

"Ah! Pamela, you silly creature!" he sighed as though in great relief.

"Silly? You dare to call me silly? Am I any more so than you, my lord? I know of no particular reason why you should fancy yourself madly in love with me after only two weeks' acquaintance. Why should my affections toward Captain Penford be any the less because of the difference of a week?"

" 'Tis a young girl's fancy, 'tis all."

"I beg to differ. But, let us no longer speak of this, as it is no matter of yours," she said coolly.

"It is if you mean to marry the man."

"I cannot 'mean' to marry him. He has free will," she said warmly. "He would need to come to admire me, as I have come to admire him. These things are a matter of affections. It is not decided in sitting rooms, by declaration of one party or another, without the knowledge of the other—"

Marchmont interrupted, "Do you love him?"

"That is none of your affair!"

"Hmm . . ." His eyes turned away for a moment as one hand went to rub his clean-shaven chin. The ruby ring winked at her, and she was near enough now that she could see the ring was fashioned in the shape of a horseshoe, the entire curve of it set with ruby red stones. The hand dropped back to hers as he looked up again, drawing her eyes back to his own. "I daresay it may be the title you are after. We all know that one day he shall be the Marquess of Waller. After all: to be a Marchioness! I could understand that desire, and *I* certainly may not promise you such a distinction.''

She would have stood, but he was directly before her, his boots pressed into her skirts. Instead she sat as straight as she might and intoned, ''Lord Marchmont, I must bid you say good day.''

He ignored her dismissal. ''Of course, there is one other solution to the matter. You might go ahead and wed this Penford, and be my mistress.''

''What?'' she cried.

''I said—''

''I heard perfectly well what you said! How dare you?''

Just then Owen leaned into the room, his eyebrows raised questioningly. ''Pamela?''

''Go away,'' Marchmont said, waving him back. ''You can see I am hardly molesting the girl. Let us have our spat in peace, if you don't mind.''

Owen retreated.

''You are quite odious,'' Pamela said with careful dignity, silently vowing to enact a revenge later on her brother for his spineless compliance with this man's dictates.

''I am not. I am rather charming. I will grant you that sometimes I speak my mind rather bluntly, but it saves so much confusion that it is well worth the inevitable censure it engenders. So you see, my dear, it is not that I am insensible to your outrage, but merely that it wastes our time. I desire you, you desire Penford's eventual title, so let us speak to the matter: why not a love affair? Penford is fully capable of finding a light-o'-love for himself elsewhere. Such an arrangement would suit us all to a nicety, I am assured.''

She glared at him, her eyes narrowing. Well, that had made the matter perfectly clear then, had it not? His "devotion" was no such thing at all; it was mere carnality on his part, apparently strong enough to compel him to first ask for her hand, but not decent enough to keep him from offending her with this contemptible offer in the immediate wake of his failed proposal. He did not love her, that was abundantly clear.

"Do tell me," she said with icy disdain, no longer able to sit, coming to her feet, her skirts brushing against his boots as she was careful to dance to one side to avoid even more contact with him, "what is there about me that makes you believe, for one moment, that I would agree to such a situation?"

She moved to stand behind the chair she had just vacated, her arms crossed in front of her defensively. She had meant to freeze him with her sarcasm, but instead he stood also, with a smile on his lips.

"Why, the way you dance, and the way you laugh. You cherish your gaiety as much as I do. A man, even be he a half-wit, can feel the life and joy in you, just by holding you in his arms for the length of one dance! I knew it the first moment we touched hands. And then, to hear your laughter is to know the strongest desire to see what other pretty noises you might make, given even more exciting reasons to do so.''

She stared at him anew, aware her mouth hung open in gaping astonishment, but she was frozen, unable to move even so little as to snap it closed.

"I have surprised you!" he announced, his grin growing wider.

Finally she closed her mouth, shook her head as though to clear it of fog, and half laughed, a sound that carried a hint of hysteria in it. "My lord, how you do go on!" she cried, for what else could a body say in such a circumstance? Her hand went to her forehead as though to check for fever there.

"I do. It is a habit of mine. I like to put thoughts into words. So few people do, you know."

"It is said you are a terrible liar," she countered. She had crossed some internal line beyond shock, and therefore found her wits returning to her. Her hands moved to the high back of the chair, which she unconsciously had placed as a kind of shield between them.

"I have been."

"What is this? You admit your own failing? Are you, then, an honest liar?" She half laughed again.

"I have no need to lie to you, Pamela. Now, some people, they require a great deal of lies. It is the way of the world, for some. Therefore, I do not consider it a fault to give such people that which they desire."

"You mean your past *amours*," she challenged. She had heard whispers that he made free with his charms, but such whispers ran rampant about any young man on the town. She had no actual knowledge whether he had *amours* or not; but the accusation came easily to her lips, and she did not expect denial.

It was not forthcoming; if anything, he smiled more. She wondered if there was a dancing light in her eye to echo the one she saw in his, for that grin of his was catching, despite everything. Was it humor, or something even more astounding that made him smile, and made her wish to smile with him?

"Among others, yes," he answered finally.

She shook her head, finally giving in to the desire to share his smile, albeit slightly. He must be the most rackety fellow: seeing mannerisms that were surely not her own, mistaking such little things as party merriment for attraction. There was only one way to respond to such amused, and clearly erroneous, insistence. She stepped from behind the chair, her arms spreading wide. "But *look* at me!" she cried then, still partly smiling. "I am horrified, angry, insulted, and furious with you! And yet you are trying to tell me that I am your very soul mate, that I am well-equipped to join you in any debauched game we may care to name! Can you not see the truth before you, my lord? *I am not* the woman you obviously think me to be!"

His smiled only increased, and he took a step toward her. It seemed he had to suppress a laugh. "Yes, you are," he said in a choked voice, which he mastered after a moment. "I know it full well. It is *you* who do not know it. Even now you smile as you tell me you are furious."

She folded her arms before her, puffing out her cheeks in a sigh of exasperation, forcing the curving of her lips to disappear. These assertions of his, they were disarming, making her doubt herself where she had not doubted in over a year. Had she not worked long and hard to rid herself of her hoydenish ways? Was there something in her still that showed the incorrigible nature that had once been hers? Despite all the effort she had made to change herself into a fully respectable young woman? What did he see, or did he indeed see anything at all? Had he any sense of how unsettling his pronouncements were to her peace of mind, or did he speak randomly, carelessly, never aware how much he upset her ordered world?

This strange moment of almost cordial revelations was swiftly dissipating, becoming annoying now. She lifted her chin and shook her head a little in denial as she declared, "I do not agree with what you say."

"It matters not. I shall show you the way—"

"I tell you, it is not so." She turned her back to him, cutting off the response he would have made. "My lord, we are at an impasse. I believe it is time you removed yourself from my home. Pray do not return."

Hands touched her shoulders, causing her to stiffen even as she uttered a small gasp. The hands turned her to face him, and she was startled to see a warmth in his eyes, all sign of humor gone. "Do not banish me from your home, Pamela. Do not do so."

"You leave me little choice—"

"You have every choice. I have taken nothing from you. I have only spoken what I believe to be the truth. For this you would never allow me to darken your doorway again?"

She stared up at him, flustered and annoyed, and also, despite herself, moved by the sudden, new humbleness of his tone. "You make it sound so very harsh, when all I really wish is some peace of mind."

His green eyes danced with amusement. "I can

give you peace of—No!'' he interrupted his own teasing, seeing the anger begin to swell in her honey brown eyes, and held up a warning hand when her lips parted to utter a harsh renouncement. "Do not speak. You have already put me in my place; I see I must restrain my tongue for today if you are not to set me adrift in a cold, lonely, heartless world.''

He had a way with words, a way that robbed her of reasonable responses. Instead she allowed another puff of air to escape from between her lips, meant to show she was not moved, but the action was somewhat denied by her following words. "I understand why you are called a rake! You manipulate every situation, every emotion. I almost feel the cur for bidding you mind your manners in my home," she scolded.

"I will mind my manners, if you insist.''

"I insist.''

"Then, I am still welcome.''

It was not a question, but she chose to treat it as one. "Yes,'' she said grudgingly, beginning to frown at her own acquiescence. How had he won that right? She knew that but a moment ago she had bid him leave and never return, and yet now here she was, granting her permission that he might stay.

"Then, I shall take my leave.''

She gave him an exasperated glance, stifling her impulse to berate him for demanding a privilege merely to cast it away. Instead she said rather tartly, "At long last!''

"You wound me! But at least you have given me your word that I may come again.''

"I have."

Now she did frown, for the amused glitter was back in his eyes.

"Then, there is only one other matter to which we must attend."

"And what is that?" she asked suspiciously.

He did not speak, instead leaning forward quickly to press his mouth to hers. The kiss lasted only a moment, but for that moment she was so startled she did not think to move, for she had never been kissed by a gentleman before. She found that her mouth responded automatically, shaping as it did when he kissed her mama and papa good night, kissing him back.

He stepped back—and she noted with a fuzzy part of her mind that it was enough beyond her reach that she would need to step forward herself if she meant to slap him—and he grinned at her anew. "I could not allow Captain Penford to best me in the area of that particular honor," he explained.

The tips of her ears began to burn, and she stared up at him mutely, amazed to find she could still be shocked by anything this man might choose to do or say.

He held up the warning finger again. "Remember, you gave me permission to return. There were no stipulations, and so this little kiss cannot allow you to change your mind as to the matter. I shall see you tomorrow, then." He made her a bow, and turned on his heel and left the room.

As she stood and marveled over the strange and mixed sensations caused by the contact—not least or strangest being the residual tingling of her lips—she heard him call a farewell to Owen, and heard the sound of his boots on the back stairs.

It was not until the servants' door closed noisily behind him that she found she could gather her wits once more, an act that suddenly had her emitting a long, high-pitched wail of outrage. Try as she might, there was no way to deny the fact that she had shared her first-ever kiss with none other than the undeniably odious Lord Marchmont.

Chapter 4

Pamela waved at the butler, Lawlton. Lawlton caught sight of the action, and turned surreptitiously to glance behind himself. Finding no one there, he turned back to the daughter of the house, his eyes widening as he saw the action repeated. He saw then that it was not truly a wave; it was more a beckoning motion. There was something about the motion that reminded him of the young lady as a child, a thought that conjured uncomfortable memories. She had been forever embroiling him in her various pranks, often without so much as his knowledge, let alone his consent. Of course, it had been some years since she had last had her ears boxed or her dinner denied, but his left leg still ached sometimes when it rained, following that episode on the waxed stairs.

He crossed with stately and deliberate steps to where she waited several steps up on the staircase to the first story. He stopped at the foot of the stairs, his heels coming together in a nice military clip as he bowed his head once and inquired coolly, "Lady Pamela? Did you wish my services?"

"Lawlton, do lower your voice! I do not wish to be overheard," she responded in a whisper. "Come up here at once, if you please, and tell me who awaits in Mama's drawing room."

He came up the stairs, allowing his suspicion to turn into nothing more than a somewhat mild shock at the young lady's manner and inquiry, as he made an attempt to erase such disturbance from his voice. "As it is yet early—"

"I know it is early. What I wish to know is *who* is here?"

Lawlton cleared his throat and inclined his head. "Master Owen . . . pardon me, that is to say Lord Powell is within, as is Lady Premington. Lady Marrelston has come down—"

"Grandmama?"

"Yes." Lawlton inclined his head again, silently acknowledging that Pamela's maternal grandmother was not a frequent visitor to the drawing room. "Lady Jane Landcove has called, and Lord Marchmont has arrived only but five minutes past."

"Marchmont?" Pamela echoed, her mouth turning down. Of course. He had said he would return, and if she knew nothing else of him, she knew that he would do as he said he would.

"Yes, miss. Shall I announce you?"

"No. I shall return to my room. I . . . I have a case of the megrims." Pamela gathered her skirt with one hand, making ready to mount the stairs.

"Shall I send Joselle or Phyllis to you, Lady Pamela?"

"No."

"Lady Premington?"

"No." She gave Lawlton a guilty glance. "I am well enough. I shall see to my own care." Really, she could not like hiding away in her room all the time, pretending to have megrims.

"Oh, there you are!" came her mother's voice.

Pamela looked beyond the butler and saw her mother emerging from the drawing room. Inwardly she groaned, caught before she could make her escape.

"I was just coming to see if you were ready to join us. Come, come," her mother called, putting out one hand in invitation.

There was nothing for it: Pamela gave a dismissing nod to Lawlton, who bowed himself away to his other duties with a quickly stifled look of relief.

Pamela took a deep, steadying breath, then came down the stairs, stretching out her hand to meet that of her mother.

"I cannot think why, but Lord Marchmont is here this morning, my dear, sitting in my drawing room and insisting upon reading parts of the newspapers aloud to any who will listen. But, then again, as I think on it, he is probably here because he is positively pining for love of you, do you not suppose? Oh, but of course. That is rather sweet, is it not? Only, it will never serve. Do try to be curt with him, dear, that he might learn to go away and make less of a nuisance of himself." Her mother put a smile on her face just as she drew Pamela into the drawing room. There was no time to reply, but even if there had been, Pamela's sentiments would have been quite similar in word and thought.

There was the inevitable pot of chocolate and plate of toast awaiting whatever morning callers her mother would have this day. "Do pour another cup for those who wish it," her mother said airily to her, waving her toward the seat nearest the tray of offerings. Pamela sat, then had to raise her eyes to meet those of the room's occupants. Owen shook his head, declining a cup; Lady Jane offered her cup to be refilled; Pamela could not catch Mama's eye, for that lady was busy naming every person who had attended the opera last night, to no one in particular; Grandmama nodded that she was ready to take a saucer now; and finally Pamela was forced to turn to Lord Marchmont, who had just moved from his previous seat to sit right next to her on the settee. He looked down into her eyes, not moving or speaking, until finally she was forced to say rather curtly, "Well? Will you have chocolate?"

"Now that I have heard that dulcet voice this morning, I am prepared to take sustenance," he said at once, smiling at her.

She all but put out her tongue at him, but managed instead only to utter in a very low voice, "Pray do not cause me to be ill."

His eyes danced as he accepted the saucer, even as his mouth pouted insincerely. "I wish only to make you very happy," he said back, not so quietly as she.

"Then be silent. *That* will make me happy," she

43

said from between gritted teeth, for Owen had turned to gaze at them, a frank and questioning expression crossing his face. Even Grandmama had turned at Marchmont's reply.

Marchmont inclined his head, taking a sip of his chocolate.

"Lady Jane, do tell us how your dear mama's health holds?" Lady Premington said, turning the conversation as a good hostess ought.

"She is well, although she still does not venture forth when the winds blow, for fear her cough could return so soon after she has begun to claim good health once more."

"How glad I am to hear it. And what of your dear mother, Lord Marchmont?"

Marchmont returned his hostess's gaze and gave a half shrug, not speaking. There was, perhaps, a slight smile hovering near his mouth.

"Lord Marchmont?"

Pamela looked at him fully then for the first time today—whatever was wrong with the man? He obviously had heard the question, but he made no verbal response. Instead, at Mama's continued silence, he stood and crossed to where Mama's escritoire stood open, removing a slip of paper from a cubbyhole, and uncorked the bottle of india ink that rested on the writing surface. He took the quill from the stand, dipped it in the ink, and scratched out a few quick words on the paper. He then returned the quill to the stand, corked the ink, and crossed the room to hand the note to Mama.

" 'She is well'?" she read, looking up from the

note with a puzzled glance. "As pleased as I must be to hear it, I now have to wonder as to your own health, Marchmont. Have you a frog in your throat that you will not speak?"

He shook his head, folding his hands before him, and turned to gaze down at Pamela.

She knew from the telltale burning that the tips of her ears had turned crimson, though whether it was more from embarrassment or fury, she could not say. A quick glance at her brother showed that fellow to be leaning forward as though in alert attention, and her grandmama was holding quite still, her teacup half-raised to her lips and a sudden expression of unlooked for awareness hovering about her features.

"That is doing it too brown!" Pamela announced with the barest hint of civility left in her voice.

"Doing *what* too brown?" Lady Jane asked, looking from one face to the other with rapt attention.

"Yes, what?" Lady Premington echoed.

"I believe," Owen said, clearing his throat, as though to swallow a smile before he went on, "that my dear sister has bid Marchmont to remain silent. He is but complying with her wishes."

"How nonsensical!" Lady Premington and Grandmama said at once, although now Grandmama seemed almost to be smiling even as she said the words.

Marchmont shrugged and then gave a little bow that implied Owen had the right of it.

"But you did say as much. I heard it," Owen argued the point to his sister.

"I am not saying I did not say as much." Pamela

flashed her brother a menacing glance, promising later retribution for this second traitorous act, then straightened her shoulders and spoke to the center of the room rather than to any one person. "All I am saying is that only a fool takes such a statement literally."

Marchmont said nothing, only putting a hand to his breast and lifting enquiring eyebrows as though to question the title he had just been given.

"Oh, you silly toad, I release you! You may speak," Pamela ground out, coming to her feet.

"As you wish," Marchmont replied, and there was a general murmur that ran through the room, as though the occupants had held their breath as he had held back his words.

She made as though to step around him, crying, "I must go! I . . . I feel a dreadful case of the megrims coming upon me." From the corner of her eye she saw her grandmama move at last, lowering teacup to saucer.

Marchmont blocked Pamela's exit, making her eyes narrow in a manner that caused her mother to gasp out a scolding, "Pamela!"

"I shall be good," he murmured, hanging his head like a penitent boy, even though he made no effort to move out of her way.

"Why do you do this?" she cried, all but stamping her foot in her agitation.

She then became far too aware of the silent, observant stares, far too keenly conscious of the fact that she ought not to have asked that question, that she did not wish him to give what would undoubtedly be an awkward answer aloud, not before such an audience.

He began to speak: "Because I lo—" but before the rest of this statement could be forthcoming, she put her hand on his arm, slipping around him and pulling him in her wake.

"We are going to see if there may be another pot of chocolate available!" she announced firmly over her shoulder.

He laughed with a delighted, surprised sound, but followed her docilely enough.

Once beyond the door that led down to the kitchens, she stood two steps below him, one hand on either hip, and demanded, "Is it your intention to drive me absolutely mad?"

He stepped down, so that he was on the same step as she. The stairway was narrow, putting the wall at her back, with only a few inches to spare between them. It was only dimly lit, for the door was closed behind them. A hubbub of sounds from the kitchens floated up to them, reminding her she was not really quite alone with him, a reminder she appreciated fully even as she pressed back into the wall.

"Of course not," he answered.

"Then why do you constantly torment me in this way?"

"In what way? All I ever do is follow your commands. You said 'be silent,' so I was silent."

"Do not play games with me!" She pointed a finger rudely at the center of his chest, to emphasize each word with a poke toward his third button. "You knew you would embarrass me. You wanted everyone in that room to hear your meaningless proclamations of affection. Well, be warned, next time I shall leave you to swing in the wind alone. I shall be impervious to your manipulations. I shall deny anything you say. It shall be you, and not I, who shall look the fool."

He caught the finger, holding it pinned in his large hand. "That seems fair," he said.

She rolled her eyes and sighed with disgust. "I declare, Marchmont, you do not seem to take me at my word."

"Yes, I do."

"Then *leave me alone!*" she cried, shaking her finger free of his grasp.

A scullery maid stuck her head around the corner, peering up the stairs. She said nothing, her eyes wide, but neither did she run away, staring at the scene in gawking puzzlement.

"Shoo!" Pamela said to her in an unusually abrupt manner. "We are having a serious discussion."

The wide-eyed maid disappeared at once.

"You have been seen alone with me," Marchmont pointed out, his eyes dancing even in the dim light of the stairwell. "Now you have to marry me; you have been compromised."

"Hardly so," she said with scorn, once again feeling the desire to stamp her foot. "Blather on if you must, but such nonsense will not distract me from making my point. I shall continue to 'comb your hair' until it parts enough to let some of my words sink into that thick skull of yours."

"I did not know you could speak so roughly, Pamela. I like it. Do go on."

She took a deep breath to steady herself. "I am," she said with hands that knotted into fists at her sides, "very close to striking you. I could hurt you, if I wished. Only ask Owen."

"But you already have," he said, and now the smile had turned bittersweet. "Hurt me down to my very marrow."

She looked away, crossing her arms in a gesture of self-defense, fists still knotted. "It won't wash, Marchmont. I know that trick already. You are no more hurt than I am the King of Prussia."

"But the words tug at you, do they not? You are not quite sure, are you? You wonder: can he truly love me?" He put one hand on the wall above her head, making her aware of his superior inches.

"Love," she tried to scoff, but it came out a little unsteady. "Pride is more the way of it, I think. I have no doubt you thought, if you thought at all, 'ah, this one shall make a nice, biddable wife,' but now that I show I have half a brain to call my own and therefore have refused you, you pretend that all along it was for love of me that you tendered your proposal."

"How do you know it was not love all along? Have I ever asked another to marry me?"

She might be mistaken, but it seemed that with each passing minute, the space between them grew smaller, that he leaned toward her by degrees.

"I am an Earl's daughter. I know why men pursue one such as myself." She drew herself up to her fullest height—quite a number of inches less than his own—and announced proudly, "I know my worth on the marriage mart, sirrah!"

49

" 'Sirrah,' you say. You chide me!"

Drat that grin of his! "Because I have some sense. Yes, you saw a pleasant enough face—" she explained, instantly chagrined when he smiled at her self-assessment, a smile that urged her to lean even farther back into the unmoving wall as she went hotly on, "a rich dowry, and a way to better the estate of your family through marriage. That is all that has been in your mind, and I can prove it: if you truly loved me, you would not make me furious at you this way. You would not embarrass me."

"Happens all the time with marrieds," he said, and now she was sure he was leaning into her. "They are forever bickering—and do not pretend you have not seen that fact for yourself! You must ask yourself, Pamela, what is it, if not love, that convinces me I must come ever closer to you?" he asked, closing the space between them to the point where the ruffles on his shiftfront brushed against her bodice.

She refused to meet his green gaze, looking down the stairwell and wishing the scullery maid would return. She lifted one foot, found the stair above, and with a quick, ducking motion slipped upward, out of the immediate half circle of his raised arm.

"The vicar calls it lust," she answered him primly.

He shrugged, an elegant, speaking habit she was becoming most conscious of, and he stepped up toward her, forcing her back another step. "Could be," he said, "but I do not think so. If it is, it is a rather powerful lust, I must say."

Something went wrong with her knees, making

them feel all loose and watery. She felt the door at her back and leaned into it, grateful for its support.

It was impossible not to be flattered by his assertions, despite every instinct that told her otherwise. No one had ever spoken such words to her, and never had a man used such a warm, caressing voice with which to speak with her. It seemed her instincts were at war, the mind and the body at opposite ends of the argument. It was quite . . . flustering.

"But . . . but now you know," she said breathlessly. "Now you know that I am not an interested party. You shall have to find another. There is no point in attempting to further attract my attention."

"I have your attention, have I?"

She did not answer, eyeing him uncertainly, recognizing that her body was near to trembling, and hating the impulse even as it formed.

He moved up one more step, and there was nowhere for her to go. Now he put a hand out on either side, touching opposite walls as he leaned toward her. "Do you know what I think?"

"What?" she said shakily.

"I think you like me—"

"I could. If you were not so abominable."

"—more than you wish to admit. I think you would not mind being courted."

"Courted? You call this a courtship?"

"I think you want me to make you fall in love with me, so it will not be your 'fault' when you do at last."

She gave a short, shaky laugh. "Such arrogance!"

"Look at me, Pamela."

"Lady Pamela, to you."

"Look at me, and tell me you want me gone forever from your life."

"I want you gone forever from my life," she echoed, meeting his gaze with an effort.

His lower lip came out, and his brows puckered together in a curious little jig that could not decide between seriousness and humor. "You do not truly mean it," he said.

"I do."

"No, you do not." His face was very near hers.

"I do."

"I do not think so."

She nearly groaned, her voice still unsteady. "You are not going to leave me in peace, are you?"

He shook his head.

Silence reigned for a moment. He was so near, so . . . expectant. It was difficult to think in his presence.

But think she must. "Then let me request a favor of you," she said in sudden inspiration, her eyes, as the thought took shape and form, now rising firmly to meet his. Her voice steadied as she spoke: "I will give you your chance to court me if you will give me something in return."

He pulled back a little. "Ah, Pamela, I find I must quake with trepidation at the light that just broke in those eyes. But, tell me anyway, for I can see I am lost, your slave in all things. What is it you request of me?"

"Mere common courtesy. No more such pranks

as just happened in Mama's drawing room. In return, I shall not forbid you my presence."

He laughed at that, and said frankly, "I can already have your company, should I desire it."

"Not necessarily. I could refuse you entrance to my home. I could never go out of doors, not even to parties. I could return to the country. If you know anything of me at all, as you claim to, you know I am quite capable of abandoning the Season."

One hand came away from the wall, picking up a tendril of her light hair, twirling it around his finger. Where it tugged at her scalp, the skin tingled. "Ah, Pamela, you are a difficult creature, are you not? But, 'tis true. I hear it in your voice, even if I did not know it before. You force my hand.

"But I cannot make a bargain I cannot keep. We must define the terms more precisely, for it is impossible for me to always display what others call 'common courtesy.' Let us say instead, that I shall make no efforts to fluster you unduly. If you shall allow me the honest chance to win your affections, then I shall not stand in your way to win those of the fine Captain Penford."

A dawning light broke over her features. "Is that what today was all about?" she marveled, for it made sense of the nonsensical.

"Oh, indeed. I am fiercely jealous of your attachment to the man. You realize that you must agree to give me exactly the same number of minutes as you give to him."

"Minutes?"

"Minutes, down to the last half a one! If you go

to the theatre with him, then you must spend the same amount of time with me the next night. And so it shall go forward, 'an eye for an eye, a tooth for a tooth.' ''

"That refers to revenge."

"In this case, battle. Like two knights, doing battle to win the affections of the princess. Princess Pamela, whose name means 'all-honey.' ''

She gaped at him, again feeling the pull of flattery to find that he knew the meaning of her name, from the Greek.

He smiled at her amazement, caressing her cheek with the tip of her own hair as he said, "Honey—your name, the color of your hair, your eyes, and the essence of your personality. You see, Pamela-Honey, I am a formidable opponent."

"I see," she whispered, wondering somewhat wildly if he thought of Captain Penford—or herself—as his adversary?

"I believe it is customary for a lady to give her knight a token before he rides off to battle."

"I am not your lady."

"Not yet." He smiled again, released her hair, and leaned forward to press his mouth to hers. She made no effort to escape him, and it was over almost before it began, two seconds of warmth and pressure and a curious tingling that leaped, lightning quick, from her lips to her toes. She managed to suppress a gasp of surprise, but she could not keep it from filling her eyes.

He said, with laughter in his voice, "A chaste kiss

to seal our bargain. You see, I can be harmless enough.''

She felt a smile tug at her own lips. ''You do not expect me to swallow that lie whole, do you?''

''No,'' he laughed, stepping down and offering a hand up to her. ''For I own I should not care to pursue a stupid woman. Come, we must fetch that pot of chocolate, or else be made to explain what use we made of our time here.''

She inclined her head with a kind of restored equanimity, accepted his hand, and descended with him to the kitchens—fleetingly thinking that this descent could be perhaps seen as a rather uncomfortable reflection of the bargain she had just struck: a descent into, what was for her, a highly uncommon realm.

Chapter 5

Pamela looked away from where Marchmont flirted outrageously with Lady Jane. Really, he was the most abominable trifler!

He had no sooner declared his undying desire to pursue *her,* and now here he was with his clever tongue aimed in another direction, spouting such flattery that he had quite turned Lady Jane's head. The girl's giggles and rapid fanning more than merely grated on one's nerves; it positively annoyed.

Of course, there *was* something of value to be had from the distasteful display: Pamela saw with her own eyes that Marchmont was incapable of accepting a rejection in any form. It could be further seen that he was unable to grasp even the fundamentals of how he would need to demonstrate his ''love,'' should she be so foolish as to mistake his protested claims of affections as being anything near to actual love.

Even in the midst of her annoyance, Pamela marveled at and struggled to suppress the emotions that coursed through her as she turned away from the sight of the two at their bantering. She knew a kind of relief, for his faithless and mercurial attention had now focused on another, but mixed with the relief there was chagrin to find her charms so apparently forgettable despite her presence in the very room in which he trifled with another. There was, too, a slow, building anger that began to tell her that she had been made to play the fool, and there was something very like disappointment, in both herself and him, at the knowing of that fact.

She had quite believed him, she realized. For a few silly, impossible moments she had believed he was madly in love with her, that he wished to court her. Now here he was, slavishly devoted to every word Jane uttered, kissing the back of the girl's hand—actually touching it with his lips, the rogue!—and sighing effusively when the girl pretended to scold him for his effrontery. It was . . . why, it was insulting! Did he think her an absolute fool? She did not know whether she wished to slap his face until it blazed red, or stand and coldly order him from her home.

She might have done both but for the fact that she was frozen in her seat when his teasing way turned from Lady Jane to Grandmama—and Grandmama fell right under his spell. Before long it was Grandmama who had a finely shaped mouth pressed to her glove, and who was laughing and denying a series of compliments of her own from the fellow.

The sight not only kept Pamela from slapping or demanding his removal, but it also kept her in her seat. It was impossible not to notice that Marchmont was just as charming with Grandmama as he had been with Lady Jane, the difference of forty years in age between one and the other seemingly unnoted by him. Perhaps . . . perhaps he simply did not know any other way to act around women. Perhaps his flirting was just flirting, and ought not to be so very damning. After all, many people flirted; it was an art, and one Pamela had always thought herself rather accomplished at. Did she not herself intend to captivate Captain Penford with her own charm and wit?

Well, perhaps she had met the Master of the Art . . . and perhaps she ought not to blame him for exercising his craft as cunningly as he did. The thought of such an art, a talent, almost made her smile, both in a kind of relief and a sense of returning comprehension. After all, what did it matter to her whether or not Marchmont wished to dally with a hundred other ladies? If anything, she ought to be relieved that his fancy had so soon shifted from her.

The time for this call was nearly at an end, she noted, as she felt a calmness return and settle over her. She sat and watched, far more wisely than she might have but a minute earlier, and waited for him to go away. Now that she knew his nature, he had no power to disrupt her life . . . and her plans for the future. Her future with Captain Penford.

His words of exit were long in coming, for he had stayed, most inappropriately, for over an hour. First he bid adieu to his hostess—this time only sketching a kiss in the air above Mama's hand, as a gentleman ought—but then he kissed Grandmama on both cheeks, as though they were long-time friends and not brand-new acquaintances. Of course, her grandmama and his had come out the same Season, so perhaps it was not outside the bounds that he presumed an acquaintance . . . and Grandmama allowed the action, smiling as she patted his cheek with one hand, even while with a funny kind of laughing asperity she called him a "gilt-tongued rogue."

He shook hands with Owen, bowed an airy kiss over Lady Jane's hand and told her her conversation "has begun the day with such radiance of wit that I despair any brighter conversation is to be found outside your company," and finally came to Pamela's side.

He bowed before her, putting out one hand. She offered her own in return, expecting the same salute he had given the others, but instead he took her hand and pulled her unexpectedly to her feet. "You will see me to the door? How kind," he announced.

She gave him a level look—meant to tell him that he had lost the ability to fluster her—and replied evenly, " 'Twould be my pleasure, my lord."

He put her hand on his arm, bowed shallowly one last time to the room at large, and pulled her from the room.

He stopped before the door, where Lawlton made a bow that acknowledged he would retrieve my lord's hat and cane, and turned to smile down at her. "What a pleasant morning! Do you know, I have discovered another good thing about you."

"And what is that?" she asked, not sure whether to allow herself to be amused by him or not. However, the oft-present amusement in his eyes—a fiery light she was beginning to accept might truly be irrepressible, despite constant attempts to extinguish it—decided her, and she smiled in return.

"I have discovered that you have been raised in a household full of newspapers."

"That is well?" she asked in some surprise.

"Oh, excellent. I adore newspapers. They may tell one anything one wishes to know about a city. Where to go, whom to see, whom to be seen with, what blood to back at the races! Do tell me you at least read the society pages, and then I shall be utterly convinced that we should wed."

"I thought you already were." Really, he was quite absurd in his "devotion," poor paltry thing that it had proved to be, she thought, her mouth twitching at the corners.

"Mostly so, although I am still willing to merely have a torrid love affair with you, recall."

After giving him a speaking look, she ignored his comment and answered his question. "I read as much of the paper as Papa allows."

At the pleased nod he gave, she could feel her own smile broadening and creating a dimple at the right side of her mouth. He was most irresistible when he gave that pleased and flattering smile of his, and that was only the truth.

"How charming," he said, his voice having dropped as he reached one finger to touch the dimple.

"Oh, charming!" she laughed even as she scoffed, batting his finger away. "I have found you out, Marchmont. That compliment just now, in fact all your compliments, have no more weight than a feather! You see, now I know that you find simply *everything* charming.''

"A great many things, but not everything. And certainly not everyone,'' he said, his head cocking at an angle, his eyes strangely sober for once.

"You seem puzzled—or perhaps, disappointed—that I have divined your character.''

"What is my character?''

"That you say very pretty things, but one is not to take such utterings seriously.''

"But *you* may take me seriously when I speak of my admiration,'' he said, and there was no mistaking the lack of humor in his voice now.

"I may *not*,'' she laughed, and then saw that he did not laugh with her, a discomfiting experience. She took a half step back, and explained further with a wag of her finger, "I will confess you almost turned my head earlier. I almost believed you; but then of course I saw you with Lady Jane, and at last I understood. Do not look so cast down! I am quite content to understand your intentions at last.''

"I had thought I had stated my intentions clearly. Do not tell me you mistook my attentions toward Lady Jane as being anything other than cordiality?''

"Mistook? No. I see that now quite clearly; it is your purpose and your ambition in life to be all that is cordial, regardless of the company in which you find yourself.''

"Is Lady Jane's behavior not all that one could wish?''

"Lady Jane is a very good friend of mine, and all that is proper. I did not mean to disparage her. I was pointing out a simple fact. To that matter, let me say that I noted you flirted just as outrageously with my grandmama as you did with Jane. But that is my point: you would flirt with a sailing ship, and just because someone once thought to call such a vessel a 'she.' ''

"Why, Pamela," he said, the disturbance on his face disappearing as a new smile dawned over his features, "I do believe you are jealous!" He caught up her hand, and made as though he would raise it to his lips.

Lawlton appeared, bearing the missing hat and cane. Pamela snatched her hand away, twin spots of color appearing high on her cheekbones. "Hardly that!" she cried in a small voice, giving a nervous glance toward the butler.

"Your blush betrays you, my dear," he drawled as he accepted the items from Lawlton. The curly beaver went on his head, the cane under his arm, and he pulled his gloves from the coat pocket. As he tugged them on, he said, "It seems clear to me that you misunderstood. Do you not recall that you and I have an agreement?"

She cast another glance at the butler, and shook her head once, denying Marchmont the right to continue.

He either did not see the motion or ignored it. "Minutes, my dear. You are to give me as many minutes as you give Penford. The same must hold for me; I shall give whomever I care to as many minutes as I give you. Now, that seems fair, does it not?" His gloves in place, he lowered his cane and leaned both hands on its silver top in an expectant posture, awaiting her answer.

Her head swam just a little—she was not used to such complexity in conversation—and she found herself nodding mutely.

He nodded, then caught up her hand again. "Adieu," he said, pressing warm lips to her ungloved hand, lips that lingered a fraction too long and made her blush anew before the servant.

"Good day, my lord," she said curtly, snatching her hand away once more, and turned her back to him with a swish of her skirts.

She strode away, not looking over her shoulder, and hoping his hand was still raised and his lips still pursed, for then there was some hope that he looked as ridiculous as he had the habit of making her feel.

Chapter 6

"There you are!" her mother said for the second time that day.

Pamela startled, almost dropping the delicate scissors she held in her right hand. She looked up from the work spread before her, her mouth tightening just a little to have her mother come into her room without so much as a knock. Mama did not really approve of the way she spent her leisure time, sniffing and assuring her daughter that "ladies do not play with toys" although Pamela always hastened to assure her she was not so much playing as constructing gifts. Not since she was thirteen would she admit that half the pleasure of making those gifts came from manipulating or admiring the end result before it must be given away. She even pretended that the doll house, the tea set, and the other games, puzzles, and toys from her own childhood that filled her room were merely being kept so that one day they might go to her own children.

Before her lay a stiff rectangle of paper upon which

she had drawn a scene of trees, now colored and resplendent in their summer green leaves. All about her, and indeed all about her bedchamber, were tiny paper clippings, cakes of color, brushes, pieces of paper, leads, bits of string, and small pots of gum arabic. She was just about to finish assembling a paper toy she was making, and since Mama had already come in and seen her at the practice, she was not about to cease. "Mama?" she inquired.

"You and your papers!" Mama scolded. "Only see how your dressing drawers' tops are forever cluttered."

" 'Twill be Liza's birthday soon. I must get this done in time."

"You need not make a new one for each birthday. You positively spoil your cousins."

"Oh, but I enjoy it, and they delight so in them," Pamela assured her mother even as she began to accordion a long, thin sheet of paper. The tree scene before her was intended to be the final card in a row of scene cards, which—when set on end, one behind the other, each several inches apart and held in place by a long, accordioned strip of thin paper gummed at either side of each card—would allow Liza to look through the hole in the first card that she might view a dimensional picture. Once all the cards were secured in place, the toy would be almost a foot long. Pamela knew how much her little cousin enjoyed a walk in the park, so she had been at great pains to recreate a lively park scene for the girl. On the first card was a carefully drawn and cut-out scene of a little brown-haired girl chasing a squirrel, and four more scene cards behind that showed people walking their dogs; carriages with fine horses driving through the park; a water fountain spouting in what she hoped was a realistic bit of artwork; and finally this scene with the tall and green-leaved trees intended for the farthest card. She unfolded the thin sheet in her hand, then reached for the nearest pot of gum arabic, intent on gumming the scenes in order, one several inches behind the other until they were in a tidy, albeit rather flimsy, upright line.

"Leave that for now, my dear. We have more callers."

Pamela opened her mouth to comment on a decided lack of need for further socializing, but her mother spoke before she could get out the protest. "Captain Penford has just come to call."

"Oh," Pamela replied, her face flushing with unexpected pleasure. She rose at once, removing her protective apron and brushing bits of paper from her skirts, as she followed in her mother's wake.

Mama was right: Captain Penford *did* have a great deal of red in his mustache. Not that it was unattractive. If anything, it was striking when one first encountered him anew, a shade that reflected well the red facings of his blue military coat. Furthermore, the multiple gold lacings on that facing brought out the golden highlights of the hair on his head, which was revealed as he doffed the black shako with its single, short white plume. The single epaulet on his right shoulder served to emphasize the breadth of his shoulders, as straight and true as the sabre he wore suspended from a white leather strap at his hip. All this, with the white breeches that completed his apparel, revealed a man in prime condition, one who had the youth, the funds, the bearing, and the family to support his military career in some style. In fact, Pamela thought while allowing herself to indulge in an appreciative glance as she entered the room, the only thing that marred his appearance was the fact that he wore but one hessian, while his other foot was swathed in bandages and a soft kid leather pump. She noted he had chosen to remain standing, leaning back a bit with all his weight on his good foot. It was as if he went out of his way not to lean on the cane, as though he refused, or resented, the need to cater to his own injury.

"Captain Penford, I believe you know my daughter, Lady Pamela?" Her mother moved forward, bringing Pamela to her side with a proud glance.

Captain Penford turned and made a half bow in Pamela's direction, and she was shocked to see a mild look of mere polite interest on his face. It was abundantly clear he did not recognize her.

Pamela recovered her poise quickly—after all, they had but met twice before, and that in the midst of a ball and then a garden party, and she had been only one young lady among many, and he with a fresh wound to distract his attention. Just because the gallant young officer had captured her notice, it was most vain to assume she had captured his. "Captain Penford," she said, making a curtsy, "how pleasant to see you again. We met at Lady Thornthwaite's garden party."

The recollection of the event showed now in his

expression, and she could see that he searched his memory for a vision of her. "Oh, of course," he said in a deep, resonating voice, one obviously used to being heard over the sounds of the Royal Artillery battalions. "Please pardon my lapse. I was not aware that you are Viscount Powell's sister."

"Did I hear my name, and was it being kindly used?" Owen said from the open doorway.

"Powell," Captain Penford acknowledged him, nodding in his direction, turning his torso to face toward Owen that he need not shift his footing.

"My dear, you are already acquainted with Captain Penford?" Lady Premington asked as Owen came into the room.

"Indeed! We are engaged to attend a viewing at Tattersall's this afternoon."

The captain explained, "I am afraid the event that injured my extremity also cost me a very fine mount."

Lady Premington and Pamela made noises of commiseration, and Lady Premington turned to lift the pot that sat on a tray near her chair. "Do you care for lemon tea? It is all the rage in Russia, and I have quite developed a taste for it myself—"

"Not at all, Mama," Owen said at once. "We are just leaving. And I shall dine tonight at my club, so I shall see you when I see you again; and you are not to put back supper on my account. Come along, Penford, for I hear this horse is a prime bit of blood with a steady nerve, just the creature a military man would require."

Captain Penford bid the ladies good day and turned,

making use of his cane, and within a moment the two were gone from the room.

Pamela looked at her mother, exclaiming in a stricken voice, "He did not come to see *me* at all!"

"No," her mother could only agree, looking most annoyed. Then her face cleared, and she said, "But nonetheless, he has made the connection that you are Owen's sister, and as they seem to have struck up an acquaintance, that can only be for the good. Do not despair, my dear. I suspect we shall see the captain many more times before he returns to his unit, and it shan't be just to call upon Owen, mark my words."

Pamela allowed herself to slump into a chair's cushions in a fashion that she never would have adopted had the gentlemen still been in the room. She sighed, though not unhappily. "Mama, is he not just the finest fellow you have ever seen?"

"Very fine," Mama agreed, not bothering to hide her smile at the signs of her daughter's first infatuation.

Pamela did not notice, lost to thought as she was. She knew that given Mama's aversion to the captain's mere military rank, this was rather high praise from the lady indeed. So, Mama would not oppose her, that was clear, and Owen seemed to hold the man in some regard. Papa would agree with whatever Mama declared to be fitting. There were no obstacles to the marital bliss she envisioned before her—except for the gentleman himself, perhaps. Really, she could wish he had displayed some remembrance of her, or if not that, then at least a little reluctance to part from her company. It was not time to surrender the field yet, however! She would have to work quickly, for the man would be gone soon—the thought of his return to a battlefield made her frown terribly—and so it was not a time for subtlety. She must see if, perhaps through Owen, the captain could be brought to many of the occasions that would put her in best light. Candlelight, dancing . . . well, no, not dancing of course . . . but gay conversation, a dozen meals enjoyed in one another's company. . . . Yes, there was no reason to suppose the captain's current indifference would maintain for long, not under the assault she planned to lead against his hopefully inferior defenses.

Pamela scratched the last entry from the list before her. No, she could not contrive to appear to faint and then expect that anyone would then take her driving, no matter how prettily she claimed to need a bit of air. She would be made to lie upon a sofa, or go upstairs to her bed, surely.

She put another line through the one she had just made, her hand on her chin as she sat at her escritoire, searching her mind for ways to maneuver Captain Penford into taking her for a drive through the park. Merely asking him had merit, of course, but then he would be free to say no. That would never do. No, she needed some way, some series of events, that would make him automatically offer and keep him from declining the opportunity. After all, he could still surely drive, despite his foot, could he not?

There was a scratching at her door. "Come in," she called, tucking the piece of paper inside her diary.

Her maid, Phyllis, entered, bobbing a curtsy. "There be a gennlemun to see yer, Lady Pamela."

Pamela felt a smile spread across her lips. "Is it Captain Penford?"

"No, miss. It be Lord Marchmont."

Pamela turned back to her desk, exasperated to find he had returned for a second time this day. Did the man have no sense of propriety? She said crisply, "Please tell him I am not at home."

"Beggin' yer pardon, miss, but he said as how yer'd say as much. He bid me say . . . well, miss, these were his words. . . ."

Pamela turned back to the girl, suspicion floating into her eyes at the hesitation the girl exhibited.

"He said as I was to say, miss, that yer be a coward."

Pamela's eyebrows shot up, and her lips narrowed down to a thin line. "The man has a colossal nerve," she said, rising to her feet, "and so I shall tell him." Which, she knew, was exactly what he had wished to happen, but she decided to face him nonetheless, for the man truly needed a set-down, and she was quite in a frame of mind to give it to him.

He was standing in the front parlor, peering down into the teapot. As soon as he saw her approaching, he made a face and commented, "Lemon tea—ugh! I detest it."

"I should order you a pot of ordinary tea *if* you were staying," Pamela said by way of greeting as she came to stand before him, arms crossed.

"You are ready to go out, then?" He smiled at

her, as though he could not hear the lack of hospitality in her voice.

"Go out?" She frowned.

"Yes, I thought we would go driving. 'Tis the fashionable hour, and the day is most pleasant. I daresay a cloak is unnecessary; a pelisse would be sufficient. I am content to wait, tea-less, while you fetch one."

"I never said I would go driving with you."

"You never said you would not."

"You never asked!"

"Pamela, will you go driving with me this fine afternoon?"

"Oh!" she cried, flouncing into the nearest settee, her arms still crossed, her expression mulish.

"Are you well?"

"I am quite well—"

"Then whatever has put that pained expression on your face? You look positively pinched—"

"Thank you"—her voice dripped with sarcasm—"for the compliment."

He laughed then, though the motion he made with one hand reflected puzzlement. "Truly, what has set your back up at me?"

"I have never in my life been called a coward before," she said with a dark look.

"Well, you proved me wrong by coming down, so I ask your forgiveness for the phrase. It worked to a nicety though, did it not?"

"I have to think your nanny tried to teach you that a lady is 'not home' if she says she is 'not home,' regardless of where her person happens in fact to be. There is nothing cowardly in claiming a few minutes' peace, howsoever one is forced to do so. But never mind your lack of training. I am here now only to tell you that your lapse in manners is not forgiven. It will, however, be forgotten if you will but do me the favor of making an exit, at once if you please." She stood, inclining her head in a sign of dismissal. She made as though to leave the room, but he caught her arm, staying her.

"You have not answered whether or not you would go driving out with me?"

"I should think that answer would be obvious."

"Pamela, what is this? Are you reneging on your word? Did you not say you would allow me to court you?" he asked seriously.

"This is not a courtship! It is a . . . a dictatorship! I am to do whatever you say, whenever you say, or else risk being called names and hounded in my home. I would have to say it is *you* who have reneged on our bargain."

"In what way? I have not embarrassed you before anyone—"

"Before my maid, you did!" she said warmly.

He waved the comment away. "And as for the rest of your claims, all I did was ask you for a drive. I daresay that is as proper as a gentleman may be, and yet you do not even deign to give me an answer." He put on an offended look, the effect of which was marred by the laughter in his eyes.

She hung her head in exasperation, shaking it a little from side to side. She sighed, then lifted her head to say, "My lord, you and I both know you never truly say things the way you claim to have done.

But—no, do not speak!'' She held up a warning hand. ''You win! I shall go with you. I have said you shall have some of my time, and so you shall, and that suits me better now than later. *My* word, as you see, has substance and meaning.'' She moved as though to leave the room and fetch her wrap, but she paused to add, ''And understand you—just so you do not think me a brainless, spineless creature—I am well aware I am letting you have your way.''

''You will let me have my way with you?'' he asked, eyes dancing as he grinned.

She threw him another dark look, belatedly realizing that she had summoned no maid or companion to serve as chaperone. She had been too ready to box his ears, and had quite forgotten the proprieties in her eagerness to give him a set-down. She could only blame herself for the oversight, and she was not about to allow him to see her discomfiture at the fact. She lifted her chin and pronounced, ''I will spend the allotted time with you, but be forewarned that I am quite prepared to ignore your various impertinences.'' He lifted an eyebrow in a kind of challenge, but she refused to further rise to the bait, saying, ''We may go as soon as I fetch my wrap.''

And my maid, she thought as she left the parlor without a backward glance, annoyed to find that the necessity of exiting in high dudgeon was becoming a common occurrence.

As she chose a pelisse, she shook her head, reviewing the scene just past and her initial response to his obviously planned goad. She ought to have learned by now that there was no winning a verbal battle with the man. Obviously, the only way to be completely free of him—for he had proved her home was no barrier to him—would be to remove herself from London altogether, and that she could not do. Captain Penford had claimed he was to have but three more weeks before he must return to his duty, and she would have to be near him daily to accomplish anything in so short a time. She did not expect a marriage, of course, in that time, nor even particularly an offer, but she was highly hopeful that he would at least pledge his heart. They could then exchange letters, get to know each other a little better that way, and then the offer would be forthcoming . . . probably the next time he was free to return to London . . . or perhaps even in writing, if the loneliness and anxiety of war became so unbearable that he must have a golden hope on which to cling. . . .

Yes, Marchmont must be endured if her plans were to go forward, but that did not mean she had to pay him the slightest heed when he was in one of his teasing humors. She had given her word, and had found a way to live up to it that should prove to be . . . well, if not comfortable, than at least acceptable.

As she descended the stairs to the front parlor, she was aware that a slight smile had come back to her lips, and she hoped above all things that the smile would give the impudent Lord Marchmont pause.

Chapter 7

As Marchmont guided the two horses pulling his curricle through Regent's Park, avoiding recent construction which partially blocked the Inner Circle path, he said, "You need not call me Marchmont."

"Of course I need call you thusly! What would you have me do?" Pamela replied with a smile and a shake of her head. She did not even look at him, instead looking about at the recent botanical installations. Here and there some items were out of place or missing, giving the park an unfinished air, but putting that aside it was truly becoming a most attractive place.

She hated to admit it, even to herself, but being driven about in a smart carriage by an attractive man on a fine spring day had quite lifted her spirits. Now that the air was clear between them, she had allowed herself to relax and enjoy not only the surroundings, but the company as well.

"You could call me by my given name, of course."

Pamela turned her head to glance back at the little maid who rode on the groom's seat behind them, but Phyllis seemed to have ceased to attend her betters, as she was busy tossing bread crumbs from a rolled paper down toward a variety of birds and squirrels as the high curricle rolled slowly along. Had the girl been attending, Pamela probably would have retreated behind primness but instead she decided to put her new strategy in place by asking him rather boldly, "But what *is* your given name, Lord Marchmont?"

"Theopholus." He shrugged at the questioning lift of her eyebrows. "Theopholus Dunmire. Yes, I am afraid it is so," he assured her.

"That settles the matter, then." She smiled.

"What matter would that be?"

"The matter of whether or not I should ever marry you."

"My name prevents you from marrying me?" he asked in disbelief, though he did not frown.

"Oh, yes. I could never marry a man named Theopholus. I should want to laugh every time I needed to call his name."

He pretended to look offended, allowing his brows to draw together as he attempted to form a frown, but he was defeated by his own grin. "But 'Theo,' now, that is surely acceptable? I daresay I prefer it myself. Scarcely a soul calls me Theopholus, but my mother when I am to be scolded. Admit it, Pamela, 'Theo' is not so very unpleasant."

"Theo," she repeated, feeling rather daring. Her eye met his, and suddenly the warmth there rather unsettled her. She turned away, pretending to be suddenly absorbed in Phyllis's task of feeding the recently returned swallows.

After a long silence, he asked, "Well?"

"I suppose it is not too atrocious a name," she said, still refusing to look at him.

"Thank you for the compliment." His voice dripped with sarcasm, an echo of the very tone and words she had given him but an hour earlier in her parlor.

She sneaked a look up at him, to see if he was as rankled as his tone implied, finding instead an animated face rather like a pixie's, she thought, if only a pixie might be as tall and broad of shoulder as he. His look invited her to join his amusement, and suddenly she was laughing, and he was laughing with her. Even Phyllis turned to smile at them, not understanding the joke, but captured and involved by their amusement nonetheless.

Several heads turned to find the location of such merriment, which only caused them to laugh the more. Pamela could feel a blush spreading across her cheeks, but she was unable to cease laughing. "Just as when I was a girl," she managed to gasp out at last, raising a kerchief to the corner of her eye to dab at the moisture there.

"How is that?"

"I was commenting on the fact that when I was a girl I used to start giggling, and then there was no stopping me," Pamela explained, still smiling.

Marchmont nodded approvingly. "And you say you are not a gay creature! I knew that to be a plumper

78

the moment I heard it. I was of that same inclination myself as a child. I was forever being pinched in church, until they learned it only made me jump and laugh all the harder.''

"I know!'' she said with an unexpected eagerness. It was a pleasant surprise to have someone else admit to having been poorly behaved in chapel. Owen had done no worse than occasionally swing his legs until he had earned a frown from one or the other of his parents. He had seemed a veritable angel next to his restless sister, who was forever whispering, or squirming, or crawling under the seats, to Mama's horror. "Mama used to fix me with the harshest eye, and then it was all I could do not to yelp with mirth. A nervous reaction, I rather suppose. If a glance could kill, I should have certainly been struck dead when I reached the age of thirteen.''

"At thirteen things changed?''

She nodded. "It was after my cousin Phillipa's wedding.''

"A wedding,'' he repeated, grinning down at her. "Tell me more.''

"Of the wedding?''

"Yes, and your reprehensible behavior there.''

"It *was* reprehensible. I shudder to think of it now.''

"You must go on,'' he urged, even as he clucked the horse to a slightly faster pace, now that the path was open and clear.

"I was giggly through the service, which was bad enough, but afterward, at the breakfast, I drank too much champagne.'' She made a face and blushed. "I recited a poem to the newly married couple. It was not quite decent, I am afraid. I had learned it from one of the stable lads. Mama boxed my ears for days afterward, every time she saw me. I had to write an apology note and deliver it myself, which was almost as dreadful as having my ears boxed.''

"And now you and your cousin are quite close?''

Pamela gave a crooked smile, well aware he believed otherwise. "Phillipa will hardly speak to me, even though it was five years ago. I suppose I am at least grateful she does not give me the cut direct.''

His mouth slanted upward as well. "Tell me more.''

"Of the wedding? There's little more to tell, except for the poem, and—believe me—I shall never repeat *that*. My ears burn in remembrance at the very thought.''

"No, I meant of your childhood.''

She blushed anew, lowering her eyes from his sparkling green ones. She could not help but note that she was forever laughing or blushing in this gentleman's company; it seemed there was no middle ground to be had with him. Now the conversation had crept toward the kind of intimacy one shared only with close friends, and she had not meant to arrive at this destination. "Oh, there is not much to tell. I daresay it was exactly the same as that of any girl. Schooling, watercolors, dance instruction, and the like.''

"Is that all you shall tell me?'' He did not sound unduly upset at her reticence.

She nodded shyly.

"Then shall I tell you something of *my* childhood?"

She looked at the birds Phyllis was feeding and clucking to, and then nodded, again shyly. She ought not to encourage this, she knew, but she could not deny a curiosity about him. And, besides, they had to speak of *something,* and at least this topic might not bring her to the blush.

"I was the eldest of four boys," Marchmont said, "which is why I was so unfortunate as to be named after my grandfather. I ought to have been the youngest, I believe, for *I* have the profligate nature, and the youngest, Robbie, has the guardian instincts. He looks after the family in a way I never shall. We all depend on him, and he only one-and-twenty years!" He hesitated for a moment, and she could not be sure, but it seemed he glanced down at the ring on his hand. He went on, "In recent years I have learned never to make an investment without first seeing if Robbie finds it an acceptable scheme. It is in part through his wise counsel that our family estates have grown considerably since my father had the good sense to finally stick his spoon in the wall."

Pamela looked up, faintly shocked at the cavalier attitude the man had toward his father's demise, but she said nothing.

He intercepted that look. "You must understand my father was a dour man. I think the poor creature was born without a sense of humor. By some strange and quite possibly unkind twist of fate, I arrived with double the normal allotment of same. I have sometimes wondered if he gave away his humor when I was conceived, or if I stole it from him at that unguarded moment.''

"Lord Marchmont," Pamela scolded, waving a hand as though the action might wave away his uncensored words.

"There I go again, speaking my thoughts as they come to me," he said, and she knew that was as much of an apology as she would receive. "My two other brothers are Caldwell—a silly pup who even now is doing his best to distinguish or sacrifice himself in the attempt to reestablish the Bourbon in Napoleon's place—and Dalton, a rather scholarly fellow with no noticeable common sense of which to speak, for he reads with one eye and gambles away piles of blunt with the other. So, you see, we are all strange creatures of one sort or another.

"In our father's eyes we certainly had flawed natures, even Robbie, who was too young when Father finally turned up his toes to have made much more of an impression than to have been occasionally snarled at. When Father noticed him, it was to snap at him for 'staring with those big, unblinking eyes of yours.' Now he never stares. Scarcely lifts his head from the estate reports, poor sot, and therefore misses a great deal of what is going on around him. Oh, not in the way of management—that is where he excels—but in life itself. He does not see the pretty girl smile, or pause to hear the end of a tune. But that is the way of it with all of us: we four chose a way to overcome our father's gloomy and oppressive rearing by excelling in our various zeals. Myself, the nonsensical rake; Caldwell, the zealous soldier; Dalton, the book-loving spendthrift; and Robbie, quiet and unobjectionable, who I fear will become as sticklike as our father if he must continue to carry too much of the weight of the estate on those young shoulders.''

Pamela shook her head, uncertain if she should comment, and surprised to find Marchmont had this much insight into his family's nature . . . and his own. It was very vulgar of them to be discussing such matters; but the stopper had already been taken out of the bottle, so there was no point in wasting the chance to sip at the usually forbidden wine.

When he did not speak, she did. ''What do you propose to do to help Robbie?''

''So he may be 'Robbie' to you, but I must be 'Lord Marchmont'?'' he teased with an arched brow.

'' 'Young Dunmire,' then.''

''That is better. We cannot have me becoming jealous of my wise counselor. But you surprise me: you seem to be able to think of me as someone who might actually provide some assistance, a kind of useful chap to have about. I cannot tell you how that pleases and encourages me.''

She made a face, speaking lightly, ''I did not mean to please or encourage you in any way.''

''Of course you did not. As to your question: I have already hired a steward to assist us with the new Suffolk estate, and tomorrow Robbie and I are meeting with gentlemen from a counting house. That will relieve the boy of some of the mountainous piles of paper, of the calculation of facts and figures involved, although it will still require quarterly monitoring, of course.'' He glanced down at her, then back at the path before them. "Will it destroy my reputation as a ne'er-do-well if I admit to you that I am attempting to learn something of farming, to help the boy? I've a keen eye for cattle and thought I might become the 'resident expert' in that one matter, and oversee that portion of estate affairs for him."

She sat beside him, surprised to find she was warmed by more than the spring sunlight. Despite the teasing quality that inevitably resided under their words, she could not help but hear, too, the rather startling fact that Marchmont cared for someone other than himself, cared enough to allow that person's welfare to interrupt him at his far more usual pursuit of self-entertainment. "Yes," she answered in a quiet voice, "it would destroy that particular reputation."

"Why, Pamela," he said in mock surprise, "do I hear something like approval in your voice?"

"Something like, though now you make me wonder if I have merely been manipulated again," she said, glancing at him from the corner of her eye.

"I daresay you have, although I will swear to you that it was not my intention when I began. Indeed, my intention was to reveal my brother Caldwell to you."

"Why?" she asked simply. The full teasing was back in his voice, and for a moment she almost could have doubted the sincerity of a moment ago. Almost, but not quite.

"Because he is the family's soldier, and in some ways more thick-skulled than Dalton. I wanted you to see his devotion is first and foremost to the army— and therefore you must see I am implying this is how it would be with the devotion of another military man, of whom we both could recall a name."

She laughed at the attempted disparagement of Captain Penford, just as the carriage rolled free of the park, heading toward her home in Mayfair. "I have already understood and accepted that fact as regards the good captain," she informed him.

"Have you?" He made a comically terrible face. "Then I shall have to think of some other condemning assessment of the man."

"You shall have some difficulty in that regard."

He merely hmmphed, giving her a patently false sour look that made her laugh again.

As they stopped before her home, a footman came forward to hold the reins Marchmont tossed to him. The Baron then jumped down, came around the carriage, and offered a hand up to first Phyllis, and then Pamela. Before she could remove her hand from his, he had gathered up the other one, looking down into her eyes. "So now you have heard how it is with my family and estate. Is it not clear to you that I need a wife to help me settle into the role of respectable landowner?"

"That is very clear. It is simply that I shall not be that wife," she said, nodding her head as though her own earnestness might cause him to accept the words.

He leaned down, to whisper in her ear, that the maid not overhear. "Very well, if it must be as you say, it must. You will marry your precious captain, and I shall marry some cow-faced creature who is good with figures and plans for the future. However, all of this can occur only if you will promise to spend every night with me.''

She just managed to keep from snatching her hands away, for that would only excite the maid's interest in the sudden tête-à-tête he had created. She forced her voice to remain calm, perhaps even slightly amused. ''You really must attempt to develop a more steadfast proposal, my lord. I vow that should I ever grant you an affirmative answer, I would not know for a certainty what I was agreeing to.''

He made as though to respond, but she did not allow it, instead going on to ask briskly, ''Now, have you the current time?''

He reached for his waistcoat, his fingers finding and running the length of a simple gold chain, which led to a fob pocket from whence he pulled his watch. He thumbed open the lid and glanced at its face. '' 'Tis six o'clock.''

''Then I gave you two hours of my time. Pray do not call again until I send a note stating that . . . er''—she glanced at the maid, who was standing patiently at hand—''er, the other gentleman has received his due time.''

''Lady Pamela, you are a hard one,'' he sighed, releasing her hands. ''But you should be aware: those of us who play all the time enjoy a hard race. It keeps us fresh, and reignites the fiery thrill of the contest.''

''Good evening, my lord.''

''Good evening, my dear. Dream of me tonight.''

She did not answer that absurdity as she walked up the steps to the front door, but despite herself she could not keep from smiling as Phyllis opened the door for her.

Grandmama came down for dinner, an unusual event. She normally took a tray in her room, for her knees bothered her a great deal and she could not like having to climb the stairs to her room any more than she must. Pamela observed this fact absently, for the dinner conversation was the same as always and did not in any wise excite her to the point of involving herself. Instead her attention wandered, returning to the events of the day. Captain Penford had come to call—a less than satisfactory call, since it had been clear he had not intended to call on her, but rather Owen. Still, he would be unable to claim a lack of introduction now, and that was to the good. The day had also brought a drive out with Marchmont—a far more pleasant experience than she had anticipated, even given his unfortunate lack of verbal restraint. That thought led her to wonder if he truly would not come to call until she had sent a missive permitting as much. It seemed unlikely, given his nature; he would do as he pleased, and, for now, it pleased him to call on her. And tease her. And make her frown to think how she might persuade him to stop. She was only glad she could not take him at all seriously, for then his attentions might form a serious dilemma. She could not like to hurt him, for all that he was quite unmanageable, for it had become clear to her that at his core there were some finer, softer feelings. Admittedly one had to search them out, but they were there nonetheless.

A titter of laughter caused her to look up, directly at Grandmama, for it was she who was laughing. Mama had apparently said something amusing, at least to Grandmama's mind. Mama herself was not laughing, but rather pursuing her lips and giving her parent a disapproving glare. "Honestly, Mama!" Lady Premington chided, "must you always color my words?"

"I did not say a word. All I did was laugh," Grandmama defended herself, not even attempting to look contrite. In fact, instead she looked over at her granddaughter, silently inviting Pamela to laugh along with her. Since Pamela had missed the moment, all she could do was give a nod and a smile.

Lady Premington turned to her husband to complain, "All I said was that he was 'well into it' with his wife, and she began to whoop as though . . . well, you know very well how one must take such amusement, when all I meant was that he was having an innocent squabble with his lady—"

"I would not have laughed, nor you blushed, if we had not both seen with our own eyes that these public squabbles of Lord and Lady Niall always lead to an absence of the same from their own parties. It is quite clear it is a form of sport for them. An Amorous Game, if you will. Your choice of words were, therefore, most amusing—"

"Mama!" Lady Premington stiffened, casting significant glances toward Pamela.

"Piffle! Young ladies are too much in the dark

these days, to my mind. Why, in my day when a girl got married she had a real sense of what it meant, not this 'swans and cupids' foolishness that exists today. Bound to be disappointed if she thinks babies are dropped down chimneys—"

"Mama!" Lady Premington cried again, coming to her feet, her expression outraged.

Pamela lowered her eyes—long since having learned that the longer she might accidentally be forgotten in the heat of the moment and thereby allowed to remain at such quibbles, the more she was likely to learn about forbidden subjects—and hid a smile. Mama would be surprised indeed to know what Pamela knew about any number of subjects, but that was a secret she and Grandmama had always kept between themselves. It had always been a source of amusement to Pamela that she was raised in a house rife with rumor and tattle all day long, but in their private sessions of an evening, suddenly there were any number of things she was expected not to know or even be curious about. Fortunately Grandmama had always answered her questions, telling her without hesitation that the more Pamela knew of men and "their expectations," the better equipped she would be to avoid the rum ones.

"I believe this meal is at a close," Lady Premington announced in a voice that trembled slightly.

Her parent did not argue, instead setting aside her serviette and rising to her feet. "Now I remember the other reason I take a tray in my room," that lady muttered as she headed toward the stairs.

Pamela stood also, a thought having just struck

her: it had been a long time since she and Grand-mama had had a chat.

Grandmama was in her favorite chair in her sitting room, before the fire with a lap rug over her legs and a lending library book open in her lap, when Pamela's knock had gained permission to enter.

"Why, Pamela! Come in, child, it has been a while since we have sat together. Come in!"

Pamela crossed at once to Grandmama's side, finding the old carved oak stool where she had sat many a time before at her grandparent's elbow.

"I thought you appeared distracted at dinner," Grandmama said at once. "You have come to discuss something of importance with me."

Pamela laughed. "Nothing escapes you, does it, Grandmama? But I would beg to differ: I do not think it too terribly important. I have a minor concern, one at which I believe you might excel in advising me."

"Oh, *love* then, is it?"

Pamela shook her head, still grinning. "Oh, yes, I do think I am in love, but that is not the source of my concern."

"In love, child? And this the first I have heard of it? You have neglected me! Tell me all." Grandmama set the book aside on the table at her other elbow, leaning forward with eagerness.

"Well, the 'love' part is Captain Penford, al-though I must own that he scarce knows I exist. But I can see to changing that, particularly since he is an acquaintance of Owen's."

"Penford? What family?"

"Waller."

"Ah! The second son, the military man—of course! A satisfactory choice, my dear. That is, if he is handsome." She gave her granddaughter a wide wink.

Pamela laughed at the vulgarism, just as she had since she was very little. "Oh, he is that, although even *I* must admit it is a rather rugged sort of handsome."

"That would imply backbone. Has he any?"

"So it would seem. He is in London for but a few weeks, recuperating from a wound. They say he was already wounded by the time of the charge, and still he led it, at least until his horse was shot from under him. The battalion went on to victory, and he was mentioned in the dispatches. It is said that some people have used the word 'hero' to describe his acts," Pamela said the last bit with pride, her eyes glittering with admiration.

"Hhmmphh," Grandmama made a noncommittal but mildly approving noise. "So you feel no difficulty toward him. What is your concern, then?"

Pamela knitted her hands together, circling her knees with her linked arms. "I have another suitor."

"And?" Grandmama obviously saw no difficulty in that regard.

"And he is most insistent. He has already asked me to marry him."

Grandmama's dark eyes, so like Mama's sharp ones, danced in her head. "And you told him no?"

"I did, but he refuses to accept my answer."

"Who is he?"

"Lord Marchmont."

"The rogue!" Grandmama cried in surprise, her hand going to her heart and a frown growing in the eyes that had been dancing a moment ago.

"Exactly so."

It was a moment before Grandmama recovered her poise, but then she sniffed, "My dear, you ought to feel most complimented. Proves your worth, let me tell you. I never thought to see *that* one propose."

"Even he owns as much. I believe that he fancies himself truly in love . . . or something like. I should tell you that even though I say no, he then immediately asks if I will become his mistress."

For a moment, Pamela thought Grandmama would rise from her chair, seize up a walking stick, charge from the house to locate the man and strike him senseless. The anger on that otherwise respectable face was quite startling. Just as suddenly the anger quelled, lost behind a battle to restrain tears. Pamela looked up into that sad, tear-haunted face, and clasped the hand that had tightened on the arm of the chair. "You are thinking of . . . ," she said in a quiet voice, not quite able to complete the sentence, not when Grandmama turned her face away, still batting her eyes furiously to keep back the tears.

"Your grandfather," Grandmama said, her voice strained and hollow.

There was an uncomfortable silence, until Grandmama could turn back to her, her lined face once more composed. She sighed, the sound unsteady. "It is ever the same with these men, is it not? Such shallow hearts they have! Your Marchmont—"

"Surely not mine."

"—he thinks one is as well as the other. Wife or mistress. Fool! Well, never mine. You have to know that he does not really mean it, not even the part about becoming his light-o'-love. He might believe he does, for now, but he does not. He is all that is fickle. All you need do is wait awhile, and he shall bother you no more. He is far too unsteady for any kind of devotion, not even the base kind."

Pamela was respectfully silent, knowing Grandmama spoke from experience. Grandfather had been the most dreadful philanderer—leaving at home a woman who had pledged to love and honor him while he went through scores of mistresses. Grandmama had had but one week of loyalty from him, although it had taken her three months to discover this terrible fact. Too late she had learned that her husband had married her out of obligation to his family duty, and that the pretty words he had used to win her had held no substance, no veracity behind them. It was those three months wherein she believed herself the only partner in his bed that had led to the birth of their only child, Pamela's mama. The whole sordid tale was another truth that Mama was not aware Pamela knew.

At length Pamela spoke, softly, so as not to accuse: "But, Grandmama, you flirted with Marchmont! You enjoyed his company a great deal, I saw that. I even thought perhaps you quite appreciated him."

"Oh, I did, I do, I would!" Grandmama said with a harsh, bitter laugh, quickly extinguished. Her voice trembled as she went on, "that ever was my downfall.

93

It is most certainly not the first time I have been attracted to such a one." She sighed. "I do so enjoy the company of a rogue, and always shall, curse me."

Pamela squeezed her hand.

Grandmama went on, "Yes, I love their witty ways. It is too late in life for me to seek a good, decent man, so I enjoy the wicked, terrible ones, for they entertain me in my old age. But you must comprehend this is not right for you. You have to understand that such creatures exist purely for the sake of enjoyment—they serve no other purpose. You must keep that foremost in your mind always when you are with such a man." When Pamela did not reply, merely staring into her grandparent's eyes once again in commiseration, Grandmama shook her gray curls with some vehemence. "Pamela," she said, her voice lowering, sounding very old and very tired.

The younger woman cupped the older woman's two hands between her own, as though to will some of the usual vitality back into her grandmother's deflated spirit.

"There is one thing you must remember, always. Never, *never* allow such a man to persuade you to marry him. For, you see, he cannot break your heart if you never let him in."

"Then I should give him the cut direct?"

Grandmama squeezed her hand in return, shaking her head. "No, that would only make him linger all the longer, striving to overcome your resistance. A challenge, you see—they cannot resist the challenge of it. No, if you would be rid of him, then give him everything he wishes: your company, your wit, your amusement, even your kisses. Just never marry him, no, nor ever take him to your bed. That is what I fear most, child: that you would give him everything, every part of your heart, for that is the only way a sweeting such as you can give your love." She made sure their eyes met before going on, her expression solemn. "Understand this: the very moment you give him all of yourself he will be gone, off to find more amusement, without a backward glance, the challenge mastered, and it would not matter to him which side of the blanket you had finally lain down upon. Mistress or wife, the result would be the same. Trust me," she said, and the tears were back in her eyes, "I know. I know very well how these rakehells go on."

Pamela looked on her Grandmama's ancient sorrow, and nodded, though rather uncertainly. "But he is not heartless. He has a care for his brother, I know. He speaks of him with affection. And he is honest enough that he names himself 'rakehell' and does not pretend to be otherwise."

Grandmama gave a bittersweet smile. "Oh, they can be honest at times, and affectionate, and caring. It is all part of the game, a terrible, cold, losing game. You do know why such ruthless fellows are called rakehells, do you not, Pamela?"

"No, I suppose I do not," Pamela said very quietly, watching her grandmother's face intently.

"It implies, my dear, that one would have to rake the many coals in hell to find such a wicked one as this."

"Oh," Pamela said hollowly, and simply, as she slid into her broken-hearted grandmama's embrace.

There was no reason to be surprised by this undeniable revelation, for it was, after all, only what she had already determined for herself.

Chapter 8

Lawlton crossed at once to where his young mistress summoned him upon the stairs, not hesitating as he had yesterday. Before she could even speak, he stepped up to her and supplied the information, "The Misses Everroad have called, as well as Captain Penford."

Pamela rewarded him with a smile and a bright "Thank you."

With a little bow and an "At your service," he turned and led the way, as she trailed behind him to her mama's drawing room.

"Lady Pamela," Lawlton announced her, then retreated to continue with his other duties.

Mama turned to greet her, even as Captain Penford awkwardly leaned on his cane in an attempt to gain his feet.

"Oh, pray, do not stand on my account!" Pamela cried, rushing to the captain's side. She made so bold as to put her hands on his arm, pressing him back into his seat. He looked up at her, allowing himself to sink back into the settee cushions, and then made her a half bow from the waist.

"Good morning, Lady Pamela, and thank you for your kindness. You must pardon my awkwardness, but I confess I am unused to being invalided, and am not so agile as I would care to be," he said in his deep, rumbling voice.

"Pray think nothing of it," she replied, smiling at him.

"My dear, you know the Misses Everroad," Lady Premington said.

"Of course." Belatedly she turned to the two sisters, nodding to the younger, and saying to the elder, "I believe best wishes are in order?"

Miss Emily Everroad sat just a little more upright with pride, her hands balanced on the handle of her parasol, the point of which stabbed into Mama's Aubusson rug. "Yes, indeed. Mister Fisher and I are to be married come June."

"Do tell us all your plans!" Mama cried.

Miss Everroad was only too pleased to comply. As the woman launched into a recitation of where and how the nuptials would take place, Pamela found herself unseated and unsure exactly where she ought to place herself. It seemed too obvious to sit herself next to the captain, but it would serve no purpose toward her goal if she sat too far from him for conversation. Instantly she decided that the elder Miss Everroad had a proper attendee in Mama, that the younger was equally rapt by her sister's announcements, and so it was clearly her duty to supply Captain Penford with an audience.

She sat beside him, feeling rather bold, and spoke in a quiet voice, so as not to override Miss Everroad. "Are you come to call on Owen?"

"Yes, ma'am. The horse we saw put through its paces yesterday at Haymarket Heath wouldn't suit. Powell says he knows a gentleman who is willing to let us look at some of his bloods, and we're for there today." Then he smiled at her, a smile that made her eyes widen with pleasure as he said, "And I was mindful that Lady Premington and her daughter were not unwelcoming to morning visitors."

"Not at all," she murmured, dropping her eyes as her heart swelled with satisfaction. So, he had not come just to see Owen again! Oh, this was beyond wonderful! She raised her eyes shyly. "I hope you find a mount that shall suit. I know a good steed is very important to an officer."

"Very."

She liked the way his mustache moved when he spoke, and briefly wondered how it would feel to be kissed by a man with a mustache. It also quickly crossed her mind that Marchmont was clean shaven and that was the only kissing experience she had known so far . . . a thought she put aside at once. "I understand you shall not be returning to your battalion for two more weeks?"

The captain's face darkened, and he frowned. "I am afraid it is so. I should be there, now that Napoleon has recaptured Paris. Every man is needed."

Pamela shook her head. "But you require time for your wound to heal. Every man is needed, true, but one must be in good health, especially those in a role of leadership." She lowered her lashes, looking at him through them as she boldly said, "I wish you did not have to return at all. I wish the war was at an end."

"Napoleon should never have escaped Elba," the captain said vehemently, apparently unaware of her coquetry, or perhaps unwilling to acknowledge it. When heads turned at his raised voice, he shook himself a little, and said, "Pardon me. I am afraid I become too excited at news of the war. It is the soldier's curse. Please, let us speak of other things."

"Of course," Pamela agreed at once, even as Mama turned back to Miss Everroad. Marchmont's warning—that a soldier loved the army first—sprang to her mind, and it seemed it was so with the good captain as well. Still, although it was true the men must do their soldiering, it was equally true that the women they left behind were in large part the reason they felt compelled to march off in the first place. The safety of one's "home and hearth" was well worth fighting for, especially if one had a wish to fill that home with loved ones. There was no reason to think this captain would not be just as willing to have someone waiting at home for him.

It was time to give her first push in that direction. "Do tell, Captain Penford, have you been yet to see *Richard II* at Drury Lane?"

"No, ma'am, but I understand 'tis a wondrous production."

"So I hear tell, but I have yet to see it for myself." There, that was as obvious a suggestion as a young lady might make.

Captain Penford rose to the occasion, asking, "Shall we plan an evening of it, then? I am persuaded Lord Powell would enjoy such an outing."

"Oh, Owen," Pamela said, just managing to keep a frown from gathering on her brow. Her brother along? But then again, Owen would do as well for a chaperone as Phyllis, perhaps even more so, as he was not overly concerned with conventions or particularly attentive to his sister's company. With Owen's benign neglect, there should be little to stand in the way of her monopolizing the good captain's time and conversation. She would be the only female on which he might lavish any of the kind of banter that such evenings tended to engender. She smiled at the captain, and said, "That would be lovely!"

To Pamela's surprise, and not some little disappointment, the captain turned to the Misses Everroad. "Pardon me," he said when the elder Miss Everrode paused to take a breath, "but we have just conceived a desire to see the latest production at Drury Lane." He turned back to Pamela for a moment to ask, "What, Monday?"

He must not have noticed the disappointment—or she was better at hiding it than she supposed—that coursed through her at the thought of including everyone, for he turned back to the others with eagerness following her reluctant nod. "The evening after tomorrow. Do you care to accompany us?" he asked the Misses Everroad.

"Delighted," said the elder.

"Most pleased," said the younger.

"It has been ages," Mama said.

"Very well, we shall bring carriages around, that we all may travel together," the captain said with a broad smile.

Pamela said nothing, bitting the inside of her lip. She told herself that if it was not quite what she had hoped for, she ought to at least take heart that she had, without doubt, begun the journey down the long, twisted road that led to the matrimonial bliss she so desired.

She knew that Captain Penford had only stayed for twenty minutes—a far cry from the two hours she had given Marchmont—but Pamela sat down that very afternoon and penned the latter a note, freeing him to once again call upon her. She was, in fact, more than a bit surprised that he had not put in an appearance all morning; she had fully expected him to disobey any dictate she ever tendered.

She did not now send the note because she was anxious to see him again or feeling in any wise guilty for having banished him, however temporarily, but rather to follow Grandmama's advice. Grandmama knew whereof she spoke: as Marchmont was a rake-hell, so he must be treated. As he meant to pursue her; well, she would cease to run from him. He himself had said a "hard race" was the thing he enjoyed most. To be rid of him was a simple matter: she must cease to make any such attempt to do so. She would bore him into abandoning her by simply being too readily available to him.

Having made that decision, it came as another surprise when he did not make an appearance all day. She had rather thought he might come around directly on the heels of the note being delivered into his hands, but by nightfall she could only accept that Lord Marchmont had something better to do this day than call on the woman with whom he had claimed to be madly in love. She found her mind wandering several times over the possibilities of what might have kept him away, even going so far as to almost call out to the footman who had delivered her note to inquire as to its safe arrival . . . only to stop herself before she spoke. That would never do. Instead she forced the question from her mind—and rather successfully, too, she told herself. She was satisfied she gave the matter hardly another thought, although she rather snapped at Mama over dinner when that lady ventured to say that Pamela seemed to be "in a pet."

She dressed for the evening's affair—a ball given by Lord and Lady Updike to begin, as Mama rather tartly said, their unfortunately rotund daughter's third season—with careful attention to detail. There was nothing like dressing well to lift her spirits, which she had to silently admit needed lifting. She did not look within to examine why that was, instead looking without, into her cheval glass. She saw a gown of the ubiquitous white that all young ladies wore their first season, although it was not a pure white, as that would have been rather unflattering with her light honey-colored hair and eyes. Instead it was an ivory satin, with a multiple of golden bows scattered over the skirt, stitched in place so as to create little poufs of the lace overskirt, with a golden ribbon wound through the lacy neckline and tied into a jaunty bow several inches below her right ear. She had not felt quite so finely dressed since she had worn her special court dress at her presentation before the Queen.

Phyllis had also taken extra pains with her mistress's hair, making use of the iron to arrange it into ringlets, which were pulled back and pinned so that they cascaded in a fall from the crown of her head. The maid had further fixed a diamond-studded comb in her hair, with a short white feather attached, as per Pamela's instructions. That lady turned her head now, watching the effect in the mirror, and smiled, for the feather was of a size and color to match that which Captain Penford sported in his shako. She had no reason to expect to see him tonight; but there was always the possibility, and she must not miss any opportunity to draw the man's attention howsoever she might contrive to do so.

A maid knocked at the door, popping in just long enough to notify Pamela that the carriage was ready. She was not one to dawdle, and so descended at once to the front hall, her mood much improved. It was lightened even more when Papa beamed at her, and turned to his wife to say, "Good gad, not a child anymore, eh, Mother? Quite the beauty, eh?"

To which Mama agreed, "Indeed." To Pamela she said, "You are a diamond of the first water, if I do say so myself," and fondly patted her daughter's cheek.

They made the brief drive, waiting inside a scarcely moving vehicle as their driver maneuvered and shouted for fifteen minutes in an attempt to bring them within a tolerable distance of the home they meant to visit. They finally found an opening, left the carriage to join a stream of other party-goers, ascended the stairs to the house, and were announced. As they moved through the decided crush in an attempt to locate a place where the three of them might stand without being jostled, Pamela looked around with careful eyes, only to find she did not see the captain anywhere, to her disappointment. Still, there were any number of people she knew, so the evening promised to be pleasurable despite his absence.

She circled at her mama's side, smiling at acquaintances, chatting with friends, and nodding to those who sought an introduction. She allowed a selection of gentlemen to put their name to her dance card, although she could not see how anyone would be expected to dance in such a crush. This mystery was solved when a pair of doors were opened at the far end of the room. A surge of humanity pressed through the opening, murmurs floating back that guaranteed Lady Updike had purposefully kept her guests crowded close so that she might make the grand impression when they finally were allowed access to her ballroom. Pulled forward by the human tide, Pamela became separated from her mama, but since she was eager to see what the "ooh"'s and "ahh"'s signified, she did not concern herself with an attempt to find that venerable lady. Instead she attached herself to a small group that contained her friend, Lady Jane.

"Oh, but is it not lovely?" that lady breathed as they came to the doorway.

Pamela stepped through the opening then, and had to agree, "It is charming."

The room was of double height, with tall Doric columns supporting the pale blue ceiling above. There was a gold leaf frieze of a faintly Egyptian design that ran the circumference of the large room, and the tall windows were hung with golden velvet curtains, now pulled back with tasseled white silk ropes. Gilded chairs were set in the corners of the room, the padded white satin seats marked with the Earl's crest embroidered in gold thread. Artificial flowers of silk, made to resemble gold and white roses, were arranged in multiple gold epergnes and oversized vases around the room. There was a long table set with refreshments, spread with a gold cloth with white tassels at each corner. A fifteen piece orchestra sat on a raised dais, where they struck up a quiet tune that would not yet interfere with conversation; the time for dancing would evidently come later, after everyone was settled and had had time to compliment the hostess.

"Do you see that Miss Updike is casting daggers at you, Lady Pamela?" a voice said near her ear. Pamela's eyes flew to the host's daughter, a rather large, round sight in pale blue across the room, before she turned to the speaker. She found she was smiling, recognizing the voice, and was surprised to find she was not particularly annoyed to learn Marchmont was here.

"My lord," she greeted him.

"Lady Pamela."

"But why do you say as much? Daggers?"

"Because your gown is the perfect reflection of this room. I daresay Miss Updike wishes she had made your choice of gold and white, although it must be said she would not carry the look so well as you."

Pamela accepted the compliment with a nod, but argued, "I must point out, however, that all this rather heavenly white and gold that surrounds us goes very well with the celestial blue the lady has chosen."

"Well enough to prove it was undoubtedly planned. Are we to believe that an attachment with the young lady would be heavenly? Why every parent believes their child to be angelic in deed and form quite escapes me. I am only grateful they did not have cherubs painted on the ceilings, for I know they would not have been able to resist using Miss Updike as the model. All those round curves, you see."

Pamela did not chide him for his uncharitable words, not wanting to be a hypocrite, for his words had made her smile despite herself.

"Lord Marchmont!" Jane said as she turned to see who had engaged her friend. She put out her hand at once when she saw who it was.

"My dearest Lady Jane, how does the evening find you?" he replied, taking the hand and bowing over it with a flourish.

"Quite well. And yourself?" she replied with a curtsy when he had straightened once more.

"Never better."

"You have come to dance, then?"

"It is my hope."

Pamela looked somewhat sharply toward Marchmont at that, for there was something in his tone that implied he was not terribly serious, but Jane did not seem to note the fact. Instead, her friend lifted up her other hand, for from the wrist dangled her dance card. Marchmont grinned, bowed again, and released her hand that she might use it to pull the card free. He accepted the card as soon as it was rid of her wrist, as well as the lead she further offered, and penciled his name on not one but two lines. He was right-handed, Pamela observed, as she once again noted the ruby ring that flashed in the light of the multiple overhead chandeliers.

"Lord Marchmont!" Jane giggled, but she did not bid him strike one of the lines as she accepted back her belongings.

He turned to Pamela, raising an eyebrow at her. She slid her card from her wrist, and offered it as Jane had done. Again, he wrote his name on two lines.

"Do you always dance twice with a lady?" Pamela asked, arching an eyebrow in turn.

"No," was his simple reply.

Jane giggled again. "You shall quite destroy my reputation, my lord."

"Shall I?" He grinned at her, making it sound as though she had offered an invitation. "I could accommodate you in the matter. You have but to give me a third dance—" he threatened good-naturedly, stretching out a hand.

Jane pulled back the arm that once again sported her card, blushed, and giggled, and then fell back on making introductions between the members of her group and Lord Marchmont. Nods and handshakes were exchanged, and then Marchmont asked to be excused, as he had seen "a friend, just there across the room."

Pamela watched him walk away, inwardly shaking her head. Well! He had certainly been at no pains to flatter or amuse *her,* and she supposedly the object of his every desire! It only proved that Grandmama had the measure of the man.

She put him out of her mind, instead noting that there were attempts being made to clear a space for dancing. Mister Cousineau, a pleasant albeit painfully thin young man, had requested the honor of her first dance, and in looking about for him, Pamela found Mama long enough to nod and smile, just as the gentleman she was thinking of materialized at her side.

She danced four dances, one right after the other, before there was a blank space on her card. She was content enough not to have a partner, for while dancing with Sir Derek it had occurred to her that perhaps Captain Penford was in attendance after all, but of course not where there was dancing. He would undoubtedly be seated, perhaps at the inevitable card tables that most good hostesses set up for those guests who chose not to dance. She would look about, just on the chance he had come.

She returned to the large main entry where a group of matrons were seated, comfortably chatting before a large fireplace, and followed a stream of people that entered and exited through another set of double doors. There were the expected card tables, the occupants mainly gentlemen, although there were several ladies scattered amongst them, but no captain.

She came from the room and saw someone disappear into a doorway down the hallway to her left, and so followed. A quick peek showed this room had been set aside for those gentlemen who wished a cognac or a cigar, or both. She withdrew at once, as some ladies might be tolerated at the tables but never here.

As she returned down the corridor, laughter met her ears, coming from the open door to her right. She glanced in, idly, but then came to an abrupt halt. Within was Marchmont, his back half-turned to her, and before him was a lady in scarlet silk. Pamela had seen her before, but never made her acquaintance. Lady . . . ? Did her name start with an "A," or perhaps it was an "O"?

Marchmont had the lady's ungloved hand in his own, which he raised to his lips, pressing a kiss there. The lady laughed and threw back her head, reprimanding him—with no real rancor at all—by crying, "Rogue!"

"You would know."

That made her laugh again, throatily. "I see you still wear my ring." Her dark eyes shone; Pamela could see that even from this distance.

"Always. I see tonight we are a match." Marchmont held up his right hand, wiggling his fingers, making the horseshoe ring sparkle in the candlelight, indicating the woman's red dress with a movement of his other hand.

"My lord enjoys me in bold colors."

"Let me say how pleased I am to hear your news. I presume Austin knows?" Marchmont asked.

Austin, yes, that was her name. Lady Austin. She

and Marchmont seemed to be more than mere acquaintances; Pamela could not fail to note the two were standing rather close.

"No, I have yet to tell him, but I shall tonight. I daresay he is not quite sharp enough to determine the truth for himself."

Marchmont shook his head, and Pamela saw his profile enough to know that he smiled. "You should not speak that way about your husband."

" 'Tis the truth!"

"I am afraid 'tis," he said, amusement in his voice.

Then Pamela stared, unable to move, her slippers fixed to the tiles, for he very boldly and shamelessly placed his hand on the lady's abdomen. "Name it Theopholus, shall you?"

"I daresay my lord would not care for the name." She laughed again, placing her hand over his.

"No, I suppose not," Marchmont laughed too. Then, to Pamela's further and utter surprise, he reached for the lady and hugged her to his chest, and Lady Austin embraced him back.

It was then that Pamela's feet fairly leaped from the tiles as though hot needles had suddenly grown up to prod her soft soles. She all but ran from the scene, her thoughts scattered by a sense of shock and—inexplicably—a strange feeling rather like disappointment.

Chapter 9

Pamela could not fail to note that Marchmont had returned to the ballroom in time for the start of the next dance. The dance she owed him, according to her card.

She hid behind the floral display of a large vase, biting her lip, mentally chasing her own thoughts in circles. She ought to leave . . . she ought not to have spied . . . he meant nothing to her, so what did it matter what she had seen? . . . what had she seen anyway? . . . she ought to leave. . . .

It was impossible. There was no way to sort out her thoughts. It was just that she felt . . . well, betrayed. She knew he did not love her, knew that she had refused to accept his advances, knew that even if she was so foolish as to be swayed by his clever tongue, there was nothing to his words, that they were nothing more than that: words. Airy, empty, meaningless, forgotten-in-a-moment words.

Still, it stung. She was not used to deceit. It unsettled her, and put her nerves on edge.

She had meant to take Grandmama's advice and be the flame to Marchmont's moth, the sooner to burn him, a nuisance removed. Now she was not so sure of that plan. If she allowed Marchmont, and the *ton,* to think she was giving in to his blandishments, and that very same *ton* knew of his . . . association with Lady Austin, what must they think of her? They would whisper behind their hands that Lady Pamela was as green as a girl could be, and was it not too sad that she had been led down the primrose path? It fair set her teeth on edge to think of such whispers, and to know that there would be no way to deny them.

Though, perhaps all these feelings of distress were for nothing, she told herself. Perhaps no one else knew of the relationship Marchmont surely had with this other woman. She herself would not have known had she not passed by at just the wrong moment. Lady Austin must needs be at least a trifle discreet, for she was, after all, married.

Yes. Yes, Pamela must hope that was the case, for she was convinced Grandmama had given her the shortest way free of Marchmont's notice—a goal that would certainly allow her life to return to a peaceful state. Even if nothing else was to be gained, that alone was worth enduring the possibility of a few whispers.

As the music for the next dance was struck up, Pamela stepped from behind the large vase, with its spread of silk flowers, and had to look no farther than a few feet to find the very man who was uppermost in her thoughts: Marchmont.

He was leaning against one of the Doric columns, his arms crossed over his chest as he gazed at her with unblinking eyes. "I was wondering when you would wish to part ways with the decorations," he drawled.

She blushed furiously. "I was mending a hem," she lied, feeling the blush deepen when he gave her a frankly doubting look.

"How remarkable, given you did not move at all for three full minutes." She stammered, astounded to find he had been waiting silently for at least that long, watching her. However, he did not wait for her response, offering his arm. "Come, it is time for our dance, is it not?"

She nodded, for there was a kind of safety in muteness.

He led her to the floor, exchanging greetings with some of the other dancers who arranged themselves for the quadrille. She nodded and tried to smile, wishing she had brought a fan so that she might fan her face, but at least she could blame her scarlet cheeks on the exertions of the dance.

Marchmont had her left hand in his right as they moved to execute the five figures of the dance. During the second he quietly spoke to her: "I shall not ask."

"Ask?"

"What you were doing behind the vase. Did I not promise I would not publicly embarrass you? So, calm yourself. Enjoy the dance."

She looked away, staring blindly at the gentleman opposite her, and blushed anew.

"Blushes are very attractive on you, my dear, but they do affect your dancing. Please, disregard that I even saw you there. I never meant to ruin your sport, whatever that may be. Smile for me, and assure me that I have not been any part of something that has spoiled your evening.''

And that was why he was not easy to ignore or dismiss: he was observant, clever, amusing, and sometimes even sweet. She could almost believe he really was anxious to make amends. And that was what made him dangerous. Just as Grandmama had warned her.

''A smile?'' he coaxed, just before he had to step forward.

When he stepped back, she had regained her balance, both in the form of the dance and in her response to him. For it did not matter: he could have his mistress, or multiple mistresses for all she cared, and the *ton* could whisper as they would, but in a short while it would all be irrelevant. He would forget her, going on to his next scandal, and she would—hopefully—be betrothed to Captain Penford. No one would be able to doubt the strength of *that* alliance. In fact, one day, when she had been devotedly married to the captain for thirty or forty years, she might even look back and wish she'd had just a little more scandal in her life, something to startle her children with, just as Grandmama did to Mama. The tiny little whispers of having once been pursued by a rake would be nothing, not even worth telling.

This knowledge was very liberating, to the point that she was able to look up at him and give him the smile he had requested.

He smiled back, but then something—she could not say what—must have given him pause, for his smile faded. His lips rearranged themselves in a straight line, and he looked away from her. For one moment a shadow swept over his face.

"Are you well?" she asked.

He nodded curtly.

She did not understand it, and was once again discomfited, this time by the unusual silence that prevailed as they moved through the dance. Really, he was of the most inconstant disposition!

This fact was proved again, she noted, for as the dance neared its ending, he seemed to relax by degrees, until at the end his bow was not stiff at all, and his smile did not seem particularly forced as she curtsied in return. In fact, she thought perhaps she saw something of a twinkle had returned to his eye as he spoke. "My dear, I was most pleased that you sent me your note, although I will confess that I was a trifle startled to find that the honorable Captain Penford actually spent two hours with you this morning."

She did not correct his misassumption. It was enlightening to learn he was aware that there were gentlemen in this world who understood it was only proper to call for a short while and not remain for hours on end as he was wont to do.

"I never thought Penford would be such a fast worker. I thought 'twould be days and days before I could once more have the pleasure of calling at your home."

"Which only proves you do not know much about Captain Penford," she said with a knowing little smile, for what it really proved was what he did not know about *her.*

116

The comment did not ruffle him. "I mark that this evening, once I have claimed my second dance, I shall have had the pleasure of your company for approximately one half of an hour. As there is every possibility that I shall not be able to call on you tomorrow morning, let us hope that Penford shall do so and thereby earn his matching time. If he stays longer than that, you will notify me, will you not?"

"In either case, I shall notify you, my lord, per our agreement. If you do not hear from me, he has not come to call." She wanted to ask why he would not be calling tomorrow, but did not, would not. This was surely a good sign, this crying off, was it not? She must make a point of asking Grandmama.

"That is well. Until our next dance." He made her another bow, and strolled away without so much as a backward glance.

Pamela watched *him* however, noting when he located his next dance partner, Lady Jane, who tittered really most nonsensically as she slid into his arms for a waltz.

Late that night, or more correctly morning, Pamela wrote in her diary:

Lord and Lady Updike's ball. Charming ballroom. Miss Updike may have attracted Mister Dunkling. Captain Penford not in attendance.

For a moment her quill hovered above the paper, and her eyes lost their focus as she thought of the

117

captain. She sighed, and then her eyes focused once more. She dipped her quill in the bottle of ink, and then in the margin near the line that held his name she wrote "Lady Pamela, wife of Mr. Roger Penford." Another dip, and then "Marchioness of Waller." She smiled at her own scribbles, then dipped the quill again, and turned back to her diary entry:

Danced twice with Marchmont. Fine dancer. Atrocious flirt. Jane is almost as bad. He seems to see all. I must get over the impulse to mind my manners with him. Instead must be as big a flirt, must be accessible.

Danced with Mr. Cousineau, Sir Derek, Mr. Boyd, Lord Gaskell, Lord Avery, Mr. Jackson (just returned from India), Sir Martin, Mr. Tewes (betrothed to Lydia Arrowsmith), Lord Brewer, Monsieur Acadia, Mr. Winter (from America), Mr. Dunkling (the one who seemed to 'ooh' and 'aah' around Miss Updike) and Lord Sygne. And, as noted above, Lord Marchmont, twice.

All in all, not a terrible evening.

She looked at her words, feeling faintly disquieted. She almost amended what she had written, for it was not quite all the truth. "Not a terrible evening" was too weak a statement. Indeed, by the time Marchmont had claimed his second dance she was actually having quite an enjoyable time. She supposed she had written the statement as it was to show the balance of the evening: one portion embarrassing and awkward, the other portion all that a lady could want.

In the latter part of the evening she had had many partners, many compliments, and even Marchmont had been all that was pleasant, going so far as to make her laugh—an honest, unfettered laugh—more than once. There had been no additional pressure from him, no weighted comments, in fact nothing to give her pause. He had behaved as well as any other gentlemen, and that was something she had not expected to see from him.

And she had written absolutely nothing concerning Lady Austin, or the fact that Marchmont wore a ring that was obviously a present from another man's wife.

Perhaps she did not write the whole of it because then she would have to admit to herself that Marchmont, despite his profligate ways, had been a part of her evening's enjoyment. It did not sit easy, that thought. It was so much easier to dismiss him when he was being roguish. Oh, dangerous, dangerous man! She knew it, and found tonight that she could sometimes forget it, and that plagued her, even down to the most private thoughts of her diary.

Choosing not to linger over the breakfast tray in her room, Pamela came down the stairs toward her mama's drawing room with a light bounce in her step. She knew that Phyllis's efforts with the braided knot of hair and primrose ribbons atop her head and her own choice of the pale, new shell-pink morning gown were as well as she could wish them. Today she did not bother to look about, to try and catch Lawlton's eye. She hoped Captain Penford was in attendance, but since Marchmont had said he would not be, she felt no need to discover beforehand who might be Mama's guests this morning.

Only one of the double doors was open to the room as she approached, blocking any callers from view. She hesitated outside the one closed door, touched the white feather that she'd had Phyllis fix close to the braids once again, then swept into the morning room.

One man sat there, unattended, bent over a newspaper that was spread on the low table before him. At one eye was a monocle. She identified him at once by his dark head and well-fitted, though somewhat somber, clothing. She called out in surprise, "Marchmont!"

He looked up with a smile of greeting. "I do like the habits of this household. The ladies rise early and allow callers every day."

"I am glad you are pleased," she said dryly, coming farther into the room. What was he doing here? He had said he would not be calling this morning— but, no, he had actually said there "was every possibility" he would not. She must remember to watch such wordplay with this particular gentleman.

"Come, sit with me and we shall read the paper together. I shall even read you sections of which your father would not approve."

She hesitated. Of course she must not be alone with him. She would have been quite content if only he were the captain—for such a situation would have been ripe with possibilities—but this was March-

120

mont. She knew better, had forced herself to learn, if not always appreciate, all of society's dictates, and this was one of the primary ones. No, she certainly ought not remain alone with a man. Particularly this man. Still, some part of her acknowledged that she had already been twice alone with him, and that he was harmlessly sitting and reading the paper in her parents' front parlor, and hardly posed a threat. And worse than all that was the certain knowledge that he would laugh quite out loud if she scrupled to remove herself for the few minutes it would take before a maid of her mama's could be found to act as chaperone.

She crossed to the bellpull, which was situated next to the doors.

Lawlton appeared almost at once, with an inquiring, "Lady Pamela?"

"Will you see that Phyllis is sent to me at once?"

"Of course." He bowed, after a quick glance at Lord Marchmont. Pamela noted that the butler hesitated at the threshold long enough to open the second door, then made sure that both doors were open wide before he left.

She could just stand where she was, barely in the room, waiting like a witless goose who couldn't decide whether or not to cross the road, or she could take a seat. The decision was made in a moment when he glanced up and looked at her expectantly with unveiled humor in his eyes.

However, she made a point of sitting exactly opposite him, with the low table between them.

She poured out a cup of chocolate for herself. "Do

you care for more?'' she asked, indicating the empty cup on the table before him.

"Yes, please. I do like chocolate. Hate lemon tea, though, if you recall. Do try not to serve me lemon tea, if you please. If your mother offers it to me, be so good as to suggest something else, will you?''

She smiled faintly at the intimation that he would be here in the future for any such offering, and proceeded to fill his cup with the rich, hot chocolate. She set down the pot, and asked, "I do not mean to appear rude, but what are you doing here this morning?''

He sat up at that, removing the monocle and slipping it into a fob pocket, its black ribbon trailing loosely. He grinned, and stood, leaning over her until his lips pressed against her cheek. He had been forced to lean quite a distance, for she had shrunk back at his approach. "Happy, and late, April Noddy's Day,'' he said, then moved back to his seat as she corrected her posture now that he no longer loomed over her.

April Noddy. She did not think anyone had played an April first trick on her in years. It had been a favorite habit of hers, up to the age of thirteen at any rate, but even she had never been eight days late in celebrating the occasion. "You are over a week late.''

"So you really could not expect a trick, then, could you?''

"Even had you the day rightly, you do not earn a kiss for a successful April Noddy's Day trick,'' she chided, even though the time to protest was already unstoppably past.

"Others may not, but I certainly have.''

She picked up her cup, placing it near her lips as a kind of shield should he decide he would take another kiss, but did not drink. Instead she said, "I did not know you sport a monocle." Once she might have blushed at making such a personal remark, but now she could only feel they had moved beyond the average conventions.

"Don't need it for driving, as I can see at a distance. 'Tis up close that I have my difficulties."

"How unfashionable of you to admit to a fault," she teased, finally sipping the chocolate, which she then set in the saucer, as it seemed he was done with kisses this morning, for he had turned his attention back to the newspaper spread open before him.

"You do not find my monocle fashionable? 'Tis rimmed with very fine gold, and the spectacle maker assured me this 'twas a very smart ribbon." He pulled it from the pocket and held it up for inspection, dangling from his forefinger, the gold thread that shot through the black ribbon glittering in the morning light. "And I am all that is à la mode. Just ask The Beau."

"Brummell?"

"Of course. Although he's not long for England, I believe, still he must be credited with improving gentlemen's attire. He always detested these dandies who have no sense of color or style. One may be well-dressed without being a tulip, a lesson many have yet to learn. Even look to your father: he still insists on all the bright, garish colors of the last century. Too French by half for my taste, my dear."

"People say you dress so somberly because you have no funds."

" 'People' say a great many things, and most of them nothing better than idiotic ramblings so that they may hear themselves speak."

"How harsh you are."

"No more than you, disparaging my taste in apparel."

She might have apologized, but he was obviously not truly offended.

She fell silent, appraising him openly. He sat patiently for her inspection as she gazed at his dark blue coat and unmentionables, and his pale blue waistcoat. His hair was brushed back, wavy, dark. His cravat was properly starched and high on his neck, but not unfortunately so, for he had a long neck that could support the structure. He wore a simple gold pin that secured the cravat in place, but other than the ruby horseshoe ring, no other ostentation. At length she said, "No, I do not disparage it. I would have to say you look rather fine."

"As do you."

She grinned. "I have to wonder at your compliment. Can you even see me without your monocle, my lord?"

He put the glass back in his pocket. "I can see you quite well enough. 'Tis printing I have a difficulty with. If your mother were to walk in right now, I should know her in a moment. It would, in fact, be difficult not to do so."

"Now it is you who disparage, and the target is my mother! But I will refuse to take offense, and will even admit she is of . . . generous proportions." An idea struck her, one she conveyed with a growing smile. "Only think, my lord, if you are still thinking of marriage with me, you must look to my mother to know how I shall look in twenty or thirty years. Can you still claim you desire such a union?"

He boldly glanced at her tidy bosom, causing her to blush at her own folly of inviting just such an inspection. "You? To ever be proportioned as your mother? Never! Not even if you eat a hundred comfits a day. No, my offers still stand, either of them."

She rolled her eyes and looked away, as if to ignore him, but also to gather her composure. She was relieved to see Phyllis come to the entry, and beckoned the girl in with more enthusiasm than she might normally have done. Phyllis bobbed a curtsy, took up some darning, and sat herself near the morning light at a window.

Pamela was under no obligation to entertain him, of course, other than good manners. He was not deserving of good manners, it was true, but now that Phyllis was in the room his company must surely be less volatile. In fact, Pamela felt emboldened enough by the servant's mitigating presence that she dared to ask the question that burned in her mind every time the ruby colors flashed on his right hand. "My lord, that ring you wear—I see it is a horseshoe shape."

"Yes, it is." He did not elaborate, although he did glance at the ring with a rather fond expression crossing his features.

"Do you wear it to bring you luck?"

"Exactly so, my dear. I have worn it every day for the past five years, and will continue to do so."

"But why a horseshoe?"

He hesitated then, giving her a level look. " 'Tis less vain than a signet, would you not say? Why are you interested?"

" 'Tis so unusual," she explained feebly.

He continued to look at her, assessing, his green eyes seeming to search the corners of her mind. At last his level look dawned into a smile. "I can only think of one reason why you should care one whit about my ring, Pamela. Did you hear something last night?"

"No," she said shortly, looking away from his penetrating gaze.

He stood, moving to the place next to her on the settee. She glanced toward Phyllis, who was concerned with her task, the girl's tongue sticking out of one corner of her mouth as she worked the fabric with her needle. When Pamela turned back to Marchmont, it was to find him leaning toward her. She leaned back into the cushions rather awkwardly.

He spoke in a quieter tone, for her ears alone: "What did you hear?"

"Nothing."

"Then you saw something."

"No, I did not." She looked away again, flushing.

"Liar. You saw me with Lady Austin."

"What if I did?"

"You heard us talking. It made you curious about this ring." He held up his hand, then lowered it to

126

the back of the settee, so that his arm half encircled her.

"It caught my eye, that is all," she lied miserably, knowing by the look in his own eye that he was anything but convinced by this tale.

"She is going to have a child," he said.

She lifted her hands, placing them on her ears. "I do not need to know anything more, my lord," she said, rather desperately.

He pulled her hands down, into her lap. "Not *my* child, you goose!" He laughed now.

Phyllis looked up, her eyes widening a little.

"Sit back!" Pamela hissed, and to her relief, he did, though he did not release her hands. Phyllis turned back to her darning.

He repeated, "Not my child. Her husband's. Oh, Pamela, you delight me with this jealous display. This is twice, love, that you have shown jealousy at what you thought were my acts."

"Why did you embrace her?" Pamela challenged. "You . . . you *touched* her in a way no lady would allow!"

"She's a lady, all right. One of the finest to my way of thinking. But since my jealous little darling has asked, I find myself wishing to explain. But first: a promise. No word of this ever leaves your lips. Promise me, Pamela, for I know you are not the sort to break your pledge."

"You are the sort."

"That's as may be, but it is you who must pledge. Now, have I your word this goes no further?"

"Of course."

127

"Not 'of course.' Swear it!"

"I swear it," Pamela said through lips that felt faintly numb. She was not sure she really wished to hear it.

He did not spare the bald truth, saying, "We were lovers, once. Five, perhaps as long as six years ago now. I was heavily into debt then. Robbie was but a boy, and I had not yet learned where his talents resided; and who would listen to a boy anyway? So, between Dalton's and my own stupid wagers, and Caldwell's military expenses, my estate was fast declining toward poverty.

"One night I met this lady, whom you know as Lady Austin, and whom I hired for the night."

Pamela might have made as though to raise her hands once more to her ears if Marchmont did not hold them tightly in her lap.

"She was of proper birth, and a beauty, too. Did you note her dark red hair, her fair skin? She should have made an auspicious marriage, but her family had gone through the very decline mine was then experiencing, ending in the death of her father before she could make her come out. It was just a matter of time after that until the creditors took everything. There was no other family, and her mother was not well. She fell on very hard times. She was forced to find . . . er . . . patrons to pay her rent and provide her with the blunt for all of life's necessary expenses, especially her mother's care. She told me once that she had never quite decided if her beauty was a gift or a curse, but at least it kept her from starving. Could she have made a living otherwise, had she been less beautiful?'' He stopped, thinking some private thought, his mouth perhaps shaped to a slight, wistful smile.

He shrugged off the thought, and went on. "In one of those odd moments life hands us all, we found ourselves talking that evening. She told me her story, not to solicit more funds, but because she needed to talk. I, in my turn, told her mine, for much the same reason I suspect. She saw at once the similarities, and wept. When I asked why—flustered, I can assure you, for my presence seldom makes a lady weep, at least from regret—she told me how foolish it was to throw everything away as I was doing. Something in the way she said it made me listen to her. That was the start of a wonderful relationship.

"I knew nothing of investing—and hardly any more of it today than I did then, I shall freely admit. However, I was even thicker in the nob then, and I was half-drunk most the time besides. That might explain why I was imprudent enough to trust her with my funds. But, as it turned out, not so imprudent. I let her invest for me, with the proviso she would have a portion of any funds she increased in my name.

"It proved a perfect union. She wished to better herself, to give up the life she was forced to, and so she was very wise with my money, as a portion of it then became her money. Before long I was no longer in dun territory, and she was no longer in need of patrons.''

Pamela said nothing, listening wide-eyed, not even aware she no longer felt the impulse to cover her ears.

"She talked to me, learned about my family, and

consequently learned about Robbie. She saw his potential. She also was sharp enough to see that our own association was waning. She did not want me to repeat my mistakes, so she convinced me to confide in Robbie, to bring him into the decision process. She was right, of course, but still sometimes I wish she had not suggested I thrust such a burden on the boy.'' He grew silent again at this, looking inwardly to memories or concerns, all trace of humor for once gone as he stared at nothing. It was a side Pamela had never seen of him before, and it was oddly endearing.

''But why a horseshoe ring?'' she urged in a quiet voice.

He sighed and gave her a sheepish look, which he at once covered with a self-mocking smile. ''To remind me never again to place my livelihood, and that of all my family, on the run of a horse or the turn of a card. Should I stretch out my hand to place a wager, the ring reminds me, chides me, stops me.''

It occurred to her that a ring could do no such thing, that the man must do it for himself, but she said nothing.

He glanced down at the ring, speaking more to himself than to her, ''So I wear it always. To remember.'' He sat up straight, his hands leaving hers. ''What I once thought I knew about racehorses, I now turn to try my hand at managing the cattle for the estate. It seems my only talent.'' He shrugged, then looked directly at her, the old deviltry back in his eyes. ''So what you saw last night, my dear, was me congratulating an old friend who had good news to relay. She is more than delighted to have resumed a respectable life with a decidedly respectable husband, and now there is a child on the way. No one knows her past, not even her slow but loving husband, and we two—now we three, Pamela—have pledged to keep it that way. She is due a little happiness, I think.''

Pamela nodded, surprised to find she was moved by the tale where once she would have found these revelations to be beyond shocking. She ought to deplore Lady Austin for what she had been, for the ''respectability'' she no longer ought to have, but there was a part of her that wondered what other way she could expect the woman to have carried on, especially with a penniless and dependent mother whose care was her sole responsibility. She found the shock came not so much from the woman's fall from grace, but rather that once fallen, she had somehow contrived to retain a nobility of spirit. She could have cheated Marchmont, could have fled with his money, but she had not. She had rebuilt her life from nothing. How many could have done as much?

Pamela had given her word she would not tell Lady Austin's tale, but it was not just her pledge, she knew, that would keep her silent. Marchmont was right; the woman deserved a little happiness, and she for one would not destroy that chance with an idle comment.

Suddenly he stood, returning to his seat before the spread newspaper. ''Let us see, what have we here?'' he murmured as he sat down before the paper, fixing his monocle in place. She was a trifle surprised that he moved away, especially as she had not bid him do so. "I see *Richard II* is being performed at Drury Lane. Shall we?"

She shook her head, speaking more kindly than she might have a day or two ago. She had not been mistaken when she had seen he had a care for his brother, for now it was obvious he felt a measure of gratitude for a certain lady who had once helped him. It seemed the rake was not completely devoid of finer feeling, not at all. "I am sorry, but I have already agreed to go with someone else."

"Your brother? Powell would not mind if I—"

"No, Captain Penford, actually."

He sat up straight, his eyes widening so that the monocle fell toward the carpet until it snapped to as it reached the end of the ribbon's length. "Penford? Good gad, Pamela, the man has more mettle than I should ever have given him credit for!"

She lowered her eyes to the hands still folded together in her lap, so that he might not see that it had been her suggestion as much or more than it had been the captain's.

A silence descended, and she felt the weight of his stare. It was as though by the strength of his personality alone he would make her meet his eye. It took a considerable effort on her part not to look up and see what his expression might be. Was he confused by the silence? Or did he suspect the reason she hid her eyes? He made a noise—rather like a growl—in the back of his throat, and he began to speak in a deep, suspicious voice, "Pamela. . . ."

It was at that moment Mama entered the room. A maid trailed behind her with a china pot that must be quite warm, for the girl cradled both the handle and the underside in a folded tea towel. "Lord Marchmont!" Mama cried as she spied their only visitor this morning; they were not the most welcoming words ever uttered.

"Lady Premington," he said, rising to his feet. He sketched her a short bow. "What a fetching turban you wear."

Her hand went to the bright violet fabric with its matching ostrich plumes, and her coolness thawed a trifle. "Why, thank you, my lord. I have always been told violet suits me, and I daresay 'twould suit you as well. You ought to try it for a waistcoat sometime, perhaps with a white stripe?"

His smile seemed sincere, but Pamela saw the flame of aversion spark in his eyes as he cast her a quick, speaking glance.

Mama took a seat next to Pamela, waving the maid forward toward the tray. "I was just having a pot of lemon tea brought in. It is my favorite. All my friends tell me I serve the very best lemon tea in all London. Would you care for some?"

This time his face never registered the slightest discomfort. He turned to Pamela with an expectant expression. "What do you say? Is lemon tea the thing at this hour?"

"Oh, the very thing," she answered at once, giving him a level look before she had to drop her eyes once more for fear she would burst into gales of laughter at the quickly stifled look of horror he gave her for her treachery.

"Do pour, will you, dear?" Mama said to Pamela.

Pamela smiled with a silent, evil humor as she handed him a saucer, and nearly—but not quite—repented of her actions as Marchmont accepted the cup with a cool and admirable grace.

He was forced to smile complacently between sips of the much-hated beverage. To his credit, however, he managed to down three cups of the brew before rising an hour and a half later to bid them his adieux. He had made himself most charming, to the point where Mama had seemed to forget how much time was passing and had even agreed that they should all go driving tomorrow.

Pamela walked with him to the door, where Lawlton waited with Marchmont's hat and cane. "A drive tomorrow?" she questioned teasingly. "You mean to match the time I spend with another tomorrow evening?"

"Exactly so, my dear. He shall have three or four hours of you then, so I note that including today's visit our little drive will make us about even."

"I suppose that is fair."

"Far more fair than being forced to drink lemon tea," he said pointedly.

She laughed, and even blushed a little at her treasonous act. "You could have said you did not care for any."

"With your mother declaring she makes the best pot in all London? I think not, not if I ever wished to enter this portal again. And well you knew it, you minx. By gad, Pamela, I dare think I have made a very clever choice in you, you must realize! Not many women have the slightest idea how to rein me in.''

He did nothing, not lean forward, not take her hand, but suddenly she wished Lawlton was out of earshot, for Marchmont's voice had warmed as he added quietly, ''Do say you will elope with me tonight instead of going to the theatre tomorrow?''

''Posh!'' she cried in a hiccuping half laugh that was perilously close to a yelp. When he spoke in that soft voice, it seemed to do the oddest things to her at the most unexpected moments. She stepped back, out of the circle of his presence, afraid her knees would soon betray her with a tremble that echoed the one in her voice.

''Ah well,'' he sighed, a mock-mournful sound as he hung his head for a moment. When he lifted it again, there was a bright and glowing light at the back of his green eyes, and his tone had deepened even more. ''One of these days you shall accept me, you know,'' he said.

She half believed him, until she physically shook herself and reminded herself he might say the very same thing to the very next pretty young lady that came into sight.

He watched her, saying nothing as the shiver coursed through her.

''Good day, my lord,'' she said, annoyed to find her voice was still altered and rather breathless. She resisted the urge to take another step back.

''Good day, my dear lady,'' he said in return as he placed his hat atop his head, accepted his cane, and exited the door.

"Is he gone at last?" Mama's voice came from the doorway behind her as Pamela put a hand to her heart, not completely surprised to find a rapid tattoo there. Mama went on, "What a curious fellow he is! I never quite know what he means when he speaks. Sometimes I think I am receiving a compliment, but an hour later I am not so sure I did. Are we to be pestered by his continued attendance, do you think?"

"You accepted a drive with him, Mama," Pamela reminded her parent as she took a deep, steadying breath. Her voice seemed to chide, but in fact Pamela was glad she had her parent to blame for that fact, for it meant she had not had to accept or decline the offer herself.

Chapter 10

The next evening Pamela frowned at her diary, not because she disapproved of what she had written, but because of the thoughts she had tried to express there. She read again:

What am I to think of Lord Marchmont? There are times when he seems the most pleasant fellow, and eager to please, and all that one could find admirable, but then a moment later he is the worst tease I have ever known, speaking to me in the lowest terms. He seems to think I should take him seriously, and sometimes I almost think that I will, but then I recall his truer nature. I cannot believe his protestations are real. How can he say he loves me, that nothing should do but that I become his wife, and then turn about and ask me to be his mistress? One surely precludes the other—and therefore his statements of love must needs be false.

And yet, sometimes when I look in his eyes, he seems all seriousness, and even a little hurt that I

*think him a liar and a mere philanderer! But he is!
He must be! He is all that Grandmama has warned
me against, and she would know better than most.
That is the only comfort that I take from this curious time, that Grandmama knows the man's measure, and that she is correct that he will soon tire
of pursuing me. The peculiar thing is that I must
give in to his blandishments—so far as propriety
will allow—and it is that which will, in a short
time, persuade him to leave my side. To rid myself
of the disease, I must be sure to do my best to try
and catch it! How extraordinary!*

She frowned again, for she had not managed to
capture all that she meant, but she could not find the
words, or even the sense, to describe this most curious of courtships, and so this would have to do. No
doubt in time, when all this was finally behind her,
she would be able to make sense of it all.

She blotted the last bit of fresh ink, closed the
diary, made sure the inkwell was stoppered securely,
and stood to remove the apron she had donned to
protect her gown from any ink stains. She crossed to
the door that led to her bedchamber, idly scanned the
children's cards she had been coloring this morning,
and went to her cheval glass.

She found that all was in order; she had only to
slip on her long gloves and then would be ready for
the night of theatre ahead. Ah, her evening with Captain Penford—how she had looked forward to it, and
now it was here! For a moment she hesitated, realizing she had written nothing at all today in her diary

concerning the captain . . . but that was not so odd, of course, for late tonight or tomorrow morning she would record the events that awaited her now.

Thinking of the captain as she looked in her glass, she surveyed herself critically, attempting to see herself as he might. He could not fail to admire her gown of palest blue silk with its underskirt of white tulle. Brussels lace—precious since the war had begun—created a pretty border of delicate triangles that ran the circumference of her décolleté bodice. There was a fringe of smaller lace triangles, too, at the little puff sleeves that just touched her shoulders. Mama had brought from the family jewel case a single, large teardrop sapphire on a silver gilt chain, and earbobs to match, the dark, rich color contrasting nicely with the pale blue of her gown.

Pamela thought her goal of accomplishing a look which was striking without being affected had perhaps succeeded. She did not desire to put the captain at any unease, for since he was but a captain, any wife he took would need to expect to live more frugally than did an Earl's daughter. He was, after all, only a second son with military expenses to be met; any woman he took to wife might very well expect no other jewels than those she could bring with her. This thought was not distressing to Pamela, who had jewels and dowry enough to sustain her as a more than credible hostess, for she felt certain that Captain Penford would not be the manner of husband who usurped all his wife's funds despite his legal right to do so.

As she pulled on her long white gloves, she examined her coiffure. Phyllis had taken her long hair and roped it, then secured the length in a twist at the crown of her head, from the center of which the curled ends tumbled, the light tendrils just reaching to her nape. Really, the little maid had created an engaging look, even managing to largely conceal the comb that held in place the single white feather that was so like Captain Penford's own. Yes, she would do, and nicely, too, she felt sure. She determined that she would slip Phyllis a little additional coinage for the extra attentive service.

She forced herself to wait above stairs, her reticule and pelisse across the room out of reach of her hand. It would never do to be awaiting him, cloaked, too eager to go. She must wait until a servant told her he had called, then rise, don her pelisse, secure her reticule, and slowly descend to the entry hall where he would be waiting for her.

She almost jumped when a rap came on the door and then opened without ceremony. "Come on, then. Horses standing." Owen threw the comment at her, turning and leaving at once.

Her eyes narrowed as she rose. Owen. Twice the traitor to her: first letting Marchmont into her sitting room, and then making free with a prattling tongue when Marchmont had played his nonsensical "silence" game before the Misses Everroad. It was time some revenge was enacted, and that revenge would suit her purposes very well this evening.

"Owen, dear, would you please be so kind as to fetch me another lemonade?" Pamela cooed.

Her brother turned to her with a decidedly frosty air. "A third? I think not. And I shall not deliver any more notes for you to your friends. I am not your errand boy."

"Oh," she said quietly, allowing a flicker of distress to cross her features. This achieved the desired result, for Owen snapped to at once when Penford's affronted gaze leveled on him. Perhaps because they were guests in his box, or perhaps because he just had a fine and honorable deportment around women, Captain Penford had kindly underscored each of the requests she had doled out to her brother by scowling if Owen demurred. This only made her all the more pleased with the good captain.

Straightening in his chair and casting his sister a quickly stifled venomous glance, Owen reached for the glass, snapping, "Oh, very well!"

"And my shawl, Owen? I left it in the coach. You do think our coachman will have returned by now, do you not? I declare there is a chill in the theatre tonight."

Owen's eyes bulged slightly, and his cravat appeared a trifle too tight. "If he's come already, he won't be letting my cattle stand, you know. I shall have to wait the devil of a long time until they drive 'round to the entrance again."

"Powell!" Penford remonstrated.

"It is quite all right, Captain Penford. I do not mind how my brother speaks to me," Pamela said with downcast eyes.

Owen drew in his breath, his face purpling, and only let it out again after five full seconds of silence. "Do not expect me back for an hour or so!" he said stiffly, turning on his heel and exiting the box.

"Posh! An hour," Pamela said, shaking her head, and smiling at the captain when he nodded his agreement that it would never be so long as that.

Pamela was glad Owen went, and not only because she had grown tired of her revenge. She would not send him on any more fool's errands when he did finally return. No, he had paid enough of a price, especially now that he had gone and there was almost no one who would interrupt her chance to have a little private conversation with Captain Penford. She would have him all to herself, for he was in the corner of the box, and she seated to his right. The Misses Everroad had left the box, spying a party of friends who had yet to hear every detail of Miss Emily's forthcoming nuptials. One of Owen's friends, a fortyish fellow, Lord Hadcombe, was absorbed in the performance. His wife, Lady Hadcombe, appeared to be entirely asleep, her chin resting on her chest, her right temple against the wall of the box, and her lips slightly parted as she breathed. She had not moved in the last fifteen minutes, and her husband did not seem to find this at all remarkable. There were also three bucks who stood at the back of the box, the combination of standing fellows and vacant chairs making for a very crowded box indeed. They were busy laying some kind of wager concerning the performance below. It was the closest thing to a private moment that Pamela could hope for.

"Your time in London is flying by far too quickly," she said to the captain.

He nodded. " 'Tis but ten days before I return to the battlefield."

"Assuming you are well."

"I shall be well enough, whether or not my foot is healed by then. It is only because I am a Marquess's son that I was brought to London at all."

"There is no hope you may stay longer?"

"No."

"Oh." She looked down at the fan that was folded in her lap. When she looked up again, she was not smiling, for she could not have failed to see the eager light in the back of his eyes. He was ready to return to battle. No one had dimmed that eagerness for him, that was clear, and there was so little time to attempt to be the one who might make him regret leaving London. She said the first thing that came to mind. "What shall you miss most?"

He thought a moment. "There's not one thing, but many. Music. Laughter." He smiled, his mustache curving at the ends. "Beautiful ladies."

Now she smiled back, accepting the compliment. "Do you know what I would miss most, were I a soldier?"

"What?"

"Pastimes."

"Pastimes?" He looked amused and baffled at once.

"To do nothing but daydream. To lie about in the warm sun, playing solitaire, or perhaps doing a needlework just because I like the way it is turning out.

To draw a picture from memory. That manner of thing." She thought of her own paper cutting, but did not mention it. Something in the way he'd said "pastimes" kept her from it.

"To be idle, you mean," he said somewhat sharply.

"I suppose I do."

"There's no time for that in a soldier's life, I can tell you."

"But that is my point! I think I should go mad if I did not ever have some quiet time just for . . . dallying."

"You are a town creature, Lady Pamela. You have the leisure to do so. But what if you did not? What if your life changed and suddenly all your time was taken up with the care of children, and bills to pay, moves to make, and little monies to make do with?"

She laughed, not quite sure what to make of his question. Surely he was not rejecting her station in life, for one day his own would undoubtedly be higher still. Or did the mere idea that time should ever be whiled away give his voice that disapproving edge? Or was he speaking of how it would be for a woman who was his wife? Yes, perhaps he was. But then she had to ask herself, did his question have a deeper meaning? Was he trying to find out how she, specifically, would respond to a change in her world, a shift to a lower daily echelon?

She answered carefully, "I should do what must be done, of course."

He stared at her for a long moment, then gave a very small nod. "Yes, I believe you might."

She stared back, and she wished she knew what that look and that comment might mean.

"Excuse me," one of the young bucks, Mister Appleton, said at Pamela's shoulder. She turned to him, at once relieved and annoyed that he had broken the moment that had riveted her stare to that of the captain.

Mister Appleton held out the play's program and went on, "I say, do you have a gleam of where we might be in this? I've been attempting to follow what they've sketched out here about whose doing what to whom in this act and then that one, but I've quite lost my place and can't tell from the bellowing below where we might be."

"He says there's a knifing or two coming up still," one of the other young men, Lord Gilbury, assured her, "but I say from here there's naught but jabbering at one another. We've a wager on it."

"We're in the middle of Act IV," Lord Hadcombe said, giving the others a dark glare. "Now hush!"

Pamela looked up at the young man and nodded, saying as quietly as she might, "There's more violence in Act V."

"Ha ha!" crowed Mister Appleton, spinning and putting out his hand to receive the blunt he had just won. The two other young men, with grimaces, pulled their purses from their pockets.

The transaction settled, the bucks looked for new sport, instantly and with unspoken agreement choosing Pamela to fit this need. They drew chairs near to hers, crowding the already crowded rim of the box, and began to speak, one's comment overlapping the other as they all tried to speak at once. They complimented her gown and her hair, pointed over her shoulder to acquaintances, calling out when the mood hit them—earning hisses of "Shhh!" from Lord Hadcombe—and debated nonsensically about what could possibly be happening on stage.

"Who's that, then? Richard? Isn't he supposed to be a humpback?"

"Sapskull. You're thinking of Richard the Third, and this is all about the Second. Besides, that's Bollingbroke."

" 'Tis not. 'Tis supposed to be Northumberland."

"No!"

" 'Tis!"

"He was in red."

" 'Tis a different scene, ninny. Can't a fellow put on a new set of tights?"

"No. It confuses the audience."

"Well, it managed to confuse you, that's a certainty."

"I say 'tis Bollingbroke."

"No!"

Mister Appleton leaped suddenly to his feet, leaning way out over the rail to peer down into the pit below, forcing Pamela to lean forward to avoid having her coiffure crushed. He screamed out, "Hallo! Hallo! Sylvie! Sylvie Carpenter. It's your old friend, Appleton. Here, Sylvie. Look up, girl!"

Captain Penford frowned, and at that moment Pamela caught his eye. He shook his head in disapproval and muttered something she could not quite catch, as Lord Gilbury was laughing rather loudly, and pointing, though at what Pamela could not have said. In fact, she found herself smiling along with him regardless, and even uttered a small laugh.

"Oh, I say, that is a pretty laugh," Lord Gilbury said earnestly at her side, his own mirth forgotten as he gazed into her face.

Pamela blushed and murmured a polite nothing.

"A pretty laugh to go with a pretty lady," said the third man, with enormous sideburns, who had been introduced as Sir Eugene, pulling his chair even closer.

"Do you care to stroll, Lady Pamela?" Lord Gilbury asked, looking eager.

"The play is still on," Pamela laughed.

"Oh, that *is* a pretty laugh." Mister Appleton turned to join the conversation, apparently having never attracted Sylvie's attention.

"But after this act?" Lord Gilbury pressed.

"The next act follows at once," Captain Penford said, his voice overriding the others'. "There shall be no break for a stroll."

"Then after?" Gilbury urged.

"If the lady cares to stroll after, I shall escort her," Penford said, and this time there was no mistaking the chill in his voice. A voice that surely was used to having its commands followed. Lord Gilbury sat back, looking deflated.

Pamela sighed silently but happily, more than content to have the captain stake a claim on her time and attention. He with a wounded foot, and yet he would have no other take her 'round but himself! How very nice of these puppies to banter with her, and how splendid that the captain seemed perhaps a little protective of her acquaintance! She was so pleased with the young men for bringing the moment about, she gave Lord Gilbury a smile, which appeared to revive his spirits as he smiled crookedly back.

"Did you hear that?" Mister Appleton cried as the curtain swayed to a close. "I say, I like the sound of that." He put a hand dramatically to his chest, one hand outstretched, and quoted, " 'I will lay a plot shall show us all a merry day.' Indeed a merry day! Quite what we have here, eh? What say we all to some champagne?"

"Champagne!" cried the two other gentlemen, and even Lord Hadcombe nodded agreeably. His wife did not stir at his side.

"I'll arrange it!" cried the tall man of enormous sideburns, Sir Eugene. He promptly popped out of the box in pursuit thereof.

The curtain below puffed in places, as no doubt scene changers darted about, setting the scene that should begin in a moment or two. Other than this action, there was naught on stage to watch; Lord Gilbury seemed to be trying to make his mouth form a comment that was never quite forthcoming; and Captain Penford was frowning slightly, staring forward. Pamela stretched out her hand, just barely placing her fingertips on his arm. He turned at the touch, slipped his hand over hers, pinning her fingers to his sleeve, and reformed his face into a slight smile. Quietly he said, "You should not laugh. It only encourages them."

Her eyebrows rose. "And so?"

"And so they become quite ridiculous."

She hesitated. It was true, they had become ridiculous, but, too, only in a playful, harmless way. Pamela had to bite the tip of her tongue to keep from smiling at the memory of Mister Appleton leaning precariously over the rail. However, Captain Penford was right. One ought not encourage them, as they rather behaved as overgrown children.

It was then that Pamela looked up and saw Marchmont in another box, far across the theatre. He was laughing, and a woman in deep blue was laughing with him. He leaned forward, whispering in the woman's ear. She sat back, raised her fan and rapped him across the cheek with it. He sat back, laughing all the harder, and then the woman again laughed with him. As Pamela stared, they rose to their feet, leaving the box.

Marchmont. With another woman. Again. Not that it mattered. *He* certainly would think little of another casual dalliance. Even at this thought, Pamela could almost hear Marchmont saying, "Minutes, my dear!" Not that she cared. He was free to spend his minutes away from her with anyone he chose.

"But look, Appleton!" cried his compatriot, Lord Gilbury. They all looked where he pointed, for the curtains had opened again. " 'Tis the girl with the large . . . er . . . that is to say, the girl. . . ."

"I see her, I see her! But why's she nattering about Caesar?"

"Caesar. King. She means Richard, you see," Gilbury explained.

"Confusing. The whole play is confusing. In fact,

all of Shakespeare's confusing. Is that not so, Lady Pamela?'' asked Mister Appleton.

"At first," she admitted.

"Not so much if you but be quiet and listen to it!'' Lord Hadcombe snapped. His wife opened her eyes at his side, but then promptly closed them again.

The three gentlemen fell to whispers, for once properly chastened. They whispered, exchanging more comments about the actors below, the appeal of Pamela's charms, and even going so far as to tweak Captain Penford for his apparent attendance on the play.

"You, Captain, you seem to fathom all this gibberish. Why do you not give us a translation?'' Mister Appleton suggested, smiling at his clever thought.

The captain fixed him with a steady glare and said nothing. Mister Appleton's smile faded, and he stuttered, "Oh, well, perhaps not, then."

"I should not mind," Pamela volunteered, to smooth the moment. She then proceeded to identify the characters as they spoke, not bothering to tell the beginning of the tale, but only illuminating what was happening now. The two bucks seemed to find that quite acceptable, though she had to admit they lost their interest in the play at once when Sir Eugene returned with a servant in tow, champagne bottles and glasses on a tray.

Champagne was poured, and toasts were made. Even Captain Penford raised his glass when the bucks cried a toast to "the fair and good Lady Pamela." She, in her turn, called out a toast to nights at the theatre, which was greeted with a "Huzzah!" and another tipping of champagne into each glass.

Owen returned just as the actors were making their bows, his sister's shawl draped over his arm and a frown set upon his face. "Missed not only the play but champagne as well! And someone other than myself paying for it, too!" he growled.

Lady Hadcombe stirred, sitting up and blinking slowly. "Did someone say champagne?" she asked, putting out her hand until one of the gentlemen pressed a glass into it.

Owen gave the woman a quick scowl, belatedly realizing his sister had not been well-attended, but then the other three gentlemen distracted him from his tardy protectiveness by handing him a glass also. A toast was made to his health, then to that of Lady Hadcombe, who promptly declared the play to be among the finest she had ever seen. Her husband agreed with her, with absolutely no sign of humor or sarcasm in his manner, and the others began to all talk at once, offering their own opinions as to the matter.

Penford, shaking his head, spoke, his loud voice ringing over the others' in the confines of the box. "Powell, does the coach wait below?"

"It was directly below a moment ago, but now I've no doubt my groom is circling Bow or Holborn or heaven knows which street at the moment."

"Then, Lady Pamela, would you care to stroll?"

"I am content to sit if that is preferable," she said, glancing at the cane that was propped in the corner of the box.

He cast a look over the members in the box. "Hardly so," he said dryly, reaching for the cane.

She hid a smile, and stood, to move out of his way. He stood quickly, having used the rail to gain his feet. The cane was in his hand in a moment, and he made use of it to slap at chair and human legs indiscriminately until they were scattered out of his way.

Once free of the box, he offered his arm to Pamela, who made a point of touching his sleeve very lightly, that she not impede his balance or his progress. He walked slowly, favoring the wounded foot, making use of the cane.

"I declare the air is fresher here. Fewer young dandies to sully the scent," he said, making her laugh.

"They are silly geese, but I confess I enjoyed their easy banter."

"Hmmph, too easy," he said. "Too frivolous by half to ever make decent soldiers."

She might have said something about the world needing more manner of men than soldiers, but just then an acquaintance called her name. She turned, recognizing the caller as her friend, Miss Tarpon, whom she introduced to the captain. Miss Tarpon then proceeded to introduce the captain to the rather largish party that made up her group. They accompanied the slowly moving group to the staircase, chatting comfortably, but at the steps offered their farewells.

There they stayed for another fifteen minutes, greeting others of Pamela's or the captain's acquaintance. The Misses Everroad stopped to say they had solicited a ride with an aunt of theirs, and asked Pamela to convey their thanks for the use—however brief—of Captain Penford's family box. Then spying the captain for themselves, they moved to offer their thanks personally. They were replaced by a young man seeking an introduction via an old friend of Pamela's from her boarding school days. Just as she turned from them, another man stepped up to her.

"Lord Marchmont!" she cried at sight of his smiling face. She had thought he had left. Truth be told, she had more than half suspected he had left with the matron in dark blue.

"Lady Pamela," he said, catching up her hand and bowing over it.

Her first impulse was to snatch her hand away, and her second was that this was the very kind of response that would only prolong his pursuit. Instead she nodded up at him and said, "Well met."

"Very well met. I would not have wished to miss the sight of you, as you are entirely lovely tonight."

She inclined her head at the tribute, aware a pleased blush had risen on her cheeks. It would have been false modesty to decline his compliment. She made no personal remark in return, although she had to confess silently that his black evening breeches and coat, and white silk hose and fawn shirt, suited him very well. She saw the monocle must be in his pocket, this time with a red ribbon attached, making a small, elegant flash of color against the silver-shot cream of his waistcoat.

Over the finely fitted shoulder of his coat she saw that the captain was engaged in a conversation that encompassed a rather large group of men, some of them in uniform as himself, and that his back was mostly turned to where she stood with Marchmont.

"I stopped to warn you, in case your grandmama had not," he said, calling back her attention.

"Warn me?"

"I see by your reaction that she did not. Your grandmama was already agreed that we shall go to the fair tomorrow, at one o'clock."

"Fair? Grandmama?" She gave him a tentative smile, not at all surprised he was apparently making plans without consulting her first.

"Indeed. She was so very kind as to reply at once to my note of inquiry this afternoon. I daresay she supped in her room, and therefore missed her first chance to speak of it to you. No doubt she meant to make mention of it later this evening, or in the morning."

"I have no reason to doubt that logic, nor even to question if such an agreement was forthcoming, for you know very well that I shall ask Grandmama if it is so."

He nodded.

She did not try to discuss whether she might wish to go or not. "So. We are going to a fair? Which fair?"

"Along the Thames, a little nothing. But it shall have jugglers, and animal acts, and all the meat pies you can consume for a few pennies. A spot of pleasure for the morrow, if the weather holds, of course."

She found herself rather hoping that the weather would hold, a fact that surprised her. Still, it had been years since she had last gone to a fair, and Grand-mama had sanctioned it, so she could see no harm in being agreeable. If anything, it fit nicely into her plans to be rid of him. That thought—that she had agreed to spend an afternoon with him to be rid of him—made her smile.

"A smile? An actual warm smile for me?" Marchmont cried, putting a hand to his heart with mock astonishment.

She went so far as to bat her eyes at him, and agreed, "For you."

He grew suddenly still before her, his face rear-ranging into softer sentiments, his mouth leveling, his dark brows smoothing, his light eyes sparkling in the candlelight. He began to lean down toward her, his intent clear. Great merciful heavens! Here, in the the-atre, with dozens of people all about, it seemed quite clear he was intent on kissing her!

Chapter 11

Pamela flipped open her fan, bringing it up near her face, hoping it might prove some sort of shield. She wondered rather wildly why she had brought the carved ivory, which might be seen through, instead of the large painted paper fan that sprang to mind now that she required an excellent cover. Then she wondered why she did not merely step back, out of his reach. Or bid him stop. Or step on his foot. No, instead she stood still, unable to move away, the man's lips only a few inches from her own now. He had no care for convention, would in fact greatly enjoy compromising her thusly. He might even believe such a public act would compel her to accept his suit.

That thought put life back into her limbs. She flipped her fan closed and said loudly, "Thank you. I believe the mote is out of my eye now." When still he lowered his head, taking half a step closer to her, she reached up with the folded fan and ran it along his jawline, applying enough pressure that he was forced to turn his head a little to the right. His green eyes watched her own, the corners slanted toward her, as she laughed aloud and cried, perhaps a little too shrilly, "Lord Marchmont, how you do flirt!"

Those eyes, so sharp and clever, laughed at her ploy even as they admired it.

She turned away from him at once, moving the few steps to Captain Penford's side. The captain was facing her now, but she was not sure from his posture, always stiff with military bearing, if he had noted any of the scene just past or not. He offered his arm at once, and she took it, saying, "Do let us tell Owen we are ready to depart."

"Of course," he said, and now she knew he had not missed at least some of the interlude with Marchmont, for he cast that gentleman a dark glance. His eyes then strayed to the single white feather in her hair, and that seemed to relax his stiff posture just a little. Had she not already been flustered by Marchmont's thwarted kiss, she might have thrilled to see that the captain had noted the sign of favor she had fixed in her coiffure.

He turned, making use of his cane, rather abruptly presenting his back to Marchmont and pulling Pamela along with him.

She half expected Marchmont to call out something behind her, but he did not. However, when she flashed a look over her shoulder, she found him staring after her, his hands folded behind his back, his gaze steady. She thought he might be amused, but if he was, it was a dark amusement; that much she could see even from this distance. She turned away, feeling flushed, provoked, and, most annoying of all, faintly blameworthy.

Owen and the captain did most of the talking on the drive home, Pamela giving in to an impulse to simply sit, strangely subdued. Her evening had not been ruined by the scene with Marchmont, now that she'd had a little time and space to consider the matter. Indeed, she thought it had gone well for her, for she could not have allowed him to kiss her in such a populated place. And it had been well, very well indeed, to be the one in charge of the situation for once. But now any liveliness she had felt this evening had been all used up, perhaps by Appleton, Gilbury, and Sir Eugene. No, that was not it. Whatever the reason, now she was content to listen to the men talking while she merely rode, enjoying the peace and quiet that moonlight was capable of creating inside a rolling carriage.

Captain Penford was last to descend, Owen having assisted his sister and then lending a shoulder to aid the military man down from the coach. They talked quietly as a servant drove the coach away on the drive that circled to the back of the house. The lad would return a few minutes later with Penford's saddled horse. Penford commented on the desirability of having enough town property to support a small stables on the property, and Owen heartily agreed. He explained that it could not support all of the family's equipage, the larger portion of which was kept at a nearby mews, but it certainly made travel more immediate and thereby convenient.

Listening to the men, Pamela learned that the captain had ridden his new horse tonight, the one Owen helped him find. She further learned that although his parents had a home in town where he could stay, one large enough to also support a stable of its own, he had chosen to reside more quietly in bachelor's quarters. His family was not yet in town for the Season, and he had no desire to bestir the servants just for his few weeks here. That was pleasant to learn, for it meant he had a courteous nature, where others sometimes cared little for the inconveniences they caused. It also meant his funds were not so limited as some might think, to be able to absorb the cost of his own lodgings. Better and better.

Two grooms came, the one leading Penford's horse, the other silently waiting by until there was a pause in the conversation. At that point he interjected to Owen, "My lord, I was wondering, as you 'ad a moment, if you'd care to 'ave a look at that bruised 'oof on Chevalier?"

"I hope it is healing well?" Captain Penford asked of Owen. He turned to Pamela to explain, "I am afraid your brother's favorite seat took a stone when we were searching for my new filly the other day."

"That I would," Owen said to the servant, then to Penford, "If you will excuse me for a moment?"

The captain nodded, and turned back to Pamela, who asked what he thought of his new mount.

The evening was cool but not wholly unpleasant, and they chatted on for several minutes. It was only after ten minutes had passed that Pamela realized Owen had not returned, quite probably forgetting about his guest while he instead coddled his favorite mount with a bucket of oats.

Aside from the groom who held the horse's head, she and Captain Penford were alone. In the moonlight.

It would never happen again, this moment of near-complete aloneness. Something—perhaps it was the success of the evening, or perhaps it was a residual effect of having someone almost kiss her—but whatever the reason, something stirred in Pamela, telling her an opportunity was nigh. She did not wait, did not hesitate, but instead stepped close to the captain, causing him to startle a little, his head snapping toward hers in a military attentiveness. His face was very near hers.

"Lady—" he started to say, but then she stretched up her neck, tilting her face, offering her lips to him, her eyes meeting his. Silence descended. Pamela was acutely aware of the stillness, of the groom watching with open interest, but she did not step away. Instead her lips parted ever so slightly—had she been about to explain with words that she was asking for a kiss?— and then the captain leaned toward her as well, and his mouth was on hers.

The kiss was warm, soft, short, little more than a shared breath, a tickle of his mustache along her upper lip, and then he stepped back, a wince crossing his features when his weight shifted to his injured foot. Two other things crossed his face: one was chagrin, no doubt that the groom stared so at them, and the other was harder to define. Embarrassment? Awkwardness? Virtue?

She stepped back then, aware that there would be no other kiss in the moonlight to follow. Of course he was right, only too right that it be so; it was difficult to imagine how she had dared to be so close to him for the first kiss, let alone another. Difficult to think she had acted so in front of a servant.

Whatever spell had brought them to the moment, it was gone for now, and they both knew it. He shifted his weight again, taking another step back from her.

Penford signed to the servant, and within a moment he was being helped to mount, his injured right foot swinging up and over the saddle. Once seated, he gathered up the reins, only then looking down at her. He sat silent for a moment, handling the horse automatically from long hours in the saddle, gazing down at her without speaking. She looked up, wanting to say something but finding no words.

At length he said, "Would you drive with me tomorrow afternoon?"

She knew she was committed to Marchmont for the afternoon. Should she defy Marchmont and not go with him? Time was far too short; Marchmont would be in London long after Penford was gone. She would be a fool to lose the opportunity to be with the captain—but scruples sometimes made you a fool, even when you knew better. Her lips feeling tight, she reluctantly answered, "I am afraid I cannot. Can you call, perhaps, in the morning?" Bold words, inviting a truth. It would be his answer at this moment that would let her know what he thought of that moonlit kiss.

"Of course. 'Twould be my pleasure."

She felt the tightness around her mouth dissolve into a relieved smile.

He gave her a serious look, but there was something less harsh in his eyes. "I should instruct your brother to tend you better, but I have decided I shall not do so tonight."

"No?"

"No. Good night, Lady Pamela."

"Good night, Captain Penford."

He nudged the horse with his heels and rode away. Pamela watched him until he blended with the night, the groom waiting with her, not meeting her eye.

One kiss. He had been a perfect gentleman, honoring her by not taking anything more than that. She knew that same honor would make it difficult for him to dismiss her entirely now: one simply did not often have the chance to kiss an unattended, respectable young lady—no less than an Earl's daughter!—in the moonlight. Still, she could have been more confident she had made a lasting impression if only he had taken just one more small kiss. A token, an opportunity of his own making, to show that he could hope another such possibility might arise. As it stood now, she could not be all that certain that Captain Penford wished to ever kiss her again. Still, he had asked to call on her tomorrow, and his words implied he had not regretted that Owen had left them alone together. Happy signs, surely.

There could be no certainties tonight; all that was to happen between them this day had happened. Now she must wait until tomorrow to see what insight the new day would bring her as regarded the good captain's feelings.

Fleetingly, as she walked toward the front door, it crossed Pamela's mind that Lord Marchmont, in the same position, would have made his feelings abundantly clear.

She tossed and turned on her bed for over an hour before she finally rose, moving with purpose to her writing table. She opened her diary and began to write:

Tonight I kissed Cpt. P. Or he kissed me. I am not sure which now. I cannot sleep. I am restless. I wish I had more experience of kisses, for I find myself trying to compare what little I know of them.

M.'s seem, well, invasive. Demanding. His always make me startle.

Cpt. P.'s showed a gentlemanly respect. He honored me. I would have to say his kisses are gentle, kind, even thoughtful. I admired his kiss a great deal. Our first kiss! It was very pleasant. Very, very pleasant. It tickled, but not overmuch. In fact, I believe I like the way it tickled. It was sweet. And just to think! I was kissed by the man I love in the moonlight! It was very romantic. I could smell the lilies in bloom, their fragrance on the night air. It is difficult to imagine how another kiss could ever surpass the sweetness of this one. It could not have been more perfect.

She put down the quill, her lower lip sticking out as she contemplated her words. She had always imagined the moment she wrote in her diary about such a kiss. Of course, Marchmont had been so bold as to have her first, and she had disdained to write anything of that. This, then, was the first chance to record her thoughts of a shared first kiss, this time with Captain Penford. She had imagined that she would write page after page, describing her feelings and her thoughts, but now these few lines were all she had written. Her mouth twisted, reflecting an inner battle, but then her truthful nature forced her to pick up her quill, dip it, and add:

"If only he had kissed me a second time."

She hesitated, dipping the quill as needed, adding:

"And, starting tomorrow, it shall be M.'s turn to be the one who is startled!"

It was only then that she was able to crawl back into her bed and at last fall to sleep.

Chapter 12

Captain Penford did not demur when offered a cup of lemon tea, nor did he seem to note the slight smile of remembrance that came to Pamela's lips when she poured.

Just as she inquired whether he would care for a lump from the sugarloaf, Lawlton entered the room and announced, "Lady Clay and her daughter, Miss Elizabeth."

Even Phyllis looked up in some surprise at the name. The maid quickly went back to her quiet darning in the corner, however, as an attractive woman in mauve entered the room. She held by the hand a little dark-haired girl whose sweet, rounded face was encircled by a charming little chip bonnet that matched her mama's down to the maroon velvet ribbons. As Captain Penford strove to gain his feet, Pamela cried with pleasure, "Liza!"

The little girl's hand dropped from her mama's, and she dashed across the room, throwing her arms about her cousin's neck.

"Sweeting!" Pamela greeted the girl again, hugging her back, then took the child up in her arms, settling her on her hip as she also stood, to make introductions. "Phillipa, do come in. I should like for you to meet Captain Penford. Captain, this is my cousin, Lady Clay."

Phillipa inclined her head and bobbed a brief curtsy, and Penford bowed from the waist as they murmured greetings.

"And this little minx is my favorite and youngest cousin, Miss Elizabeth Anne Locke, whom you must call Liza."

Phillipa's lips twitched in a mild disapproval of the nickname, but Pamela was used to the expression ever since she had performed her singing *faux pas* at Phillipa's wedding, and paid no particular attention to it now.

"Please, do have a seat. Do you care for lemon tea?" Pamela asked, returning to her own seat, the child on her lap.

"Yes, I would," Phillipa replied as she sat on the nearest settee.

"But, do tell, what brings you this day?" Pamela asked, mostly of the child.

"My birfday," Liza said, her eyes growing round with pleasure as her grown-up cousin smiled back at her.

"But tomorrow is your birthday, sweeting! You have come a day early."

"Knowing Lady Premington's morning parlor is frequented daily by guests, I was hopeful that our coming unannounced would not be a difficulty,"

166

Phillipa said a trifle stiffly. "But we are having a small gathering in the nursery for Elizabeth tomorrow and would not be able to come otherwise. She insisted her birthday would be quite spoilt if she did not see you by the day thereof."

"But of course!" Pamela cried, setting the little girl from her lap. She bent down so that she was eye to eye with Liza, and added, "You knew I should have a particular something for you, did you not?"

"Pamela, you ought not encourage the child to be forward," Phillipa scolded softly.

"She is not being forward; she is being clever. She knows a child's birthday must not pass without something special from Cousin Pamela, do you not, sweeting?" Pamela's smile encompassed the room, causing the captain's lips to turn up briefly, and even Phillips had to respond with a short smile.

Lisa nodded enthusiastically.

"Wait right here and I shall fetch it, shall I?"

Liza gave another enthusiastic nod.

Pamela turned to her guests. "If you will pardon me for just a minute or two, I shall be right back."

"Of course," the captain and Phillipa said together.

When Pamela returned to the parlor, she found Mama had joined the scene. Her parent looked up and made a tsking sound when she saw the papercuttings in Pamela's hands, her expression making it clear she wished Pamela had not chosen this moment to flaunt this peculiarity of hers.

"Liza has come for her birthday gift, Mama,"

Pamela explained in the face of her parent's unspoken censure.

"Ah. And how old are we today?" Mama asked, turning her attention to the little girl.

"My birfday's tomorrow," Liza explained.

"Yes, I see. And just how old shall you be tomorrow?"

Four fingers were held aloft.

"Four! Well, I daresay Pamela has created something that a four-year-old would like." She turned to Captain Penford, clearly pleased with herself to have thought of a way to turn her daughter's quaint custom into a virtue, as she brightly told him, "Pamela has an understanding of children and what they should like, you see. She shall make an excellent mother one day."

Pamela shot her parent one quick, speaking look, but would not be distracted from the pleasure of seeing Liza receive her gifts. The stacks of cards she placed facedown on the tea tray, out of Liza's immediate reach, and handed forth the peep show.

Liza knew what to do with the creation, for she had received one on her last birthday, as, for years, had every cousin they shared in common. "Hold the end for me, Cousin Pamewa!" she cried.

"What do you say, Elizabeth?" her mother prompted.

"Thank you," Liza said automatically and with no hint of sincerity, but her eagerness was sincere enough a thank you to make Pamela smile. She took the end piece, extending the accordioned papers so that the length of her construction was over twelve inches, as Liza held the front piece, pulling it to her eye. "Oh, Cousin Pamewa, 'tis the park! Green Park!"

"So 'tis. Do you see the little dark-haired girl chasing the squirrel?"

" 'Tis me! 'Tis me!" cried the four-year-old, bouncing up and down, the peep show bobbing between the two of them.

Pamela laughed at the display, Lady Premington appeared tolerant, Phillipa frowned—possibly thinking of the child's overabundance of enthusiasm come tomorrow's party—and Captain Penford scratched his eyebrow, smiling benignly.

"Gently now, gently," Pamela advised. "We must be as careful of this peep show as with the one you received last year. But do not fret, for I have a second gift for you, one that you need not ask your nanny to help you with." She gently extracted the paper toy from Liza's hands, setting it on the table, and turned to the tea tray to pick up the stack of hand-colored cards. "You may play with these all by yourself."

She knelt down to turn the cards over on the low table, revealing the drawings on the other side. There were six sets of three cards each, each third containing a portion of an animal's body. She arranged the six sets so that six animals were revealed: a giraffe, an elephant, a crocodile, a parrot, a badger, and a cat. All of them were drawn standing upright on their hind legs.

"Pretty!" Liza cried, clapping her hands together.

"And see here: you may exchange one part for another and invent your very own new animals,"

Pamela explained, moving the giraffe's head away and placing the crocodile's in its place.

Liza squealed with delight, and she reached to re-arrange the configurations before her. "Look, look!" she cried, laughing, pointing at a creature made up of a parrot's head, a cat's body, and a giraffe's legs.

" 'Tis a par-cat-raffe." Pamela stumbled over the pronunciation, which caused her to laugh along with her little cousin.

Liza pointed to another combination. "What's dis called?"

"That would be a . . . um, badg-ele-dile."

"And dat?"

"Oh, let me think . . . ! I suppose it must be called a gir-rot-ephant."

Liza laughed again.

"Did you draw them, Pamela?" Phillipa asked with mild curiosity.

"Yes. They are called metamorphosis cards. I saw the idea in a periodical for children, and the moment I saw them I knew they would be just the thing for Liza!"

"I like dem very much," Liza pronounced.

"Do you think Cousin William would like some? Some with soldiers, perhaps?"

"No, he would get mad if their uniforms were not always just right," Liza said seriously. "He wanted to frow away his wooden soldiers because dey had da wrong hats now, but Uncle Llewellyn said he would carve dem and paint dem differently."

"That is true, I suppose. He is always quite the one to inform us what is the latest in style and manner

170

for the soldiers, is he not? Well, perhaps just 'people' then? Butchers, bakers, and candlestick makers?''

Liza nodded. *"Dat* he would like.''

"Is that the end of the gifts?'' Mama prompted.

"Yes.''

"Then, Liza dear, it is time to take your things away above stairs to play with them. Phyllis, do please escort Miss Elizabeth to Mrs. Hart above stairs, and then you may return to your darning.''

Phyllis put the darning aside and came to take the little girl's hand.

"The peep show will remain here with Cousin Pamela,'' her mama decreed.

Liza was content with this decision, the metamorphosis cards safely guarded by the tightest grip her little hand could create—lest, perhaps, some other adult say she may not take these with her. However, she could not be led away before flinging her arms around Pamela's knees to give her grown-up cousin a big hug of thanks. Pamela, trapped by the embrace, patted the girl on the back and smiled down at the child, and told her, "You are welcome. It was my pleasure.''

As the little girl was led away, Captain Penford spoke. "You seemed to have pleased her, Lady Pamela.''

"Pamela is the sort who knows how to please,'' her mama interjected before she could speak. At the comment, Phillipa's brows rose for a moment, before her eyes settled speculatively on Pamela, then the captain.

Pamela could feel a blush stealing over her skin,

but fortunately Mama chose that moment to change the subject by inquiring after the health of Cousin Phillipa's parents.

Conversation was desultory until, ten minutes later, Phillipa announced she was leaving. Liza was brought, engulfing Pamela in another hug before executing a sweet but inelegant curtsy to the captain and Lady Premington. With Phyllis once again tucked into her sewing corner, Mama rose to see Phillipa and Liza to the door, leaving Pamela to entertain the captain alone.

"She is a dear." Pamela smiled after them.

"Undoubtedly so, though in need of some training," Penford said when they were quit of the room.

"Liza?" Pamela asked in some surprise.

"She is far too inclined to throw herself about. It is not seemly for children to thrust themselves physically upon others."

"Oh, but she is only just now four, and we are close friends," Pamela explained.

"It is never too soon to begin instructing the young in their manners."

Pamela's hand went thoughtfully to her lips, as though to hold back the comments that formed on her tongue. Perhaps she ought to have taken the child aside to give her her gifts, instead of thrusting her on the company of the adult guests. Although Pamela could not fault the child's demonstrative nature—having had much the same nature herself once upon a time—perhaps the moment should have been kept private.

Penford was speaking. "You have an artist's eye," he said, pointing toward the peep show.

For a moment it crossed Pamela's mind to ask how he could judge that fact, given he had not stirred to see the cards from any closer vantage point than his chair, and had never put his eye to the peep show, but she did not. Instead she said with her mouth, "Thank you," even as her mind was busy thinking that Mama must be right: this papercutting hobby of hers ought to be kept to herself. Others did not share her enthusiasm in the construction of the devices, or find them particularly clever. Of course, one did not often think of a soldier as the sort to care overmuch for art for its own sake, so perhaps she ought not to judge the captain's apparent disinterest in her efforts. Perhaps he might be as sedate even if he was gazing at the Elgin Marbles, or a Turner, or the Sistine Chapel. And perhaps that was one of the things a wife could bring into his soldier's life: an appreciation for the arts and things of beauty, rather than destruction.

That thought struck her as being an inspired one, and she asked, "Have you seen the Marbles, Captain Penford?"

"Elgin's?"

"Yes, they are really most wondrous. I believe you would be intrigued by them, as many of them reveal ancient battle scenes."

"Indeed?" He sat up, leaning forward.

Marchmont was right: the captain was a soldier, through and through. A soldier in need of a wife, Pamela added.

173

"Do you care to visit them?" she asked. "Lord Elgin has made them available for viewing."

"Visit what?" her grandmama asked as she came into the room.

"The Elgin Marbles," Pamela answered as the captain leaned forward, attempting to gain his feet.

"Do remain seated, Captain," Grandmama told him moving to the tea tray. She lifted the lid of the pot, saw it was lemon tea, and made a face. She put the lid down, turned her back on the pot, and settled next to Pamela. "Child, do send for some chocolate, will you?"

Pamela rose dutifully, crossing to ask Phyllis to see to the chocolate, while her grandmama and the captain spoke quietly. When she sat again, her grandmama informed her, "I have told the captain that we should be happy to accompany him to view the marbles tomorrow."

Pamela dared not flash her grandmama a look of gratitude, instead allowing her pleasure to be heard in her voice. "I have but seen them once, and I should so care to see them again. They are not well-arranged, I fear, in their present location. Though I have no doubt the captain may be able to shed some light upon those pieces we shall be able to see."

"I do not know that my ancient history is all that it could be, but I daresay we may contrive to recognize some of the artist's representations." Penford nodded.

Just then Lawlton came to the door, announcing, "Lord Marchmont." The butler stepped aside, allowing the caller to come forward, dressed all in shades of moderate blue, with the exception of a white silk shirt. For him, the powder blue of his waistcoat served to be almost dashing, especially with a gold chain connected to his watch tucked in one fob pocket, and a midnight blue ribbon to his monocle in the other. Pamela glanced at the long case clock that stood near the fireplace, seeing that it was indeed already one in the afternoon, which explained why Grandmama had chosen to come down.

"Ah, Marchmont, come in and be seated. You already know the captain, of course," Grandmama said, coming to her feet, Pamela following her example. She waved Penford to remain in his seat once more.

The two men exchanged nods as Marchmont moved before a chair. He held up the beaver he retained in his hands, and explained, "I have not surrendered my hat, as I thought we might be away at once?"

Grandmama graciously inclined her head. "Of course." She turned to their other guest. "You must excuse us, Captain, as we are promised to Lord Marchmont this afternoon." She motioned toward the maid. "Phyllis, do send a footman to the stable and have Captain Penford's horse brought around, please."

The maid left, and the captain finished his tea. The occupants of the room fell awkwardly silent, still enough that the long case clock could be heard to be ticking. There was no missing the fact that the captain and Marchmont had developed no great desire to be in each other's company, as neither made an effort at small talk. Pamela gave Marchmont a speaking glance, one that chided him for not being his usual ebullient self, especially as her own mind was stubbornly empty of any conversational tidbits, but he only smiled innocently in return. Grandmama made an effort saying, "Have you been to see Lord Elgin's Marbles, Lord Marchmont?"

"Yes."

"Did you care for what you saw?"

"Very much so. 'Tis a shame that so many of them have been lost, and we must commend Lord Elgin for rescuing what he could of those which remained."

"There are some who felt he had no right to take them from Athens," Penford said.

"I find that a difficult argument, given the continuing destruction of the very sites from which he rescued these," Marchmont said, his eyes filling with animation. Penford frowned.

"It matters not," Pamela soothed, wondering why she had wished the silence gone. "Since they are here, it behooves us to appreciate them."

Penford opened his mouth, whether to agree or disagree never to be known, for the maid returned and bobbed a curtsy that implied the horse was ready. Grandmama said to the captain, "May we see you to the door?"

Marchmont put out a hand, which Penford either did not see or did not care to take, for he rose by himself, using the high arm of the settee to stand from his seat. He gathered his cane and was escorted by the ladies to the door, Marchmont following in their wake.

"Tomorrow, at two?" Penford said to Pamela, giving her a direct look that excluded all others.

Marchmont looked on with a frank regard, making the moment a trifle uncomfortable. Pamela nodded and murmured, "That would be all that is delightful."

The captain caught up her hand and bowed over it, graceful despite his bandaged foot. Pamela could not quite decide if she wished he would execute a continental kiss over her hand or not, but with Marchmont's sharp eyes watching and quick tongue waiting, she decided she was glad when he did not do so.

As he exited, Grandmama said, "Let us fetch our bonnets and our pelisses."

"I shall await you ladies here," Marchmont assured them.

As soon as they were free of the room, Grandmama asked Pamela, "You have been doing your best to persuade Marchmont there is no challenge in pursuing you, have you not?"

"A little, last night. It does not come naturally to me, I own. Most of the time I wish to stomp upon his foot or pinch his ear—quite the opposite of your advice."

"Today is a perfect day to do as you must. He will be expecting me to guard you within an inch of your life, but if we are clever, we can do the opposite, and terrify the man by making him believe we have now settled upon him and mean to bring him to the altar. There is nothing that will unnerve a rake so much as to believe he has achieved his spoken goal, even while we make sure he does not achieve the unspoken goal that underlies it all.''

"Hardly unspoken in his case. He is quite direct with the idea that he would take me howsoever I might come to him,'' Pamela said with a dry humor.

Grandmama frowned briefly, and murmured, "Odd fellow.'' She looked up at that, and added, "But so are they all. Irresistible, of course, but scoundrels nonetheless.'' She shook her head. "I wish I did not enjoy men's company so well as I do.''

"Well, enjoy away today, Grandmama. There is no penalty to pay for this day's sport.''

"So we fervently hope,'' was Grandmama's reply.

When they returned to the entry hall, so had Marchmont's good humor and spirited tongue, for he told them, "You must realize I dare not take you out, for great crowds will throng my carriage to see such beauteous ladies to the point that we shall never arrive at the fair.''

"Oh, you!'' Grandmama scolded, visibly pleased with the flattery.

As the day was pleasant, the hinged tops of the landau Marchmond had brought had been lowered, making an open carriage. Pamela and her grandmama sat facing forward, Marchmont on the opposite seat, a driver in gray and silver livery mounted on the box. Marchmont pointed out other acquaintances they passed, although they only stopped to greet the occupants of two other carriages, merely waving or nodding at others. There was no need for haste; but Pamela could see by the light in Marchmont's eyes he knew a kind of eagerness for the activities ahead, and

Pamela had to admit she felt a small thrill of such emotion herself. There was nothing like a fair for entertainment, after all.

She told herself her eagerness had nothing to do, of course, with the fact that she was supposed to do her very best to spend the entire afternoon flirting outrageously.

Chapter 13

It did not take long to drive to the site of the fair near Blackfriar's Bridge. Marchmont handed the ladies down, agreed with the driver as to when they should meet in this same spot later, then offered each lady an arm.

They had not walked twenty feet before they came to a Punch and Judy show, already in progress. "Do you care to watch?" Marchmont asked, looking to each lady to gauge her response.

" 'Tis started already," Grandmama pointed out. "No need to pay a penny for half a show."

Pamela did not answer, for she was already listening. Punch had been clasped by a watchman, who stated, "Mr. Punch, you are to be placed in prison!"

"Am I? What for?" cried the voice of Punch.

"For having broken the laws of this country," came the answer.

"Why, I never touched 'em," Punch replied.

A large guffaw rippled through the crowd, and when Pamela turned to glance at Marchmont for guidance on whether they would stay or go, she was smiling along with the crowd. He looked into her eyes for a moment, then declared, "Half over? Or perhaps it has just begun? It matters not, for already it has made my Pamela smile. Ladies," he said firmly, then went before them, using his shoulders to secure them a place nearer the little stage. There was an attendant, who may well have been the proprietor or hired as a herald between scenes, and to this man Marchmont paid three pennies.

Grandma leaned close to Pamela and, under cover of the noises of the play and the crowd, whispered quickly, "*My* Pamela?"

The younger woman colored and shook her head, gazing intently at the puppet show.

Her serious expression lasted all of one minute, however, for then she was laughing again at the antics of the puppets. It was difficult not to smile, and even laugh, as the hangman puppet—here known by the name of Jack Ketch, after a true hangman of that same name—attempted, as was his perennial rite, to hang poor Punch. Prior to this occurrence, he attempted to force Punch to give a final, badly scrambled speech of repentance.

" 'I regret having been a cruel and a vile man,' " prompted the Jack Ketch puppet.

"I want a pot of gruel and a slice of ham," Punch recited, causing the little children watching in the crowd to howl with laughter.

"No, no! Say, I wish to confess my sins against my fellow man."

Punch said, "I wish to protect my shins in bellows and pans."

In the end, Punch was rescued by Joan, or Judy as she was called of late, with a great deal of misspoken instructions by one to the other, which usually resulted in the hangman being struck on the head, this battering egged on by the children's cheering.

When it was over, Pamela applauded her appreciation and turned to thank Marchmont. "That was delightful! It has been years since I last saw a Punch show, for Mama does not approve. She says it is all nonsense."

"Rather the point, I should say," Marchmont replied, once again offering each lady an arm.

The fair was scattered along the Thames road, with hawkers crowding into any available space that was not already taken by a songstress or a fire-eater, or wandering through the crowd, calling their wares and their prices as they went. Flower sellers offered posies at every turn, and jugglers offered shows for a penny. There were two hand-walkers, each challenging the other to perform a longer, more difficult set of tasks, all the while calling to the audience to challenge them both onward to greater feats by dint of their coins. To a fellow who went up and down a set of portable wooden stairs on his hands, performing a backward flip from the top step at the end of his endeavor, Marchmont threw a sixpence. The lithe young man caught it in his teeth and grinned to show the reward even as he accepted it with a bow. Pamela clapped her hands, and even Grandmama smiled indulgently.

They saw a pair of swarthy young foreigners walk

a tightrope suspended six feet above the ground. They saw dogs that had been trained to perform tricks of walking on their hind legs and appearing to dance a jig. A man walked by with a pegged stick, from which hung dozens of caps. He tried to sell one to Marchmont, but not with any real hope of success, for that gentlemen already sported a very fine beaver. A globe walker, a woman in a gown made of bright-colored panels with a jester's cap on her head, rolled by, balancing atop a large round ball. "This way to a reenactment o' the Battle of Waterloo! Follow me! This way to see Napoleon's surrender!" she sang out, even as she avoided colliding with a cart loaded with hot crossed buns.

Marchmont spied a man with a tray full of meat pies. "Nuncheon, ladies?" he inquired.

After receiving pleased nods, he bought one for each of them. Pamela bit into the flaky shell, leaned forward to keep the contents from dripping on her dress, then cried, "Oh! 'Tis very hot inside. Do be careful."

Marchmont reached over, wiping away a drip of gravy from her chin. He then put his finger to his lips, all the while holding her vision with his own. Grandmama looked away, and Pamela looked at her pie as though it had suddenly become intensely interesting. There was no mistaking the kind of hunger that Marchmont was experiencing, and it had nothing to do with the gravy he now licked from his finger.

After a moment she realized a perfect opportunity for flirtation had been created, and she knew she must respond in course. She forced her eyes to rise, and smiled, and managed to keep her vision level with his only by effort of will, for something sparked deep in his eyes that unsettled her. He seemed to search her face, which grew warm under his scrutiny, but still she gazed at him, only allowing herself to blink twice.

At length his gaze left hers as he turned to her grandmama, who was still half-turned away. He inquired, "Shall we take these away with us to the 'Battle of Waterloo?' "

"Let us do so," Grandmama agreed as she turned back to the young people.

Marchmont looked from one lady to the other, a contemplative look crossing his features, replacing the open appetite that had resided there only a moment ago, and then he led the way, parting the crowd before the ladies.

They followed at a leisurely pace behind the elevated and gaily garbed globe walker, who led them, and a score of others, to a row of rickety benches set before a raised platform that had four upright poles on which hung rather tattered draperies. Marchmont paid for the privilege of sitting on the short, foremost bench, but would not allow the ladies to sit on the cracked, dusty wood until he had taken off his coat and spread it for them to sit upon.

"Oh, no, my lord, you must not!" Pamela protested, her eyes darting about to see if anyone was staring at the coatless Marchmont.

"Alas, unlike Sir Walter Raleigh, I have no cloak to lay down for you. My coat shall have to suffice."

Pamela opened her mouth to protest again—a gentleman simply did not walk about in public in his shirtsleeves—but a speaking look from her grandmama stopped her. Her chin rose, and she said instead, "Why, Lord Marchmont, how chivalrous."

One of his eyebrows rose questioningly, but he said nothing, instead indicating to Grandmama that she should sit. "Lady Marrelston?"

She sat on one side of his spread coat, leaving room for Pamela on the other half. The short bench had just enough room for the three of them, and even so Marchmont's left leg stretched out at an angle to help him keep his balance on the narrow strip left for him at his end of the bench, his right thigh pressed close to Pamela's own.

"I could not have asked for a better seat," he said quietly near Pamela's ear.

This time she refused to look up, instead staring down at her gloved hands in her lap. Grandmama would have none of that, however, and that worthy's elbow nudged Pamela in the ribs rather sharply. Pamela forced her chin up once more, wondering fleetingly why it was so difficult to play the coquette with this particular man, and gladly found that he was busy watching the crowd and not her for once.

He truly was a sight, this man in his shirtsleeves. His title was certainly several stations below her own, and the scent of the shop still clung to his name; and yet here in this crowd of men he stood out as no other. There was no doubting he was fine to look upon, seeming especially tall now that they were sitting side by side, the sun glinting off the dark hair visible under his hat. His new-leaf green eyes seemed almost peculiar when compared with the blue of another man's eyes: the one filled with unholy mirth, the other with the sobriety of the battlefield, yet they were stunning to behold. One had but to look into their green depths, and suddenly it could become difficult to remember what one was speaking about. His chin was not so strong as that of Captain Penford, whose chin lent his face a forcefulness to go with his deep-chested voice. Marchmont's voice was more moderate, the kind of voice that could manage a whisper as perhaps the captain's might not. He did not have the straight lips that Penford had either; instead Marchmont's mouth was all curves, as though he had been born to smile. He claimed as much, so perhaps it was true, but at any rate his nature showed in his face. There were laugh lines just beginning to form at the corners of his eyes, and his nose was an ordinary affair, not at all patrician. He was handsome, yes; noble, no. A man who could be comfortable without his coat, and yet a man who was no more common among all these common men than the Prince of Wales. Perhaps this was because he held himself straight, not afraid to meet any man's eye, and not afraid to laugh at what amused him. That was something he shared with the captain, this confidence. Both men knew who they were, and neither blinked when faced with a challenge. If anything, they thrived on such challenges. Perhaps it was this commonality, this forceful trait that he shared with Captain Penford—to whom she was so very attracted— that made it difficult for her to banter easily with Marchmont.

She suddenly realized he was looking down at her

once more, assessing her as openly as she did him. "Do you like what you see?" he asked at length.

She answered simply and honestly, "Yes."

His hand, heretofore in his lap, slid over hers. "So do I."

She did not move her hand away. Grandmama would expect no less, as it was a harmless way to encourage him.

Just then, a small cannon boomed, causing the occupants of the audience to startle and gasp in surprise. Marchmont's hand tightened over hers, and she allowed it to stay that way.

The tattered curtains were drawn back, and the Battle of Waterloo—consisting of a cast of eight—ensued. The threesome watched, not speaking to each other, their bodies pressed together, Pamela's hand still captured under his.

When the fifteen minutes production was finished, and an amusingly tall yet appropriately humbled "Napoleon" was led off the stage, the ladies rose.

"Did you see the fellow with the long face? The one that always died by falling off the back of the stage? By my count he came on with a different bit of costuming and died at least ten times," Marchmont said as he donned his coat once again.

Pamela grinned as she noted, "He died very poorly when he was supposed to be French, but made an effort at a glorious end when he was supposed to be English."

"Oh, but 'tis dusty!" Grandmama cried, pointing to Marchmont's coat as he settled it about his shoulders.

"It matters not."

"Let us dust you off," Grandmama offered, reaching to pat his sleeve in a sweeping motion. Around his arm, Grandmama gave Pamela a telling look, one that said she was to join in the activity.

Pamela pulled off one glove and reached out, tentatively dusting the shoulder of his coat, refusing to look about for fear someone she knew might be watching her place her hands about the Baron's person. Marchmont laughed, lifting his arms straight out to his sides to aid them in their task.

"Turn," Grandmama ordered.

"Your wish is my command," he laughed.

It was the work of a minute, with Marchmont grinning all the while, and then they were done.

"Finished? Already?" he asked, pouting openly, when they stepped back. Funny how one may pout and grin at the same time, Pamela thought, her own mouth twitching, reflecting the fact she was not quite sure whether to laugh or frown herself.

She went to pull on her glove, but Marchmont's hands came up, capturing her hand between his own two. "But wait," he said, "your hand will be dusty, and we would not wish to sully your glove. Allow me." So saying, he pulled a kerchief from his pocket, tucked the glove he took from her under his arm, then proceeded to wipe her fingers one by one with the lacy cloth. She watched his hands as he did so, remarking silently to herself on the largeness, the curious foreignness, of a man's hands. Strange how something so simple as a touch could give one pause even as it did her now—and she struggled to suppress a sudden shiver that coursed her length.

The cloth was put away, the glove produced and before she knew it he was pulling the glove into place upon her hand for her. It went on smoothly, slowly, and his fingertips tickled the skin of her wrist. For a moment she blinked, the lids of her eyes staying closed a moment longer than necessary, and she fought to keep her features free of reflecting a sudden turmoil that ripped through her very center, stealing breath and words and thought. For a brief moment it seemed she might swoon; but that sensation passed at once, and she felt a tremble come into her fingers, like an echo of the shiver just passed.

She pulled her hand away, pressed together her lips, which had parted, and turned from him. She spoke suddenly, her voice sounding thick and muddied: "Where next?"

She thought perhaps there was a short, deep chuckle from Marchmont, but she could not have sworn as much.

"Do you ladies care for a lemonade?" he asked, even as he lifted a hand to signal to a passing vendor.

The lemonades were purchased and quickly consumed, for they were in naught but waxed paper rolled into cones, and would quickly disintegrate. Refreshed, the ladies then agreed that they should stroll to see more of the fair.

They passed a juggler who tossed colorful silks through the air in graceful arcs. They listened for a while to a man who stood on an upended crate, predicting that the members of the populace present this day would all end by tumbling into Hades' deep recesses, much to Marchmont's obvious amusement. He was quick, however, to turn the ladies away when members of the Watch appeared to drag the fellow off—for after all it was neither Speaker's Corner nor Sunday.

"That is too bad of them! I should have preferred to hear what all he had to say. He was simply filled with descriptive phrases, rather as though he had been there himself, do you not think?"

The comment had a desirable effect, easing any stiffness that may have sprung up among the party. Grandmama and Pamela exchanged amused glances, and Grandmama even gave a short and rather undignified bark of laughter.

They stood in the crowd for a while, watching a sword dueling display given by two actors in Elizabethan garb. The actors shouted bits of disjointed Shakespeare at each other, causing two young swains to call out which play they thought had originated the dialogue. At first the actors were annoyed; but pennies began to clatter in the cloth hat set upon the ground before them at the sport, and so they entered into the spirit of the moment by calling out whether the young men were correct or not. Others joined in, causing the actors to point toward the correct speaker with their swords, that was if they were not busy defending themselves with them. The one actor was superior to the other in his ability, making a play of flourishing his sword when he could, yet the other led the way with new speeches for the crowd to determine.

"Richard the Second,." Marchmont called once, and was rewarded by a pointed indication of the actor's sword. After he threw a coin, a reward to the actors for their cleverness combined with his own, he turned to beam down at Pamela, remarking, "Seems I saw more of the play the other night than I thought."

Pamela knew an opportunity when it came so easily. It was a simple thing to appear possessive, the very thing that Marchmont claimed he wished her to be, but which Grandmama assured her would dull his quest. For a moment she hesitated, though, for she knew he would gleefully accuse her of being jealous—which he had already accused her of being twice before. It did not seem to her that these "jealous" displays of hers had cooled his ardor one bit, but perhaps that was because she had always then become retiring, unwilling to challenge his claims.

When she looked up at him, she had made up her mind. "You *were* rather busy," she said with an assumed tartness.

"Oh-ho! What is this I hear in your voice? Do you chide me? I take it you saw me in a certain box last night?"

"You were with a lady in dark blue."

"Ah. Lady Calridge. You would like her, I think," he said smugly.

"Would I?" she asked with some asperity. She glanced at Grandmama, who was watching the duelling but also nodding her head ever so slightly, silently encouraging her granddaughter onward.

Now she was sure he chuckled. "Well, perhaps not."

"She is a particular friend of yours?"

"Sometimes."

"Sometimes?"

"We have a . . . casual relationship."

Pamela frowned; this was just another sign of his faithless nature.

Grandmama spoke suddenly: "Do you know, I am most weary of standing about. Let us find me a seat. There, just over there is a bench." She led the way, not bothering to solicit their agreement.

She settled on the ironwork bench, leaving no room for Pamela to sit beside her, and looked up at the young people to say, "I should be mortified if my weak nature kept you children from enjoying yourselves. There are some vendors' carts, just over there, which you may enjoy looking at, and I shall be able to watch over you well enough from this vantage point. Do run along."

Pamela glowered ever so briefly at her Grandmama's obvious manipulation—she had just made it absurdly easy for Marchmont to have Pamela to himself for a short while—but did not argue with her grandparent.

Marchmont gave Lady Marrelston a bow in agreement, a smile hovering near his lips. He offered his arm to Pamela, who took it, and led her toward the indicated carts.

"Oh, do but look!" she cried as they neared the displays.

"What have we here?" Marchmont asked as they gazed down at the various toys on display. There were sets of teaching cards. Some depicted the alphabet with elaborate illustrations to emphasize the etched letter for each card; others detailed facts regarding a number of subjects, from military leaders to botanical names. There were flip-flops, which changed pictures when one side was turned to the other, painted building blocks, and wooden peg dolls.

"Oh, look." Pamela smiled, reaching to connect two wooden toys carved to look like circus animals and set on wheels. The back of one had a metal ring set in it, and the front of the other had a hook that slipped through the ring. There were more, with the same hook and eye connectors, and soon Pamela had strung a number of them together to form a line of animals which marched along as she pulled the leader by the string tied about its neck. "I should care to make something like this if only I could work with wood, but I have no talent in that regard." She sighed.

"Do you wish me to purchase these for you?" Marchmont offered at once.

"No," she half laughed and shook her head. "I did not mean them for myself, but for my cousins. I should not ask any man to make such a purchase, for I have eight cousins that are under the age of ten, you see."

"Ah, I see. But I am not loathe to purchase a gift for any young cousins of yours. Allow me—"

"No, no. It serves well enough that they get nothing more complex than paper toys from their older cousin," she said as she picked up a peg doll and examined the painted-on shoes under its simple skirts.

"Paper toys?" Marchmont questioned, leaning one elbow on the cart and smiling an inquiry at her.

She ducked her head, belatedly remembering she had just this morning determined that she ought to keep that information to herself. "Oh, 'tis nothing. I like to color and cut, and my poor little cousins are the unfortunate victims of my peculiar largesse."

"Really. I should like to see some of your efforts. Do you keep any for yourself?"

She waved a hand. "No, not really," she said dismissively, but honesty forced her to add, "except what I am working on at the time. And a few favorites. Silly of me, I suppose—"

He cut in, saying, "Not at all. You forget to whom you speak. If you thought collecting mud pies was fun, I should be the first to sit down in the dust with you and a bucket of water. 'Sport' is my middle name, did you not know?"

"Theopholus Sport Dunmire?" She grinned.

He nodded in mock solemnity. "Quite so. Do you know, I have been working all this morning on nothing but making an inventory of the tack for all the estates' cattle. I now am the possessor of such stimulating knowledge as the fact that the Barony of Marchmont has in its possession no less than five-and-twenty curry combs, seven-and-twenty saddle blankets—thirteen of which have the family crest woven into them—and sixteen hoof picks. My very, very dearest Pamela, need I explain that now I am all but dying with the need for some amusement? I do not care if it comes in the guise of pretending I do not see some deep planning in the back of your grandmama's eyes, watching men misquote Shakespeare, or playing with toys, paper or otherwise! So, please, divert me howsoever you might, at any time, any place, with no apologies, for I foresee a terrible and growing need for diversion in my future.''

It was as if Grandma nudged her in the ribs again, for Pamela found a coquettish comment rose at once to her lips. She gave a mock sigh and said, ''So I am naught but a diversion for you, my lord?''

His mirth did not wane, but his eyes turned a deep green. ''Oh, Pamela. Have you not heard from my own lips how you could be so much more?''

Her ploy had backfired, and she retreated at once from the warmth in his gaze, turning to gaze down at the contents of the cart in some agitation.

''Speaking of diversions,'' she said inanely, ''is this not charming?'' She felt a need to busy her hands, so she reached out to touch a dissected map of the globe, only belatedly seeing it in truth enough to note that it was of a rather fine quality. It had two pictures on it, so that both hemispheres of the world might be seen. ''Look how cleverly they have cut it,'' she said to Marchmont, pointing to the neat wavy lines that divided the puzzle into parts. The artist had cleverly surrounded his globe halves with ivy vines, along which the cuts twined.

She almost gave a sigh of relief when Marchmont turned to observe where she pointed. ''I had not seen one before with anything other than straight cuts,'' she went on, glad for the diversion, fingering the path of one wiggly cut.

"Then please allow me, this time, to purchase it for you."

"Oh, no, I could not do that," she said, still flustered. It was one thing to have a man spend pennies on one for a day's entertainment, but such an attractive gift seemed . . . well, it seemed dishonest of her to accept such a thing. If they were betrothed, or even if she had a care for him. . . .

"Why not?" Marchmont asked even as he pulled forth his purse. He pointed to the dissected map as the vendor eagerly caught his eye.

"A gentleman does not buy such a gift for a lady."

"Again I ask why not? 'Tis scarce more expensive than some posies I have bought in my day. 'Tis not terribly personal. And do not tell me it would shock your grandmama for me to buy you a gift, for 'twas that very same grandmama that just now gave me a perfect opportunity to steal away, alone, with you."

Pamela blushed a deep red, clearly demonstrating that the same thought had crossed her own mind. "Oh, I am sure not. Only look, she can see us perfectly well—"

"And knows perfectly well that any man worth his salt would take the chance to slip into the crowd with you. No, that bubble is burst, Pamela. You may not call out the rules of propriety at this point. And see here, I have already bought you your map, so there is no turning back." He handed the proper coinage to the vendor and accepted the puzzle, now wrapped in brown paper and tied with a string. He returned his purse to his pocket, then offered the packet to Pamela, who had clasped her hands before

her, her lower lip caught between her teeth in inde-
cision.

"Please take it, Pamela," he said quietly, holding
out the packet toward her.

For one heart-stopping moment she could not decide what to do, but then her hands came up and she
took it. She flashed a brief, shy smile up at him, and
murmured as sincerely as she might, "Thank you."

She turned away, then made a pleased noise, for
now she had spied a peep show cart across the way.
It would serve very nicely as a means to get beyond
this awkward moment. She turned to Marchmont.
"May I bother you for another couple of pennies, my
lord? I see a peep show just over there, and I daresay
it could prove a diversion."

"Lead on," was his immediate answer.

The cart bore one big wooden box, six feet deep,
cut with numerous eyeholes. Marchmont paid for the
privilege, and then they bent to put their eyes to the
holes. Inside was a scene, set up just as were her
own, only on a larger, more formal scale. At the very
back was a glass screen, on which was painted the
final scene, and on the outside of which glowed a
series of small lamps that provided the illumination
that they might see the contents within. It was an
aquatic scene, complete with ships, waves, dolphins,
fish of every size and color, and other denizens of the
deep, as well as a pirate's treasure chest that glittered.
Pamela gave a cry, for after giving them a moment to
look and admire, the cart's owner must have pulled a
string or a lever, for the waves swayed back and forth,
animating the scene. This was followed by another

manipulation: three dolphins leaped out of the "water," happy grins on their painted faces as they disappeared once more from sight.

Pamela called to Marchmont, "Look, there to the left? Do you see the swimmer?"

"Do you see the shark coming at him?"

"Oh, yes!" she laughed.

They stayed at the box for over ten minutes, while she asked the owner four times if he might have the dolphins leap "just one more time," and they pointed out to each other every facet of the artistry within until there was nothing left unseen.

When she at last pulled her eye away, she was laughing with pure pleasure, and Marchmont laughed with her. He pointed toward the box and asked, "Do you, in your paper workings, do anything like this?"

She did not wish to speak of it, but neither did she wish to lie. "Well, yes," she answered, shyly. "And sometimes panoramas."

"Then I truly must see some of your works," he asserted. "Perhaps when I take you home today?"

"Oh, no! No, not today," she cried at once, thinking of her untidy bedchamber. "Another day, when I have had a chance to move them out to my sitting room, perhaps."

"Perhaps?" he echoed, shaking his head, but then he said nothing more on the subject, instead offering her his arm.

"Back to Grandmama?" she asked, relieved the topic was left behind.

"Not at all! We both know the dear Ancient has arranged it that we might become so very accidentally separated, so we must comply with her wishes. Come along!'' He did not wait for her consent, but closed his hand over hers where it rested on his arm and pulled her forward, into the crowd.

"Oh, I do not know—"

"Hush now. We shall come back to her shortly, I promise you. Even I am not so evil as to abandon an old woman in the midst of such a crowd for long,'' he told her, hurrying her along.

"Where do we go?''

"There,'' he answered, pointing to a narrow doorway. He pulled her toward it and through it, and they quickly walked the length of a long, narrow path that ran between two buildings. It suddenly opened up, becoming a miniature courtyard garden, overhung with dense greenery and fragrant blooms. Windows, half-obscured by the garden plants, looked down into the courtyard, but there was no sign of life behind them; everyone was at the fair, no doubt.

He stopped just under a small balcony that hung from an old stone wall, turning with a sudden movement that pushed her back against the wall, pinning her length there with his own. She gasped and dropped her packet.

"Do you know today is Hock Tuesday,'' he told her, his face only a few inches above her own. "I have every right to bind you and demand a forfeit.''

"You are not my landlord, and I owe you no rents,'' she said breathlessly.

"At this moment I am. I am master of this deserted courtyard, and you must pay me rent to pass through it.''

Her heart began to pound. Flirt, yes, she must take the chance to flirt with him. "What manner of rent?" she asked.

"Oh, something very simple: a kiss, 'tis all. A traditional Hock Tuesday kiss." His eyes bore down into hers, and she was grateful for the wall that gave her some support, for her knees trembled of a sudden.

"Very well," she said shakily, half wishing she had slapped him or done something to cause him to release her, that she might be away from him, from this sudden impulse that made her actually want to kiss him.

"But not with this in the way," he said, one hand reaching for and untying the bonnet ribbon at her chin. He grasped the bonnet and flung it aside. She heard it land several yards away, but he was so close she could not see where it had gone.

He lowered his head, slowly, so slowly she could think of nothing but the mouth coming toward her own; and then that mouth touched hers, and she heard herself make a small sound.

His lips were questioning, not insistent, and she knew she could slip out, now, suddenly, from under his pinning length if only she would make the effort to do so. But she did not.

She needed to now more about kisses, and his was soft and sweet and gentle, and left her unable to form a clear thought in her head; all she knew was she wanted more of it. When his arms came to her waist, encircling her, pulling her to him, she came to him, not resisting, not even thinking of resisting.

The kiss deepened, and his hand came up to caress her neck, his fingers curling in the hair at the nape. She had not really known it was possible to be so thoroughly kissed, though one part of her had to marvel that she could ever have been so blind as all that. It seemed so very natural, and even necessary in its way. Like singing or dancing. Somewhere inside her there formed a desire to do nothing but go on being kissed, and to kiss in return. Her arms did not come up to his neck of their own accord; she put them there, wanting to touch him, wanting to keep that mouth on her own.

It was only when his mouth trailed to her chin and down her throat, when she found herself arching her neck that he might kiss her as freely as he wished, that she saw a small child looking down out of a window with a mild curiosity on its face.

What a sight they must appear, she realized with a start. A kind of sanity slowly returned to her even as she formed the thought. What was she doing? This had gone far beyond flirtation! If she had entered into this to compare his kisses to another's, she had utterly failed to do so. His touch, his surely meaningless and ephemeral male desire, had overridden her senses. This was not what was supposed to be happening. She was supposed to be frightening him away with her own eagerness. And . . . and the captain would never treat her this way, would never cavalierly take a kiss in this demanding manner.

The captain. Yes, she must think of the captain, and imagine it was he holding her in his arms instead, and kissing her. The captain, with the mustache that tickled . . . she remembered that quite well. . . .

Suddenly Marchmont's mouth paused on her throat, and his hands stilled in her hair. He pulled his mouth away from where it caressed her skin, and for a moment his arms tightened around her. Then his grip slackened, and he bent his head, pressing his forehead to hers. He gave a low, mournful chuckle that lacked any humor, and said hoarsely, "Pamela, that was cruel."

"Cruel?" she echoed, still half-lost to a sensual fog.

"To leave me like that. I believe I am most grievously wounded to have been so easily displaced by a man not even present."

She flushed a deep scarlet and stepped out of his arms. "I do not know what you mean," she stammered.

"Yes, you do," he said simply. His arms, still outstretched as though she might step back into them, fell to his sides. He shook his head, expanded his chest, and sighed.

"I think we should return to Grandmama," Pamela said, beginning to walk backward, away from him.

He advanced toward her, one slow step at a time, his expression making her want to run away and keeping her from doing just that, all at once. "Before we go, you must admit one thing," he said.

She shook her head, even though she had no idea what he was going to say, glancing over her shoulder for fear she would trip as she continued to back away from him.

"You must admit that for a minute there you felt

something for me. For a moment it was me that you were kissing, and wanting to kiss.''

She looked around, as though the stone walls would inspire a response in her, for she had none, and saw her bonnet lying discarded a few feet from him. ''My bonnet,'' she said stupidly, pointing.

He stooped, retrieved the bonnet, stepped forward and picked up the packet, and handed them both toward her, finally bringing her retreat to a halt. When she reached for them, he did not release them, instead using them to pull her close once more. She let go at once, but did not step back, frozen in place by the look he gave her, a stubbornly demanding look.

''Admit it,'' he said.

''I admit nothing,'' she said in a whisper.

He held the wrapped puzzle toward her once more. ''Take it and that shall be your admission. You need only take my gift and I shall know it is true, even if you will not bring yourself to speak the words.''

She stared at him, hesitating. There was something in his voice that made her think perhaps he was truly wounded. There was a harsh edge, meant to cut her in turn for thinking of another while in his arms. But, too, there was a pleading of some kind, a wanting that was hard to ignore. But wanting was not enough, and she could not allow him to make more of this gift than it was.

She put her hand firmly on one edge of the packet. She did not shrink away now, and she met his gaze levelly. She drew herself up, and said quietly, ''I shall take it, Theo, because you are my friend.''

For once he had no immediate response, if she

discounted the astonishment that crossed his features ever so briefly. He looked into her face, belatedly releasing the packet into her hand, then reached to take the bonnet from her other. He settled it on her head and carefully tied the ribbon under her chin. He stepped back as though to admire his handiwork, only then speaking. "Do you know, this is the second time you have offered to be my friend. The first time I was most insulted."

Somehow everything had turned heels over head, and he had lost control of the situation to her—he knew it, too, that was obvious. "A curious response, most would think," she said, half-prepared to smile if only he would smile first.

"Not if they, like myself, had just proposed."

"And so, my lord, what say you now?"

"You ask me: are we to be friends?" He put his head on one side as though he were pondering one of the great mysteries of life. He offered her his arm, which she took, and led her toward the narrow path, allowing her to step a little ahead of him so that there was room for both to make their way out together. As they emerged back into the fair crowds, he looked down at her, for she was looking expectantly up at him, awaiting his answer. "My dearest Lady Pamela," he said, almost smiling, although there was something unusually sober in his expression as well, "I should be delighted to be counted your friend."

"And I, yours," she said, and smiled at last.

He smiled in return, took up the hand that was on his arm, kissed the skin near her wrist, and with a wry shake of his head, moaned, "Friends!" as he settled the hand back on his arm, to lead the way back to Grandmama.

She walked beside him, the smile still on her lips until they approached the seat where her grandparent waited. The elder woman looked up and scowled, and not from disapproval of their disappearance. That she had intended, and planned to let Marchmont know it. No, it was suddenly quite clear to Pamela that Grandmama did not approve of the sight of them walking arm in arm, smiling at one another. She would be, of course, expecting Marchmont to have a sour or hunted look about him, if only she, Pamela, had done as she ought. This good humor of his meant he had turned their time away to his own advantage instead of the other way around, so Grandmama would think. Pamela could see the conclusion clearly radiating from the woman's narrowed eyes.

Too late to undo the deed, she realized she had just done a very dangerous thing, the very thing Grandmama had most warned her against: she had been so very foolish as to allow the rogue into a tiny corner of her heart.

She had allowed him to be transformed into a friend.

Chapter 14

"That was a curious carriage ride home," Grandmama said dryly as she laid her reticule on the pier table in her sitting room.

Pamela trailed her grandparent into the room, and agreed in a soft voice, "Quite so."

"It was most evident that he kissed you."

One of Pamela's hands flew to her lips guiltily. "Was it?"

"Yes. There is a certain way a girl has of avoiding a man's eyes right after he has kissed her, and you could not have looked at Marchmont to save your life. I should not mind one bit if it only meant that you had put the fear of the parson's mousetrap in him, but it is quite clear you did not. Really, Pamela, all it would take is a show of enthusiasm from you, a few whispered words about a future together, about a household full of children with runny noses, and the man would rather expire than suffer a moment longer under the threat of such domestic bliss. You are entirely too sweet! You can only tempt him further by behaving at all maidenly. You must overcome such scruples, my dear, for it is that very kind of shy and retiring manner that so attracts the male. At least until they have crawled into your bed, and then such charms are the very last thing they want anymore."

"I am not so sure, for he does say, over and over, that he wishes to marry me," Pamela said.

"Well, of course he does! For those are the words any girl wishes to hear, so he *would* say them to tempt you to his side! Do not pay the slightest heed to a word the man utters. No, my girl, it is his actions you must watch!" she pronounced as she drew a shawl about her shoulders. She hesitated a moment, then looked off into the distance as her hands smoothed the fabric she folded over her breast. "But do you know, there was something about Marchmont that was odd," she said at length, as she drew off her bonnet and in its place settled a cap from the vanity. "He ought to have been all smug, attempting to make assignations for the future. I own I scarce know *what* he was thinking, just sitting there and making conversation so nice and proper as he was. I will tell you this, my girl: Marchmont plays a deep game. You must not forget that. Do not take him lightly, or he'll sneak past your defenses. Heaven knows, it is tempting to take such scapegraces at their word, for their word is ever charming, but you must always remember underlying it all is a false heart."

"You are right, of course," Pamela whispered.

"What is that, my girl?" Grandmama asked as she settled in her chair by the fire. She patted the arm of her chair to indicate Pamela should take a seat at the stool that was set nearby.

"I said I think I have put entirely too much thought toward Lord Marchmont and not nearly enough toward Captain Penford," the younger woman said as she settled on the stool.

"That is a very true thought, my dear. Do you feel you have made any inroads with the captain?"

Pamela gave a silent sigh, gratified the conversation had turned. "Yes, I can honestly say I believe I have. He asked you, did he not, if we would be interested in going to see the Marbles, rather than you suggesting it?"

"Yes."

"Then that is surely an encouraging sign. And we went to the theatre together and had a great deal of conversation. I even venture to think that perhaps he was a bit annoyed that we had several other gentlemen in the box, who possibly took up a little too much of my time? I do not think I am being vain to think as much—"

"Oh, of course not," Grandmama agreed.

"I should tell you that last night he kissed me."

"Did he? After the theatre?"

"Yes."

"That is well, very well!" Grandmama beamed, then asked eagerly, "Where?"

"Before the house, while we waited for his horse. I am afraid Owen left us alone to see after one of his own horses."

"Nodcock! But at least his neglect went to good

purpose. Here, hand me that bit of stitchery, will you?''

Pamela stood, retrieving a hooped piece from a small nearby table. She handed it to her grandmother and sat again as that lady began to ply her needle.

"Did you care for it? His kiss, I mean?'' Grandmama asked as she stitched.

"Oh, yes,'' Pamela said at once, but then her mind leaped from that memory to another: a kiss just shared today. She began to shake, just a little, and had to bite her lip to keep it from quivering. She must not let Grandmama see that she was perturbed in any way. She did not want to admit, out loud, that today's kiss had been far more moving than any previous one. She did not want to acknowledge to herself that she had become quite mindless in the midst of that kiss, that she had wanted nothing but that the embrace should go on and on. She did not want to recognize that there was still a reckless side to herself, a side that she had struggled to put aside for years now. She could not admit any such thing to Grandmama, for she knew she had inherited from that lady the very temperament that had led Grandmama to marry so unwisely.

She had thought she had learned from the lessons at her grandparent's knee. She thought she had at last become all that Mama wanted, all that a proper young lady ought to be. Even given her penchant for making toys, she thought she might be behaving in a largely acceptable manner, for it could be said that many people made toys; it was not something to be ashamed of . . . at least not for most people. Of course, most adults probably did not have a second wardrobe in their room, one that the servants had been ordered to leave be, filled with nothing but toys.

There were the works she had made for her cousins, but there were others as well: ones hidden away in the wardrobe because they pleased her so, or were old and filled with memories, or had some facet that she doubted anyone would enjoy but herself. She blushed even now to think of the peep show she had made some years ago, a scene where winged unicorns flew and grazed on golden grass, or lay in beds of opulent flowers. She had spent months, and not some little of her birthday monies, on decorating it. The golden grass really had been golden, for she had purchased ground pyrite and mixed it in her paints. The flower bed had been made up of little scraps of cloth she persuaded the maids to surrender from their mending or ribbons she bought herself. The feathery wings of the flying unicorn that leaped near the upper edge of the peep show had been made from real bird's feathers, carefully clipped to shape and gummed in place with care.

No, she must be honest with herself; there could not be many grown people who not only made, but also kept hidden away such things, a secret vice.

As a child she had always been told she was an unruly hoyden, and now she was terribly afraid to think that perhaps she still was. If she wished to prove otherwise, she ought to throw all her works away, the secret ones that were hers alone. Yes, that would show she had gone beyond such silly things.

But no, she could not bear it. It would be like

giving away all her dreams, her hopes, her happy memories. What did it mean that her silly collection of toys seemed like old friends, and that she could not enter these years of her own adulthood by abandoning them as others had done long since?

Had she laughed too much today? It seemed to her that perhaps she had. There was no excuse for it, for she knew other young ladies who were terrible coquettes, such as her own friend Lady Jane, and yet one *never* found them laughing too loud or too much. And what young lady of her acquaintance would have ever gone off with Marchmont, leaving her chaperone behind? No one. No wonder Marchmont had dared to kiss her so thoroughly, with her so mindless as all that! And, if she needed more proof, had she not taken advantage of her isolation with Captain Penford? She most certainly had; she could not pretend otherwise. Would Jane have stood so close to a man she hardly knew, lifting her face for a kiss, in the moonlight? No, Jane, for all that she liked nothing better than a man's compliment, never would have allowed herself to be in such a situation in the first place. She knew better, and behaved better than that.

Pamela almost groaned aloud, sickened by the knowledge of her own clearly juvenile, unrefined nature. It seemed that merely having a strong desire to be changed was not enough to make that change occur.

Yet . . . perhaps, just perhaps, with someone who was strong of character, someone whom she could wish so very much to please, she could finally make

that change. If that someone was of a serious nature—
not as Marchmont, who would only encourage her to
more and more infantile behavior such as would mirror his own—a solid and sound man such as the captain, she could learn a woman's seemliness, learn to
face the world without a need for playthings and idle
diversions. For such a man, surely she could learn to
be correct and gracious and all the things Mama had
so often despaired her only daughter would ever grow
to be.

Realizing her need, the worst part was knowing
what Captain Penford must think of her. If he had
thought well of her, it would not have been outside
the bounds for him to offer for her after taking that
moonlit kiss. Looking back on it, she realized she
had been in a most compromising position. That he,
the honorable captain had not offered for her said
much.

"Pamela, my dear, are you crying?" her grandmama said, laying a hand on her shoulder.

Pamela blinked back her tears and attempted to
steady her voice where it caught in her throat. She
shook her head. "No," she managed to say. She then
gave a hiccupy laugh, almost a sob, and added, "not
much anyway."

"Whyever for, child?"

"Because . . . because the captain is leaving in
nine days," she said brokenly. It was not even close
to the whole reason for her tears, but served well
enough as an explanation.

"Nine days," her grandmama tsked, patting her
granddaughter's head. "Do not cry, Pamela, sweet-

ing. After all, you have heard of a Nine Days' Wonder, have you not? That is what we shall have here, make no mistake. A Nine Days' Wonder. The *ton* will be simply amazed when the captain announces your betrothal before he leaves,'' she said with a confident air. "Hush now, dry those tears."

A reluctant laugh surfaced once more from under the tears. At least there was this one last advantage of having been always too quick to laugh: it was possible to rally swiftly now when such a rally was needed. "Yes, I like that," Pamela sniffed. "A Nine Days' Wonder. That is what I shall have to be, indeed." After all, it had taken God only seven days to make the heavens and the earth, so why should it not be possible for her to make a whole new self, one not only acceptable but desirable to a military man, in nine days?

She lifted her head and added resolutely, through the tears that marked her face, "Perhaps not a betrothal, Grandmama, but I swear to you, absolutely, that the good captain will not leave London without knowing that Pamela Elise Thorpe has set her cap for him."

Grandmama looked into her granddaughter's tear-marked face, a flicker of something . . . doubt? . . . concern? . . . crossing her features, but said nothing more. Pamela rose and kissed her grandparent on the cheek, then made her way to her room, to wash her face and get through the dinner hour.

When she returned to her room after the meal she readied for bed, not bothering to summon a maid to help her. She then sat at her escritoire and there in her diary poured forth every emotion, every thought, she had experienced this day. She left out nothing, writing by the light of a lamp until well after dark. She did not spare a word, not even concerning her clinging participation in Marchmont's kiss.

She wrote of her fear that she had done a perilous thing by allowing him to become a friend. By acknowledging what he had become, he grew suddenly—and painfully—dear to her. Marchmont . . . Theo . . . who liked her very well, who would change nothing about her, it seemed. How powerfully intoxicating that was: to be sought out for no other reason than being one's self.

She wrote how terrified she was to think that by reaching for the future she so craved she would need to sacrifice the present, would have to relinquish him, the only friend who would have her as she was this day, this hour.

She explained, as she wrote, that she had discovered what made a rakehell so very dangerous: how it would be simple to forget herself with him, to fall over the edge into—she hesitated and then wrote the word that came too easily to her thoughts—love. If the raging, aching, throat-constricting storm in her breast when she thought of losing his friendship could be called love. But no matter, for by whatever name that delirious state could be called, she knew it could consume her, take her whole, leaving her as nothing when—oh, surely not *if*—he decided to be done with her. Today she had learned he had a fondness for her, in his fashion, she was sure of that, just as she was sure his words of devotion far outstripped his ability to actually demonstrate just such a lasting devotion.

Which left her with but two choices, and two choices only, which she wrote of in a frantic hand in her diary: the first, to cut the man cold, never see him again, never allow him to speak a word with her, let alone steal a kiss. She could be far crueler, far more cutting, far more resolved never to see him again, if that was what she determined she must do.

But the second choice was to refuse to give him up, this newfound friend of hers, no matter the consequence. To see if it was possible to keep him truly as a friend. To be kind and gentle in her rejection of his curious suit, while enticing him to remain her bosom beau, despite marriages, despite the fundamental differences of their genders, despite anything. Given what she knew of him, it seemed unlikely such a man would ever accede to such a relationship, but she found as she wrote along in a crazily scratched hand that she could not bear to think of a future devoid of his company, any more than she had been able to give up her collection of toys, and realized now that she never would, not even for the captain.

She had to try to hold on to some small part of the relationship she shared with Marchmont, that which might survive the thwarting of his urges. She had to have some secret little part of herself that could occasionally be allowed a taste of levity. She would allow Theopholus Dunmire, Baron Marchmont, to entertain her, and, if he was willing to play the game she proposed, he would be entertained by her. And if the subsequent marriage she was determined to make proved too much a barrier to any kind of friendship between them, at least she would know a few last days of childhood freedom, of time spent unmonitored, uncontrolled, in the company of one who wished her just the way she was. With Theo, she need be neither proper, nor well-behaved, nor mindful of anything. . . . That is, anything but keeping herself from believing she might have the same lasting kind of future with him as with a man such as the captain.

It was decided, and she did not think twice when she wrote her decision in the diary. She would marry the captain, or some man if the captain could not be brought to the altar, who would provide her with the stability that she had been so often reminded she needed. But, that decision aside, she would spend the remaining days of the Season, of her youth, doing exactly as she pleased with the one who would be willing to assist her in one last wild farewell celebration of that same youth.

She knew it would be no difficulty to persuade him that such an alliance must be a discreet one: he would revel in the fact. The Baron and the Earl's daughter in a secret alliance—oh, yes, he would have a care for that! She would make her memories, as Grandmama had made hers, even though it was abundantly possible they would prove to be bittersweet or worse. She did not care; hang the emotional cost until it was done and over!

She pulled a piece of vellum from a slot in her escritoire and penned a note. It read:

Dearest Theo—

I shall be out tomorrow afternoon, but I hope you shall call upon me come the evening. I believe I should like to attend Vauxhall Gardens with you. Please come for me at eight. My maid and I shall wear dominoes.

Your friend,
P.

She folded it in third, addressed the outside, and sealed it with a wafer. She would have it delivered by a footman early in the morning, that it might arrive at Marchmont's home before he ventured forth to her own. Of course, he might still call come the morning, but she almost hoped he would not. She could not let Mama have any notion of her desired goal for the evening. It was a shocking thing to attend Vauxhall Gardens—Mama would not allow it if she learned of it beforehand—and for that reason, the Gardens seemed to Pamela to be an entirely inspired destination, a place for making memories. Ah well, as to that, if Marchmont came in the morning, she would merely take him aside for a moment and secure his word he would say nothing to the matter. He would comply, she was sure—although he might take a kiss or a fondling as payment for his acquiescence. Even as he might, indeed, at the Gardens. But, she admitted truthfully and with a flurry rather like mice feet scurrying in the pit of her stomach, that was exactly what she wanted until her betrothal, to whomsoever that should be.

The lamp was burning dimly when she finally

snuffed the flame, making her way to her bed in the dark. The poor light it had provided had allowed her to leave her task without ever quite realizing how many tears had hit and streaked the words that had flowed from her pen. The words were difficult to read up to the passage wherein she had penned her decision, and then no more tears had marked the pages.

The Marbles were beautiful. Broken; in pieces; heads, legs and arms missing—but beautiful all the same. The artistry was breathtaking, no less so because this was the second time she viewed them. One could not but be moved by the elegant portrayal of so simple a thing as the flaring of a horse's nostrils as it charged into battle, or the agony on a soldier's face, or the lifelike posturing of a woman's hand outstretched. The occasional nudity of a piece here or there did not disturb her, for the pieces were of a beauty that transcended modesty. One could see the flexing of an arm, as though it were the working of bone under flesh, the artistry so fine that it seemed impossible it was mere stone before them. They would have been even more spectacular, only there was not enough room here at their fourth London home, made in a timbered outhouse behind Burlington House; some pieces had been left outside, with the grass growing up around them. Most of the items inside were piled one on top of the other, like a strange puzzle that needed sorting. Even as the works awed her, they also made Pamela ache, deep in her chest to see such battered, misused beauty.

"There is talk that Elgin may sell to the museum," Captain Penford said at her side.

"There has been talk of that for years. It is said he has money difficulties," Grandmama agreed from the captain's other side.

"There has been talk of that also for years. At one time, do you know, he had said any marbles that arrived on a British ship would be given to the museum in Montague House, but that promise is long since reneged. Bad show, that! This manner of thing belongs in a museum, not piled as cast-off stones. Any difficulties the man has had with expenses are of his own making, I say," the captain said.

"I thought you said they ought to have remained in Greece," Pamela said in a quiet voice.

"Well, perhaps they ought to have, but what's done is done. Now I say it behooves Elgin to *give* the collection to the British Museum. I do not see why the government ought to have to pay."

"I have always felt rather sorry for Lord Elgin," Pamela said. "I think he has been misunderstood. I think he saw how beautiful these were and, profit or no, could not bear to see them left to destruction."

"Still, one must acknowledge that profit has been ever high in his desires."

"I acknowledge no such thing," Pamela said, her lips thinning.

The captain looked at her with some surprise, and parted his lips to respond, but Grandmama overrode him, saying, "Well, I do believe we have seen them all, or at least what we may, arranged so haphazardly as they are.''

"Yes. Do let us return home," Pamela said.

"Or, would perhaps you ladies care to have an ice at Gunter's?" the captain proposed.

Pamela had no desire for ice; but Grandmama agreed, so she murmured her assent. The captain settled the ladies in the carriage he had brought from his family's home, leaving them alone for a moment while he informed the driver of their destination.

"Good gad, girl! What are you thinking of to be arguing with the captain's opinions that way? Do you not know you shall draw more flies with honey than with vinegar?" Grandmama scolded in a whisper.

"I did not realize I was arguing," Pamela said, frowning.

"You most certainly were! And there were quite a number of more gracious ways to accept an invitation to an ice than to mumble a nearly unintelligible 'all right, then.' Now he returns; attempt to be all sweetness."

Pamela mentally shook herself. Grandmama was only right, and it was not the captain's fault that she had awakened in a cantankerous mood for some reason. Disagreeing, mumbling, and grousing about were no way to demonstrate one's desire to be in a man's company for a day, let alone a lifetime.

She forced herself to become lively, entering the conversation with what she hoped was sparkle. They ate their ices while greeting acquaintances, and Pamela could not help but be aware that those same acquaintances looked from her to the captain, assessing what the situation might be. That was all to the good, for the captain could not help but note these assessments as well. Did they cause him to begin to think of himself as part of a couple that involved her as the other half? She could not say for sure, but he did not seem to take the general pull of the conversation amiss.

A friend of her mother's, Lady St. Clair, put her thoughts into words as she approached their table. Captain Penford rose, making use of his cane, as she asked, "So what do you think of our delightful Lady Pamela? Expectations are that she shall not see a second Season before she sees a wedding, and I think we all may agree that is a decided possibility, would you not say?"

"Indeed, my lady," the captain said, neatly offering no personal opinion as to the matter. "Will you join us?"

"I do not mind if I do," Lady St. Clair responded.

The captain saw her seated, then seated himself once more. And so it went for over half an hour, with the poor captain forced to rise more than half a dozen times as other acquaintances came to greet their party.

When at last they made noises about leaving, Lady St. Clair would not let the captain go without attempting one last time to pry a more definite answer from him. "Have you made plans for Lady Pamela and yourself, Captain, for the next little while you remain in London?"

Pamela blushed even as she attempted to appear as though she thought it a conventional question.

"Nothing definite, my lady, although it is my wish that I may occupy more of the lady's time," the captain said. At that moment he offered his hand to Pamela, to assist her to her feet. She may have been mistaken, but it seemed, for a moment, that he squeezed her hand. She could not look at him, and she certainly could not look at Lady St. Clair, not without blushing furiously again.

On the drive home she was not quite sure what to make of that comment of his, but she knew from the rather self-satisfied set of Grandmama's mouth what that lady thought of it. She made a mental note not to mention the possible squeezing of her hand to her grandparent, for Grandmama might be tempted to predict wedding plans for the near future herself.

Before their home they bid him please not to descend, to give his poor foot a rest, letting the driver instead hand them down. The door of the coach remained open, and he leaned out of it to say, "Lady Pamela, I meant what I said to Lady St. Clair. I am hopeful you would wish to spend tomorrow evening with me. I thought we might go to the opera. Do say you wish to go with me?"

"I do so wish," she said. "Grandmama?"

"No, I have no desire for it. You have to take your mama, or better yet, the little maid, Phyllis. By gad, Pamela, your mother was right this past winter when she said we ought probably to hire a companion for you. You shall wear the rest of us out with all this traipsing about town, day and night!" She turned to

222

the captain to add, "Such a popular girl, our Pamela." She did not wait for a response, not even the slight knowing smile the captain turned on Pamela, but turned away, hobbling a bit from the discomfort of her bad knees as she made her way to the front door.

"We are alone again," the captain pointed out when Grandmama had disappeared into the house.

"Except for the driver and at least three passersby," Pamela said, almost smiling. He truly was a pleasant fellow, for all that he never seemed quite relaxed, but that was only to be expected given his profession and the short amount of time they had been acquainted.

"And it is bright daylight still. Pity that. There are things one simply may not do in the fullness of daylight." He looked at her mouth.

All he had to do was lean forward just a little more, just give a tiny sign that he would take a kiss despite these obstacles.

He sat back.

"Good day, Captain," she said, reaching to close the coach door for him.

"Good day, Lady Pamela. Until tomorrow evening."

She watched his carriage roll away, then turned slowly, idly looking at the front of her home where Lawlton waited with the door open for her. She wondered—rather traitorously, she thought—what it would take to make the captain do anything improper. She sighed, nodding to Lawlton, the movement of her head causing her to note that there was a dark shape in one of the first floor windows; it could not help but draw her eye, for she was perfectly aware that window was in her bedchamber.

As she stared, her mouth falling open in surprise, she saw that it was Marchmont.

Chapter 15

He lifted a hand in a motion that signaled she should come up, then turned from the window.

Suddenly her feet were flying through the door, Lawlton staring at her in great surprise, so that as she approached the stairs she threw over her shoulder, "Thank you, Lawlton. I must hurry if I . . . if I am to be ready!" She had nothing to be ready for, but it was as handy an excuse as any other. If he shook his head over her return to the kind of commotion she had always created as a child, it only served the purpose of having him accept her haste as relatively normal behavior. She forgot the servant, and dashed up the stairs.

Before she could form a thought as to why Marchmont would be in her private chamber, she was past the top of the stairs and standing, breathing unevenly, in the open door that led from her sitting room.

Marchmont was now sitting on her vanity chair before the two large dressing drawers that served as her work space. He had one eye pressed to one of her peep shows; the other eye squinted closed. Behind him was the second wardrobe, the one that held all her toy collections from throughout her life, the doors wide open, the interior all but emptied. On the bed, the floor, the surface of the dressing drawers, and indeed every surface were scattered her things. Along with his discarded hat and gloves, her dollhouse was to his right, a game of Fox and Geese at his left. Her first several sets of metamorphosis cards, ones she had first experimented on to learn how to align the three sections, were arranged in neat piles to one side, and one was arranged so that it was obvious he had played with the combinations.

"Theo!" she cried, coming into the room. She did not think to add "how dare you," for of course he would dare.

"Pamela. I have a favor to ask. May I keep this?" He held forth the peep show. She knew from the drawing on its frontispiece that it contained a scene meant to be that of Robinhood and his Merry Men hiding among the trees, awaiting the oncoming Sheriff of Nottingham's soldiers. "I have taken rather a fancy to Friar Tuck. 'Tis very clever how you made his brown tunic blend with the tree. I can see how cleverly you made that big belly of his rather appear like a bole."

She came into the room, standing before him, staring down at him. She knew what she ought to do and say, were she the same young lady she had been yesterday, but any anger she might normally have felt had been burned away in the night. Instead of ordering him from her room, she reached back, her hands on the surface of the dressing drawers, and pulled herself up onto its surface, her feet dangling several inches from the floor as she made a seat for herself.

He looked up at her expectantly, his eyes dancing. "Yes, you may keep it. It is one of my earlier ones. I thought Robin turned out rather ugly."

"I only get it because you think Robin is ugly?" he cried in offended humor.

She nodded, grinning. "I shall make another with a handsome Robin, and Maid Marian, too."

"Ah yes," he said, putting down the peep show and leaning toward her. "Make it a forest idyll, verdant, thick, and green, with butterflies in the air, birds in their nests, and the two lovers lying in the tall, warm grass between the trees, clasped in each others' arms. Make them look as do you and I. Do that, and I shall pay you good coin for your efforts."

"What do you in my chamber, my lord?" she asked, swinging her feet a little as she laid her hands flat against the surface beneath her and settled comfortably.

" 'My lord?' I'll have none of that, not when you have three times already called me 'Theo.' I like the way you say my name, you see," he said, stretching out a finger. With it he caught the edge of her skirt, lifting it up to view the lacy shift underneath. "Very pretty! Is it as pretty a few inches higher?"

She batted his hand away, unable to summon up any real indignation. "You did not answer my question."

He leaned back—*out of harm's easy reach,* the thought crossed her mind.

"Your note said you would not be here this afternoon, so I knew it would be a perfect time to see this collection of yours which otherwise you would never make the effort to show me."

"How did you get in? No, you need not betray him, for I know it has to be Owen who admitted you, the traitor."

"Maybe I sneaked in."

"Maybe my brother is a toad. Someone needs to kiss him and turn him into a prince."

"I have that very same need," he pointed out, grinning.

"You have had too many kisses in your life. You have been turned from a prince to a frog and back again so often that now you are both at once, never to be separated again."

He gave a shrug that conceded the point, then balanced an elbow on the top of the dressing drawers, resting his fist against his temple as he listened to her speak.

"But, so then, here you are, howsoever you came to be here. What think you of my cuttings?" She made a self-mocking face, prepared for any comment but the one she received.

"I think they are magnificent."

"Magnificent? That is a curious word! Are you gammoning me?" she said as her feet ceased to swing.

"Not at all. Have I not made you surrender one to me that I may keep it all my days?"

"Now there is a hopeful sign." She rocked back

and forth playfully, balancing on her hands in place of swinging her feet, smiling again.

"How is that?"

"That you think to acquire something by which to remember me. If you must remember me, then that surely means you must be doubting that we shall ever marry."

"I never said that. I said I wanted to own something you had made. It does not mean I do not wish to own you as well." He sat forward again, at the edge of the seat, a little too close to her now.

"Own me? Oh, well, that is flattering." She spoke with an asperity that had no real rancor behind it. She ceased to rock, instead bringing up her hands and crossing her arms before her, a way to keep him some small distance from her.

He may have been moving to stand, but did not when his booted foot disturbed a pile of cards at his feet. "Ah, I have missed something during my exploration. What are these?" he asked, bending to pick up the long strips.

"Learning cards." She uncrossed her arms to leap down from her seat, taking the cards from him. She bent down, her skirts billowing around her, arranging the cards on the carpet. "See? There is a letter on the lefthand side of each card. If you put the cards in the proper order, the letters spell out the name of what you are seeing, in this case 'barnyard.' The picture, assembled in order, corresponds of course. 'Tis a simple way to practice one's spelling, without it seeming so very dull."

"Your cousins must adore you."

She blushed. "Oh, I just hope they enjoy what they receive."

"*I* adore you. I need a gift as well."

"And so your gift shall be that peep show."

"Not what I had in mind, but I do thank you most sincerely for it nonetheless."

The words made her twist to look at him, searching his face for mockery, but there was none. She turned away quickly, picking up the cards and stacking them carefully.

Hands encircled her waist, and with a little startled cry she was pulled onto his lap, the cards flying from her hands. One flew straight up, coming down on his head, then falling to the floor. He paid no heed, his expression questioning and less amused than it had been a moment before. "Now, my fine lady," he said, his large hands encircling her waist firmly so that she could not rise, "you will explain to me how it is that you wish me to take you to Vauxhall Gardens."

She ought to peel his fingers from her waistline, but instead she gave in to impulse, settling against him, her torso fitting into the curve of his body, forcing his one hand to move away from her waist, though the other remained, fingers splayed as if to hold her in place.

"Because you are the only man I know who would be willing to take me there."

One free hand came up to wind a bit of her hair, gone errant from her chignon, idly around his finger. "I suppose that is true. But why go at all?"

"Because I wish to. I have never been. If my maid

and I wear dominoes, no one shall ever know who we are. We should not appear completely odd in dominoes, should we?''

"A trifle, but I daresay there are enough dominoes to be seen there from time to time that none would question the disguise. But, to my regret, I am afraid I must inform you that I shall have to forego this delicious proposal, as I already have a prior commitment tonight.''

She felt a keen sense of disappointment.

"Tomorrow evening?'' he suggested, his finger leaving the stray lock of hair, that his arms might enclose her in a loose embrace.

She did not resist, even putting her head against his shoulder. She sighed. "No, tomorrow I am going to the opera with the captain. Who are you with tonight? Lady Calridge?''

"No.''

"Who, then? Come, you know of every moment I share with Captain Penford. If you know where I am at all hours of the day and night, it is not too much to ask that I should know where *you* spend your time.''

"That is fair, I suppose. And I have no objection to telling you: I am invited to dine with Lord and Lady Austin.'' She could see a portion of his mouth from where she lay upon his chest, and now that mouth quirked in amusement. "I have been invited to inspect the newly fashioned nursery. They are both extremely pleased with it, so they tell me, but I am to offer my opinion as to any improvements.''

"That is amusing, to think of you inspecting a

nursery," Pamela said. She could hear his steady heartbeat where her ear pressed against his waistcoat.

His fingers laced together, his clasped hands coming to rest on her hip. "You are in a curious mood this afternoon, my dear," he said, quietly, as his mouth hovered not far above her ear.

"Yes, I am," she agreed. She was averse to breaking the moment's comfortable spell, but she had to make of him a willing conspirator in her plans. "I should explain something to you," she said, reluctantly sitting up.

His hands fell away. Their eyes were almost on a level, and he gazed into hers, a hooded look coming into his own. "What is it?"

"I have decided that come what may, I do not wish to become a matron without first having experienced a deal of the gaiety that surrounds the Season. I want to be just a little bit naughty. Nothing drastic. Nothing that shall ruin my reputation forever, but to enjoy the sport that so many others enjoy so freely. I believe I ought to be in a carriage race at least once, and there are the Gardens to be seen, of course. I should like to sip a little too much champagne, just once, and I would like to see a risqué farce. That would mean telling Mama that I am going to one theatre when I intend to go another instead. So, you see, that is part of it indeed: I have a desire to pull the wool over her eyes in just such a way, once."

He did not nod or shake his head, listening and watching her mouth and her eyes.

"That is where you come in, Theo. I have no other acquaintance who would be willing to help me in such endeavors. What do you say?'' She smiled at him.

Only then did she realize how still he had become, how lacking in humor his expression had grown.

He put her from him, coming to his feet as well. Tugging on his coat sleeves, he said pointedly, "I must tell you I do not care for this language of 'once.' I do not believe I have ever done anything but once. It is not in my nature.''

Disappointment rippled through her again. He was going to refuse her! The one thing she thought would earn her a measure of contentment in her days to come, and he was not going to give in to it.

There was a soft sound, a tiny clink, that rose to their ears from the carpet. He bent, picking up a few pieces of a miniature tea set that had been disturbed by one of his Hessians. He looked down at them, not speaking. When he stood again his expression had turned serious. He said, "Although to be fair, for there is something about you that forces me to it: I must admit that I have never before sat in a woman's room, uninvited, and toyed with a collection of playthings. I suppose I must admit that is a 'once.' ''

He turned, moving to one of the wardrobe shelves, upon which he placed the pieces.

In silence she joined him, also retrieving some of the pieces. She felt a curious need to burst into tears, whether because he was rejecting her proposal, or because he had unbent enough to soften the blow, she could not say. She swallowed repeatedly, keeping the tears just at bay.

They worked wordlessly, until everything had been

restored to the wardrobe. He closed the doors as she took a seat in the chair. She knew her shoulders slumped and her chin touched her chest, but her dejection was too complete for her to care to put on a bright face.

A hand touched her shoulder, but even so she could not bring herself to raise her head.

"Very well," Marchmont said, bending so that his voice was a soft breeze across her ear. "What harm can it do? I shall squire you to the frivolities you profess to desire."

She looked up at that, tears teetering on her lashes even as she formed a smile for him. Unable to speak for a moment, she made a gratified noise, her hand coming up to cover his own.

"Perhaps if you are forever in my presence, you will come to realize what a truly fine fellow I am, despite first impressions. You might see that stiff-necked captains are the most tedious fellows on earth and would never be able to amuse you as I shall."

She managed in a watery voice, "But, Theo, that is why I asked you, do you not see? I already know that you are a fine fellow. You do not molest me— well, not unkindly or overmuch, that is—despite numerous opportunities. I see that I am safe from any lasting harm in your company."

"Are you so sure of that?"

"Absolutely."

"But, Pamela, are you not aware that I have just compromised you?" he said in a soft, low voice as he came around to one knee in front of her, clasping her two hands in his.

"By being in my room?" She found she could laugh, and even tease a little. "Let me tell you, it is not the first time I have been compromised this week."

He appeared startled by the words, but she went on, leaving him no chance to comment.

"I am growing quite used to being compromised. It is, however, true that you have also done as much. So how is it that you have not finished the job? Why do you not call out to the servants, that our scandalous meeting might be witnessed? Why do you not go to my father and insist we must now wed?" she challenged, but in a manner that held no malice.

His eyes darkened, and he released her hands, standing and stepping back from her. She rose from the chair to face him.

"I shall tell you why. Because you do not wish me that way. It is no victory in this game of ours, not if you win everything but my acquiescence. You want me to come of my own accord, and not by some manipulation of yours."

He stared at her, until he could no longer do so, looking away toward the door.

She said nothing, not needing to point out that she was only too right, that she understood him very well indeed.

Finally he looked back at her. "That is, I think, something that a man could only do once, and it would be to his regret. I have no desire for such regrets," he said, a muscle near his jaw twitching.

"Theo, your scruples are showing," she teased ever so gently, her voice little more than a whisper.

Suddenly he was moving, snatching up his hat and gloves in one hand, the other snaking around her waist. She was pulled suddenly to him, and his mouth was on hers. It was a short, deep kiss, one that bent her backward so that she had to hold on to his shoulders. She did not try to fight it in any way, even though she tasted anger on his lips. It was over too soon as he stepped away from her, leaving her off-balance in more ways than one.

"I believe my scruples are safely hidden once again," he said almost harshly as she grasped the dressing drawers, the better to steady herself.

Now that his second hand was free, he scooped up the peep show. In the work of a moment he had collapsed the pleats so that it would be not be crushed, made her a swift, stiff bow, and then stomped from the room with no backward glances.

It was not until after dinner that she discovered her diary was missing. In its place was a note that did not fold flat for there was a small wrapped something inside it. She did not know Theo's writing, but the moment she laid eyes on the bold, slanted script she sensed the note was from him. She picked up the cloth without opening it, instead unfolding and reading first the note:

My dear,
   You already know I am capable of nearly every kind of violation, and so now I have committed another. I have your diary. For blackmail? That is

236

a tempting thought, but, no, I take it now that I may understand, hopefully, what it is about myself (or the good captain) that keeps you from me. I shall return it intact once I have read it. Lest you loathe me for trespassing into your privacy, I in turn leave behind a bit of my own soul with you, to show my goodwill. I believe you comprehend that this is not easily nor lightly done, as I admit to you that I feel quite naked and exposed. I leave this to show that I am, indeed, willing to risk a great deal to learn how I may be held dear and close within the circle of your heart's affections.

Ever yours,
Theo

She set aside the note and unfolded the fabric, revealing his ruby horseshoe ring.

Chapter 16

The next morning after she had dressed and the maid had gone, she placed the ring on a chain, a chain long enough that when it was placed around her neck the rubied ring dangled from sight, hidden between her breasts. No one must see it, for she could never explain how it was that she had the ring.

She had not slept much last night. At first she had tossed and turned, fretting over the absence of her diary. She tried to recall every word she had written in it, especially the latest entries, but the more she tried, the less she was sure what had been her thoughts and what had actually been put to paper. What would he make of her words? Would he take them as they were written, or would he read between the lines, extrapolating meanings she had not intended? Had she written more than she thought, and if so, what had she written concerning him? Worse yet, what if he found her thoughts infantile? What if he determined she had a small, closed mind? She had no way to explain her words, no way to watch his reaction to them, facts which left her in an agony of suspense.

Somewhere around midnight her fevered distress had shifted into something quieter, more reflective. What was done was done. He would think what he would, and she had no control over it. She ought to have stormed his home and demanded he return her property. A solid plan, if only she had executed it hours ago, but now he had no doubt long since read what he would and was abed, or out upon the town searching out the pleasures of the night. The only thing she could do past midnight was to attempt to foresee what tomorrow might bring.

But tomorrow had been still hours away, and the deepness of the night led her to other thoughts: did he run the breadth of the town or was he sleeping peacefully? In bed or in sport, was he restless as she was? Did he feel the absence of the ring? She knew what it meant to him. He was a man of appetites, appetites that tugged constantly at his civilized mien. The ring had become a talisman for him, a thin thread tied to the shreds of his self-respect, a tentative bond that kept him from plunging once again into the world of ruinous debt and, even by his own standards, untenable behavior. Its tiny weight must be hugely noticeable to him in its absence. Did being free of it mean that tonight he lost control? Did he go whoring? Was he at the tables? Did he perhaps drink to overcome any such impulses? Or did he think of his brothers and guard his ways, realizing the ring was only a ring?

Of course he did. The ring held no magic, he knew

that. No magic, except indeed for the most powerful of all: the ability to hope again. Hope: that was everything, the center of his world. When he had written that he had left behind a bit of his soul, she had to see it now for nothing less than the truth.

For his own strange reasons, he had entrusted her with something far more precious than the gold and rubies that made up the ring. So if he was even now looking into her soul, she was carrying a piece of his in return.

When she had lain down to sleep at last, her hand had clasped the ring placed beneath her pillow. Even in sleep she had desired to keep it safe, as she did this morning by wearing it close to her heart.

The morning brought two gentlemen callers, neither of them the men foremost on Pamela's mind. It was pleasant to see Lord Gilbury again, although he was a bit tongue-tied until they began to discuss the play they had "seen" together that night at Drury Lane. He brought with him a Mister Nisbet, who fortunately made up in his knowledge of Shakespeare what Lord Gilbury lacked. Mister Nisbet was friendly, but Pamela got the impression he was—not unlike herself—not wholly given over to the conversation.

She soon saw that Mister Nisbet might have had an ulterior motive in accompanying Lord Gilbury today, for when it was announced that Lady Jane had come to call, as she frequently did, the man brightened visibly.

The morning passed in pleasant conversation, although it might have been more pleasant if Pamela had not felt a need to survey the doorway every ten minutes or so.

When Mister Nisbet and Lord Gilbury rose to leave, Pamela was happy to see them go. Jane had given herself over to simpering ways, obviously having become aware of Mister Nisbet's regard, for she gave a particularly annoying giggle every five minutes regardless of whether or not Mister Nisbet said anything at all clever. Pamela found herself judging her friend rather harshly by thinking that she herself would far rather laugh too loudly at something than too much at nothing, and at once felt abashed that she'd had such an unkind thought. She truly was capable of a foul temper this day, make no mistake about it—no doubt due to her lack of sleep.

Jane departed at the same time as the gentlemen, making use of the excuse to have Mister Nisbet hand her up into her carriage. Pamela did her best to dismiss the thought that here was another entirely proper, albeit utterly cloying, demonstration of the womanly art of coquetry as so ably practiced by Jane. She suspected it grated only because she was jealous of the woman's ability to be so light and gay even as she was all that was proper.

As these guests left, more arrived, and still Pamela saw no one that she truly wished to see.

When finally the last caller—Lady St. Clair, who gushingly told Mama about their encounter in Gunter's—departed, Pamela went to her room with a sick headache.

She spent the day in bed, thinking of nothing at

times, at other times worrying her lower lip as she tried to recall just how thoroughly she might have exposed herself in her diary. Eventually she just lay there, fully clothed, staring at the plasterwork ceiling until she drifted into sleep.

Phyllis woke her in time for dinner, and then it was time to ready herself for her evening with Captain Penford. Phyllis helped her unbutton and remove the dress she had worn down to dinner, and Pamela made a point of keeping the ring hidden below the line of her chemise. She chose a pretty ivory gown with partial overskirts of pink silk, ivory ruffles adorning the sleeves and deep flounces that made up the hem. A two-inch-wide row of tiny stitched pink flowers created a vertical line from the top of the neckline to her toes. A glance in the cheval glass proved her choice to be at once both fashionable and demure, for she had chosen a gown with a high neck to hide the fact that she wore a chain. The ostrich feathers that plumed from her pearl-studded bandeau suited her, or so Phyllis was quick to tell her. She thought, momentarily, to replace the ostrich plumes with the short white feather the captain had admired before, but then decided that, no, this would give him another look to admire.

She waited in her room, watching from one of her bedchamber windows as the dusk faded into evening. She saw several carriages coming and going down the street, their lamps lit against the gloom. She thought she recognized the one, and decided that, yes, it was the captain's coach, for it slowed as it approached her home. It was then that she noted another carriage slowed as well; Owen must be planning an evening of his own.

She did not wait for her mama or her maid to let her know the captain had arrived. She pulled on her cloak, picked up her reticule, and descended the stairs.

The captain was not awaiting her in the entry hall as she might have expected, but candlelight and the sound of voices quickly made it clear that he had been asked into the front parlor. Pamela crossed the room's threshold before she realized there were more than two voices to be heard.

"Theo!" she cried, then blushed hotly, for all eyes had turned to look at her, and only a set of green eyes did not look at her with either censure or displeasure at her outcry. Indeed, it was impossible to read any emotion in Marchmont's eyes.

"Pamela," he said in return. Was his lack of use of a title meant to cover her own gaffe, or to make the situation worse?

He crossed to her, extending his hand. In it was her diary, or so she must assume, for it was something of a diary's size, wrapped around with brown paper and tied with string. Instead of snatching it back, as she might have thought she would, she stared at it, unable to move.

"I will not keep you, as I know you are on your way out," he said, his voice cordial. "I was passing by, and thought to stop and return the book I borrowed."

She stared at him, as if by the power of her will alone she could divine what he was thinking. No revelation came to her. "How did you find it?' she asked with numb lips, having to know something of his thoughts.

"I found it interesting reading."

Did he smile? Sneer? Stifle a yawn? Or an oath?

She finally reached out, accepting the parcel.

His back was to the others, and his voice dropped very low as he murmured, "Pity we have so many spectators. I was almost looking forward to the colorful denunciation I should have received from you otherwise."

She did not respond, unable to think of any words that would properly sum up her mingled outrage, her fear of trusting him in any way, her relief that the diary was in her possession once more, and something oddly close to amusement at his words.

Her silence seemed to be comment enough, for he lowered his lashes and folded his hands penitently together as if she had given him a thorough upbraiding. He said softly, "A denunciation which, I might add, I very much deserve."

Was he truly contrite for his misdeed, or did the words relate to something he had read in the diary? She could not think, nor did she particularly care. It was enough to see the man humbled.

"Are you off to view more nurseries tonight, my lord?" she asked. If he wished forgiveness for his sin, he would have to do more penance than merely to show a moment's worth of guilty conscience, feigned or otherwise.

As she spoke, the captain made his way across the room, frowning.

Marchmont turned as the man approached, making his answer to both of them. "Not at all. I am going to Covent Gardens."

"To the opera?" Captain Penford barked.

"As are we," Mama said with a certain sourness.

"Are you?" Marchmont's eyebrows rose as though in surprise.

Pamela gave him a steady look, but one corner of her mouth tilted up despite herself. That was what she got for roasting him.

"Then I must make a point of calling upon you in your box," Marchmont said, one corner of his mouth rising as well.

"As you please," Pamela said, putting paid to the conversation by adding, "It is unfortunate that we may not offer you a seat in our coach, but I know you would not wish to discommode our host by crowding his wounded appendage."

Marchmont's slight smile, combined with a light in his eyes, suggested little to the others perhaps, but to Pamela it was clear he would be more than pleased to not only discommode the captain because of his foot, but would most happily trod upon that extremity with relish, if only given an excuse to do so. Her reaction to that knowledge was a sudden, overwhelming need to either laugh or strike him with her reticule, but fortunately at that moment the captain stepped before her. "My dear lady," he said, "should you not return that book to your room, that we might be on our way?"

"Oh, yes, of course," Pamela said, her voice pitched higher than usual. She took a deep, steadying breath, murmured, "I shall return at once," and fled from the scene before she disgraced herself by acting on her impulses.

In her room, she ripped down one corner of the paper to ascertain that it was indeed her diary beneath. Satisfied, she crossed to her escritoire, placing the diary in its usual place; only now she bothered to lift the folding writing platform upward and, used the little key she had stored in a drawer to lock it in place. She slipped the key into her reticule. It was only when she turned from the task suddenly that the ring, still dangling between her breasts, shifted, reminding her of its presence. She had not returned it to Marchmont despite his return of her diary! She must do so, somehow discreetly, before he left. It was only fair.

She slipped the chain over her head, careful not to disturb her coiffure, and slid the ring from its length. She put both in her reticule, and left her room to descend the stairs.

When she attained the front parlor again, she found Mama and the captain ready and waiting to go. "But where has Lord Marchmont gone?" she cried.

"He has left already," Mama supplied.

"Oh," Pamela said, feeling strangely hollow at the news.

Ah well, as to that, no need to feel she had somehow left him adrift. She would just have to return his ring tomorrow when he came to take her to Vauxhall Gardens . . . or, tonight.

Yes, she would have to attempt to find a way to slip it to him tonight at the opera. Of course that would mean having to be alone with him, somehow, for a moment or two. She was not concerned that she could contrive to do that in some feasible manner, but rather found herself fretting that if they did find a moment alone, he might then reveal what he had made of the writings in her diary.

She had to admit even to herself that while she was desperate to know, she was not so sure she could bear to have him tell her.

Chapter 17

Pamela did not understand a word of Italian; but the music was familiar and beautiful, and she could not fault the company by which she was surrounded. Mama and the captain had discovered a mutual interest in the game of battledore, he in playing the recquet game, she in observing it as it was played by others. Pamela thought to herself that he spoke in terms that made it seem more a battle than a game; but Mama matched his enthusiasm, so perhaps she judged too harshly. Lady Jane had made an appearance, bringing the latest *on dits* with her, couched in her usual blithe and charming manner. Pamela spent some while watching her friend be gay and charming, and wondered if she would ever master the skill of being both without also seeming forward. She arrived at no conclusion before Jane was swept away on the arm of Mister Nisbet, whose absence was no loss for he had spoken to no one but Jane. Lord Gilbury stopped in, sitting down next to Pamela without invitation to do so. Captain Penford frowned at him, but did not abandon his conversation with Mama.

Pamela was grateful Lord Gilbury had come, for here was one more person to keep her from looking across the way to where she knew Marchmont was seated. She had ascertained, early in the evening, that he was in Lady Calridge's box, and had done her best since to keep from looking that way. What he did was his business, and she had no desire to be caught watching him. She would approach him during the strolling that invariably occurred between scenes, and would contrive a way to return his ring. How she would get him alone, she had no idea, but something would surely occur to her.

At first Lord Gilbury said nothing, simply sitting next to her, rather awkward in his silence, staring down at the stage.

"I never can decide if I care for sopranos," he said at length, making a face at the woman who sang below.

"Why is that, my lord?"

"Well, if they all sang the same, then I could decide, but some of them sing like angels, and others as though they wish to bore a hole through your head. There ought to be some kind of regulation, don't you think?"

She laughed. "There are times I could agree."

He looked at her out of the corner of his eye, a sudden color flooding into his face, and he began to stammer. Finally he formed a word, and then another, "M-my . . . lady . . . that is to say . . . er . . . could you be persuaded to . . . er . . . join me, one day . . . er . . . that is to say, for a ride through Hyde Park?'' It was only then that he turned to face her, the color of his skin growing redder still.

Flattered, she looked away. She knew a certain gratitude, too, for it showed that even should the captain decide she was not the lady of his choice, there might be others willing to take a silly young thing such as herself to wife. Of course, Lord Gilbury would never do, for he was almost as impossible in his behavior as she was herself. Still, there could be no harm in being seen in his company, she thought, and parted her lips to agree to the plan, but was interrupted.

''She is promised to me tomorrow afternoon,'' the captain said.

She turned to look at him in surprise, for this was news to her. He met her gaze, returning it levelly, daring her to deny him. It was not an unpleasant presumption on his part, she decided.

''The day after that,'' Lord Gilbury blurted, flushing an alarmingly deeper shade of crimson yet.

The captain stared hard at the man, belatedly giving a peremptory nod as he growled, ''Very well, I suppose. That is, if the lady agrees.''

Pamela gave him a speaking glance that said his acknowledgment of her role in granting consent had come a little late, but then she turned to Lord Gilbury. ''I should be honored.''

He let out a breath of air, and the color began to recede from his face. He all but slumped in the chair, recovering from the obvious exertion his offer had cost him. ''That is well,'' he said, taking a deep breath and letting it out again. Then he leaped to his feet and made her a deep bow. For a moment she wondered if his sudden movements would cause him to collapse, but apparently Lord Gilbury was made of sterner stuff than he looked, for he stood upright without difficulty despite all the blood that had gone to his head to turn his face such a ruddy hue. "It shall seem a week until we may go for our drive," he said, a hand to his heart. "Good evening, my lady."

"Good evening, my lord," she replied, smiling even after he exited the box.

With everyone else already engaged in conversation, she watched the singers below, completely at sea as to what the scene was about. The music, for all that it was pleasant enough, did not particularly engage, and so she found her gaze, almost as if of its own volition, rising to look across to Lady Calridge's box.

Lady Calridge sat there, viewing the singers, or perhaps someone in the pit, with her opera glasses. Behind her sat two ladies, busily chatting, but otherwise the box was empty. Marchmont was gone. Fetching wine, no doubt.

Here, then, might be her opportunity to return his ring.

Pamela stood, catching her mama's eye. "I shall return at once," she said quietly, shaking her head when it appeared that Mama would join her. "Do keep the captain entertained, will you not?"

The captain turned to look at her, asking, "Do you stroll?"

"No, no," she assured him.

He was gentleman enough not to press her further, for after all she might be going to find a necessary. Instead he nodded and turned back to Mama.

Pamela slipped out of the box, opening her reticule long enough to slip the ring over her thumb, holding it tight with her fingers wrapped over it.

She moved down the corridors, nodding to acquaintances and murmuring excuses to keep moving, searching for the sight of Marchmont's dark head among the crowd.

After fifteen minutes she had not found him, and knew she had to return to the box.

He was seated in her chair when she returned. She could not help herself: she gave something perilously close to an oath when she saw him sitting there. Penford had a stiffness to the set of his shoulders, and Mama was frowning outright, clearly annoyed to have Marchmont in the box.

He rose as she entered, even as the captain did, and she used his length to hide her from the captain's line of vision just long enough to give Marchmont an exasperated look.

He gave her a questioning glance at the reproach and stepped aside to offer her the chair he had just vacated. She sat down, and he pulled over another chair to sit beside her.

"Lady Pamela, how do you find the opera?" he asked, looking for all the world as if he cared to hear her opinion on the matter.

Caught between the two men, she could do neither of the things she wanted to do. She wanted to return his ring, and she wanted to scold him for being here and thereby not making it a simple matter for her to do so. Instead she spoke the truth: "I am afraid I have not followed it at all well."

"Neither have I." He grinned at her.

The captain leaned toward her, taking up her gloved hand, fortunately not the one clutching the ring. "Then let me explain it to you," he said, not releasing her hand as he went on to do just that. Marchmont never looked down at the clasped hands, but his polite and still attendance to the captain's explanation said well enough he was aware of it.

"Perhaps we should return tomorrow, to view the opera again, now that we are in possession of this intelligence," Marchmont said to Pamela when Penford was done.

"She is promised to me," the captain said.

"No, sir, she is promised to me," Marchmont said quietly.

"Is this true, Lady Pamela?" the captain asked her, his mustache bristling.

"Yes, it is."

"Pamela, you never said a word to me!" Mama cried.

"I meant to take Phyllis."

The captain lifted his chin, and pronounced, "Then perhaps I should speak now to reserve your company for the evening after."

"Perhaps we should alternate evenings," Marchmont suggested, a devil leaping in the back of his eyes as Penford gave him a hard look.

Pamela had no chance to state her opinion on this

suggestion, for Mama stood, putting her hand on Marchmont's shoulder. "I have taken the notion to visit with Lady Calridge, and you may escort me to her box."

Marchmont gave in to the obvious maneuver with grace, rising without ado, rather to Pamela's surprise. "Good evening," he said as he bowed to the box's occupants. As he straightened he caught up Pamela's free hand, the one that still held the ring. He bowed over the curled fingers, pressing a light kiss to her glove, only then releasing her hand with something of a flourish. There had been no opportunity to slip the ring into his hand, even had he been prepared to receive it in such a fashion.

As she and Captain Penford murmured fare-wells—in differing degrees of sincerity—Marchmont offered his arm to Mama and indicated the doorway of the box. As they departed, he made a comment, one that Pamela saw the captain heard as well as she did: "Do you realize you have left your daughter alone with a man?"

Mama's reply came to them also: "They are chaperoned by the hundreds around them. Now, Marchmont, much as I am loathe to speak out of turn, I must say something about your continual visitations—" The rest of her comment was lost as they moved away.

The captain looked down at Pamela. "It appears your mother shall put a flea in the man's ear."

"So it would appear."

"About time, I say! He is forever about, smiling in that knowing fashion of his, taunting, offering his corrupted opinions. I cannot see how you tolerate the man, for he is quite the boor—"

"Oh, no," she said, squeezing her hand against his.

His oration ground to a halt. "What?"

"I say that, no, he is not a boor. He is many things he ought not be, but certainly not that. Captain Penford—"

His other hand came atop hers so that her hand was clasped between his two. He spoke before she could continue: "Lady . . . Pamela, do I presume too much to ask that you should call me Roger?"

She hesitated only a moment before she agreed, "Roger, then." She looked up at him, firmness coming into her eyes. "Roger, I should tell you that Lord Marchmont is my friend. I know he is a difficult sort, but he is my friend for all of that. You must not speak poorly of him to me."

He cocked his head at her, surprised, but she could see from his startled expression that he knew she meant it. "Do not tell me you have a fondness for the fellow?"

"I do. A fondness, and only that. I am not such a fool that I would ever expect more than friendship from Lord Marchmont," she said softly.

He was silent a moment, absorbing this information. "But could you expect more from some other fellow?" he asked, his blue eyes fixing on hers.

"I could," she said, and then had to look away, for it was impossible to mistake the light in his eyes.

A hand touched her chin, pulling it around so that she must face him once more. The captain stared down at her for several beats of her heart, which pounded uncomfortably against her rib cage, and then he lowered his mouth to hers and kissed her.

She knew at least a hundred people might witness the kiss, knew that by kissing her thusly he had all but declared himself. Her heart careened wildly, then seemed to land in the bottom of her stomach, where it throbbed. For a moment she felt dizzy, just as he released her lips, his hand coming away from her chin. She sat still, waiting, her upper lip tingling where his mustache had brushed.

"Must you go with Marchmont tomorrow evening?" he asked huskily.

It was not the question she was expecting. She blinked her eyes, striving to clear her head, and responded breathlessly, "Yes. I said I would."

He sat back, his one hand coming away, although he left the other still entwined with hers. "Pardon me," he said, looking away from her, discomfort flooding his features. "I ought not to have kissed you like that. It was precipitous, and far too public. I hope you may excuse me. I admit I was momentarily swayed to it by your beauty."

"Captain—Roger," she gasped, alarmed by his withdrawal. "Is it that I . . . ? I mean to say, I promised—"

"I understand. A promise is a promise. Of course you must fulfill your promises." There was a long pause while his shoulders worked under his coat, but then his hand squeezed hers. "After all, I expect you to keep your promise to me that you will accompany me for the evening after your drive with Gilbury?"

She sighed with relief. He was annoyed, but not lastingly angry. She thought perhaps she had not been mistaken that he had come very close to proposing. Perhaps, in two nights, he just might after all. Two nights. Not such a long time away, not at all. Two nights from now there would still be five more before he left London. A world of time, now that he had kissed her where prying eyes could see the act.

It was as that thought formed that she looked up, meeting Marchmont's stare across the way. He looked directly at her, and she knew in a moment from the way he held himself, staring and so still, that he had witnessed that kiss. His ring, still clutched inside the fist she made with her curled fingers, seemed to burn against her skin.

Pamela looked away, feeling color flood her face. She did not look up again, despite the fact she believed the eerie sensation of being stared at was undoubtedly based in reality.

When Mama returned they agreed the opera had lost its appeal. While the captain came to his feet, Pamela took the opportunity to slip the ring into her reticule.

The captain escorted them down to the theatre's portico, where they waited only three minutes before his coach was brought around, and then it was a short drive home.

After the driver handed the ladies down, the captain leaned forward on his seat, reaching out of the open door to take up Pamela's hand and half bow over it. He pressed a kiss upon the spot where another kiss had already been pressed this evening. The action made her shiver in response, although she would have found it difficult to say if the shiver was from pleasure or some other emotion.

"Good night, Lady Pamela. Do not let that puppy, Gilbury, make you late for our evening together."

She noted he said nothing about the evening she was to spend with Marchmont, and perhaps that was all to the good.

"Good night, Capt—Roger. I shall not allow it, be assured."

He nodded, pulled the door closed, and his coach rolled away.

As she came into her room, she remembered the ring. She retrieved her reticule from her sitting room, removed the ring and thought about placing it under her pillow. She considered this course of action for a moment, and then decided it might be better to have it on her person at all times. She felt sure Theo would be grieved should she lose it. She retrieved the chain from her reticule, her fingers also finding the little key that opened her escritoire. Where to keep the key, and so her diary, safe? She smiled at the thought, for who else but Marchmont would ever want to see the thing? She could not imagine the captain ever reading her writings without permission first. She knew she was locking the barn door after the horse had escaped, but nonetheless she examined the key and found it had a bit of decorative metalworking that formed a space through which a chain could be slid. She put down the reticule, placed both the key and the ring on the chain, slipped it over her head and under her clothing, and then moved to her vanity. The chair that Marchmont had used earlier today had been replaced before the mirrored table. That was where she sat as she pulled pins from her hair, reaching for a brush to begin absently counting the one hundred brush strokes required each night.

She was just about to ring for Phyllis when there was a knock at the outer door. "Enter," she called, setting aside the brush. She leaned toward the mirror over her vanity, not terribly surprised by the weary, thoughtful face looking back at her. She had been through a great deal today.

"You did say to enter," a male voice said quietly.

She spun around, "Theo!"

"At least this time I was invited in," he answered, standing in the bedchamber doorway, his hat in his hand.

"What do you here?" She stood, pushing her hair back over her shoulders, feeling half-undressed with her hair down.

"There is not a great deal of time for explanation, I am afraid. I have set Lawlton to look for Powell, and I fear it will not be very long before he discovers that unlike what I have just told him, in truth your brother is currently not returned home yet this evening. We must act quickly."

"Act quickly? In what way?"

He stepped toward her, turning the hat in his hand. He looked down at it for a moment, but when he looked up again, there was a sheepish grin hovering at the corners of his mouth. "I had me a thought. I thought tonight might not be too early to begin our foray into frivolity. Come, let us cast off caution and go forth.''

''Oh, I do not know if I could . . . ,'' she said faintly, a hand going to her throat.

A spark lit in his eyes, and he said in a controlled voice, ''You said it was what you wished.''

She thought about the truth of that, thrilled despite herself by the very fact that she was even considering it. Her hand, poised at her throat, then traveled to her hair. ''My hair . . . I could not possibly—''

He tossed the hat to the surface of the vanity, put two hands on her shoulders, and said, ''Sit. I can do your hair in a trice.''

''You? What do you know of women's hair?'' she cried, startled, even as she sank onto the chair.

''Not a great deal, I own, but I can make a braid, and then you can pin it.'' Even as he spoke, his fingers pulled at the length of her hair, smoothing it back. ''It is really too poor a thing that it needs to be put up at all,'' he said as he worked, ''for I quite fancy it down like this.''

She sat still, not relaxing as she usually did when someone worked with her hair. She watched him in the mirror, wishing he was done, amazed that she was letting him do it. She could not be sure, but it seemed that his hands ran the length of her hair for an unnecessary amount of time before he separated it into three sections and began braiding.

''There is still some curl there around your face,'' he pointed out, catching her eye in the mirror as he worked. ''You shall look well,'' he said, then handed the end of the completed braid over her shoulder.

She took the end and reached for pins. She wrapped the braid three times around itself, securing it with a dozen pins or more at her nape. She looked in the mirror and realized it was not the most elegant style she had ever sported but that it would do.

"Find a cloak and a bonnet, and we shall go," he said, still looking at her reflection in the mirror, daring her to refuse his offered entertainment. Her second dare this evening, in fact. Well, she would not back away from the one any more than she had the other.

"And Phyllis," she said, accepting.

He shook his head. "No Phyllis. I have to think that once this night is over and done with, she would not be able to keep our little secret. And I have to tell you that earlier this evening your mother forbade me to call here at your home anymore." He frowned at the words, and perhaps a flicker of pain crossed his features.

"Oh, no! Did she?" Pamela cried.

"She did. If we are to do as you ask, our assignation must be kept secret. I doubt your little maid could accomplish that."

She put her hand to her mouth, thinking hard and swiftly. " 'Tis true," she agreed finally, thinking she would have to rouse the maid from the above stairs chamber Phyllis shared with two other girls. When she did not return soon, the others would be sure to question her quite thoroughly.

"What say you, then? Do we go, alone?"

"It shall be all right if I bring my domino, should it not? That would make it possible?"

He smiled warmly down at her. "That would make it all right, love. Fetch it at once, for I doubt your mama would approve of our little adventure, so we must go before she finds us at our task."

How true that was. It was not to be wondered at that her heart began to pound; he was offering the very chance she had asked him to give her. They were going to flout convention, do something for the spontaneous joy of doing it, unplanned, unsanctioned. "How will I get back in the house unnoted?" she asked.

"That will not be a problem."

He spoke with such certainty, she believed him. He would have a contingency in mind, for he always did. She rose, coming to his side long enough to put her hand on his arm. "Thank you," she said.

"You are welcome." He lowered his lids over his green eyes for one long moment, but then raised them again to say, "Hurry now, or the plan shall be undone. I shall slip away and await below in my coach."

"I shall," she said, then almost giggled because of the exhilaration that whipped through her at the thought of her own daring.

She found the domino where she expected to find it in the wardrobe, the mask hanging on the same hook. She donned the cloak and held the mask at her side, under the cloak, hidden from sight until she could slip from the house. She could explain a cloak, but not a mask. At the last moment, she recalled the ring. She slipped the chain over her head, leaving the chain and the key on the vanity once she had pulled the ring free. She found a pocket in her cloak and put the ring there, where it would be simple to retrieve. She hesitated for a moment, wondering whether she ought to take the time to find a pair of gloves; but then a sense of urgency overcame her, and she abandoned the requirement for fear she would be caught by her maid or worse if she was not soon quit of the house.

She descended the stairs, saw the entry was deserted, and let herself out the front door as quietly as she could.

There was the coach, exterior lamps not lit while a faint glow came from inside the carriage, and Marchmont, a dimly outlined shape, standing beside it, motioning her forward. Her heart somersaulted, and for a moment she quailed. She ought not do such a thing. She never would with the captain. Oh, yes, she never, never would—unless she did it right now. Had Grandmama been like this? Had she craved the excitement of adventure, and admired the vitality of a man willing to participate? Yes, no doubt she had, for she had married Grandpapa. But Pamela had the advantage over Grandmama, because she had chosen to act without forethought. She had planned this. This was a moment she had diagrammed for herself. To run from it now was to be craven, and to be filled with that many more regrets in the years to come.

She stepped forward and allowed Theo to hand her up into the dark carriage.

Chapter 18

He rapped on the roof of the coach to signal the driver, and they were away. The small interior lamp provided enough light for them to see one another, but the color of their clothing was soft and muted.

Marchmont spread his hands. "So, we begin our adventure."

She laughed, letting him see her excitement. "Where do we go?"

"Ah, as to that . . . ," he said, moving from the opposite seat where he had settled, to sit beside her. "Will you allow it to be a surprise?"

She thought about that, then answered with eyes that glittered even in the dim lighting, "Yes. But I shall have three guesses first. Let me think. As it is so late, I cannot conceive that we are going to a performance?"

He made no response, smiling softly at her.

"Unless perhaps you have arranged some special performance after hours. I have heard of patrons doing such things. Are you a patron to any of the arts?"

"No." He slid an arm around her shoulders, pulling her to his side.

She hesitated, stiff a moment against him, but then she allowed herself to relax, leaning into him much as she had done yesterday in her room. "How unfashionable of you!" she teased. "So then, where could we be going? Could it be a . . ."—she lowered her voice, as though to say the words too loudly would be to make them worse—"a gaming hell?"

He smiled widely at that and nearly laughed. "No."

"You are not supposed to answer! Recall, 'tis to be a surprise," she cried, striking her hand gently against his chest in reprimand.

He caught the hand and raised it to his lips, making her glad he probably could not see her face flush with color at the boldness of their bare hands touching. He kissed it just above the knuckles and, when she did not snatch it away, went on to kiss each of the knuckles themselves.

Something broke loose inside her, slipping around her interior with a curious melting sensation. It was really too much, and she ought to tell him to stop . . . but he was not doing any harm, not really, and it was pleasurable, and it was his way to tease . . . like this. . . .

"Um," she said, her voice shaky. "Um . . . I . . . let me think . . . I have another guess."

Now he kissed each of her fingertips, his mouth warm against her skin. "Mmmm?" he said, watching her over her hand.

She looked away, unable to meet that warm regard. "I . . . well! If not a gaming hell, then . . . ah . . . perhaps a race of some kind? Oh, yes!" she said, perhaps a little too brightly, her words tumbling together. "I had said I should like to be in a carriage race without seeming too shocking to society, so having it take place in the middle of the night, that would certainly serve the purpose, would it not?" Her voice had gone up an octave, and on the last, rather squeaky word, she pulled her hand away, unable to allow the caress to continue.

There was only so much one could allow in the name of adventure and friendship, after all, she told herself. The unfortunate part of it was that she did not want to call an end to such "play," but knew she had to. She never should have allowed him to pull her close. She should forbid him to do the like again. She ought to sit away from him. The problem lay in that she did not wish to do any of those things.

As she sat in a cloud of confusion, hands reached for her and pulled her onto his lap. "I think," he said, his voice thick, "I really do need a kiss from you."

"Oh, no, we mustn't! Theo, this is too much. I do not mind a bit of fun, but—"

"Oh, I think we must. One kiss, Pamela. One kiss to keep me sane for the next five minutes. 'Tis not a great deal to ask."

She was not sure if she nodded acquiescence or not, but suddenly he was kissing her.

There was no mustache to tickle her lip and nose, only a gentle touch, reverent almost, seeking some answer. A shared warmth from mouth to mouth. A friend's kiss.

No, it was more than that, for suddenly it overflowed, coursing down her throat into her belly, casting out caution, inviting more, no longer a friend's salute. Something more. Something extraordinary.

Her hand came up, needing to touch him, finding his hair, his neck, her thumb tracing the line of his jaw. His kiss deepened, no longer questioning, now fulfilling a requirement, a necessity; soothing an ache even as it created others.

He released her mouth from his own, and for a moment she thought she felt a tremble beneath her.

Silence reigned, and she could hear her own heartbeat, and perhaps his as well. Face-to-face, they looked into each other's eyes, breathing unevenly.

Then he was kissing her again, his hands defeating the order of her coiled braid, smoothing the line of her throat, his arms encircling her to pull her up, deeper into his kiss. Thought was abandoned, sensation ruled. She did not tell him no, for she could not form the concept. She felt the beginning of a beard on his cheeks, felt his buttons pressing into her, smelled an essence of shaving soap on his skin, and that was all she wanted to know. That, and an endless stream of kisses; caresses on her lips, her chin, her cheeks, her eyelids, her forehead. Caresses she returned, amazed by the contours of his face, by the texture of his skin. She had never felt before how vital each second was, even while she was suspended in time. How small the world became when it was made up of no more than two people, how expansive the interior of a coach was when you were with someone and he was all you ever needed.

Unbidden, a memory surfaced. A memory of another more public kiss, just a few hours earlier. A kiss that more than likely would lead to an offer of marriage.

She pulled back her head, and his kisses trailed down her throat. "No," she moaned, raising heavy, limp hands to push at his chest.

He stopped kissing her, but for a moment did not release her. His hands opened and closed on her clothing where he touched her. "Perhaps you are correct," he murmured, sliding her from his lap to the seat beside him.

She sat on something hard, and only then did she remember the ring was in her pocket. She pulled on the cloak of her domino until the pocket was out from under her, her arms strangely weak, and then pulled the ring from the pocket, holding it up before him. "Your ring," she said, her voice unsteady even to her own ears. "You returned my diary, so I need to return your ring." Then she looked away, wondering how she could have forgotten about the diary.

He did not reach for it. "Ah yes, the diary."

"Tell me, then," she ordered, sitting up straight, making sure no part of her touched him now. "I shall not mind what you say, for I have thought the worst and you cannot surprise me."

"I knew tonight when you agreed to come with me that you had forgiven me for that particular trespass."

"I have, for I know what this ring means to you."

She handed it toward him, but he made no effort to take it.

"Keep it," he said.

She turned to look toward him in astonishment. "Keep it?"

" 'Twill serve our purpose well enough."

"Our purpose? I do not understand. Theo," she said, suspicion creeping into her voice. "Where do we go? We have traveled some distance, I believe. Do we go to some distant race course?'

"No."

"Where then?" she cried, still holding the ring out to him.

"Gretna Green."

Her eyes widened in shock as her hand sank to her lap.

"You asked me what I thought of your diary. I found that things were much as I suspected—I hoped!—they were. Pamela, can you look at me and tell me that you do not have a care for me?"

She threw back her head, not quite able to look him in the eye. "I do have a care for you, but that does not mean I shall elope with you. You must take me home at once."

"I will not. Pamela, you say yourself you care for me, and I say I adore you. What is to stand in our way?"

"Everything! We should be miserable together—"

"Your diary confesses such fears, but they are mere echoes from your grandmother's past, Pamela. Her fears have nothing to do with our happiness." He leaned toward her, his palms turned up like a beggar's. "Come, sit on my lap and practice calling yourself Baroness Marchmont. 'Tis a long way until we find an inn this night, and we may as well pass the time agreeably."

"Take me home," she said from between tight lips that struggled to keep the panic out of her voice.

" 'Tis too late for that. How should I return you to your father's home without creating a scandal? We should have to marry in the end anyway, so let us instead enjoy now our daring."

"I said earlier today that your scruples were showing. I was mistaken, for obviously you have none."

His mouth tightened and his eyelids lowered. "What good are scruples if they bring only misery, keeping me from the thing I most desire—the thing you most desire, too, if only you would be brave enough to admit it?"

"I will not."

"Will not love me? Pamela, you already—"

"I will not marry you. Even in Scotland, you cannot make me say the words. I must say the words or else not be married. I must be willing. I am not willing. I will not make the wedding promises."

He sank back into the squabs, silently watching her, a sadness in his eyes. At length he asked, "Why not?"

She stared at him, her anger making her shake.

"Why not, Pamela? Am I so unlovable as all that? Am I beyond all redemption? Is it so impossible that I could love?"

Oh, the rogue, the blackguard!—still he managed

to worm his way around her sensibilities. Still he made her want to soothe him and tell him what he wished to hear. She wanted to reach out and pull his head to her bosom, murmur kind words, assure him he had done nothing so terribly wrong. But he had! He had tricked her, just as he always tricked her, just as he always would. It was his nature, and she would be a fool to surrender to that nature . . . to surrender to her own. . . .

She breathed heavily, torn despite the fact she knew better. At last she cried out the only words that made sense to her: "Get out!"

"What?"

"Get out of this carriage! I will not be alone with you for another moment."

"Pamela—"

"Get out!" she cried, her voice rising, tears slipping unbidden down her cheeks. She threw the ring toward him, saw him flinch when it bounced off his chest. She covered her face with her hands, and sobbed, "Captain Penford will make me an offer, I know it! I shall be his wife. I shall be his wife!"

A heavy silence fell, broken only by her sobbing.

She only looked up when there was a rap on the ceiling over their heads. She raised her eyes in time to see Theo open the coach door as it slowed to a stop.

"I go because you asked it of me," he said in a soft, sad tone. "Only see, even now that I find I shall not have you, I do my best to give you everything you ask of me."

He did not await an answer—perhaps he sensed

that she had none to give him—before leaping from the carriage. He closed the door, and a moment later the carriage turned in the road; and they were heading back the way they had just traveled.

She sank down, lying cross the squabs in misery, her knuckles—so recently kissed—pressed to her mouth. Across from her, on the opposite seat, the ruby ring gleamed at her in the light from the lamp.

She began to sob again, soaking the plush fabric with her tears even as she used it to try and muffle her cries, not wanting her anguish to be heard by those who rode outside the coach.

Chapter 19

She watched out the coach window. The coach sat some distance down the street from her home, so it was difficult to see much, despite the nearly full moon, as Theo climbed a trellis toward the first floor of her home. She did not realize that she held her breath until she let it out in a huge sigh as he obtained her grandmama's balcony. He appeared as little more than a dark shadow as he opened and slipped through the unlocked balcony door. She fleetingly hoped that Grandmama would not be frightened to death by the sight of a man in her rooms.

Five minutes later, a dressed and cloaked Grandmama accompanied Marchmont from the front door of the house. The coach lurched forward, bringing her to where they waited.

Grandmama pulled open the coach door. Perhaps it was a trick of the moonlight, but she looked quite pale. "Pamela!" she cried, her voice a whisper. "Are you well, my child?"

"Yes," Pamela answered shortly as she gathered

her cloak about her, the domino's mask in one hand, preparing to descend.

Then Grandmama astonished her by laughing loudly, though the sound was a trifle hollow. "Marchmont, how you do go on!" she trilled.

Theo said nothing, offering Pamela a hand. She allowed the touch for only a moment, as she might that of a stranger, coming quickly down the carriage steps and moving at once to her grandmother's side.

Grandmama went on, speaking loudly, even as she reached to attempt to restore some order to Pamela's hair. "We had a wondrous time. I confess I have never before taken a midnight drive. Although I doubt it shall ever be all that is fashionable, I found it enormously entertaining."

Theo still did not speak, standing with his hands now clasped behind him.

A candle floated into sight in the windows near the front door, and then the door was pulled open. Grandmama's hand fell away from the hastily pinned knot at Pamela's nape. Lawlton stood in the doorway, candlestick in hand, and hastily dressed to judge by his less than usually pristine appearance. "My lady?" he questioned as he saw Grandmama.

"Ah, Lawlton, just the man I wanted to see. Would you be so kind as to arrange a pot of tea—not that dreadful lemon tea, mind!—to be sent up to my room as quickly as may be. Pamela and I have just returned from a midnight drive, and I own we are not only chilled but parched!"

"Of course, my lady," Lawlton said, looking on the scene with a hint of disapproval.

Grandmama turned to Theo. "Marchmont, as . . . entertaining as this evening has been, I believe I may say we have had quite enough such sport from you for quite some long while, eh?"

He stiffened momentarily, but then he inclined his head. "Indeed, my lady. Quite enough. Good evening, or should I say, good morning." So saying, and without a word to Pamela, he climbed back into his coach and signaled the driver to pull away.

Grandmama sailed into the house, pulling at the tie of her cloak as she walked with unusually hurried feet. "The tea, if you please, Lawlton?" she ordered as she headed for the stairs, signaling with the crooking of her finger that Pamela was to follow.

A branch of candles and a small lamp lit Grandmama's room, leaving the corners in shadows, echoing the state of Pamela's mind. As soon as the ladies were behind the closed door, Grandmama whipped the cloak from her shoulders and tossed it across a chair. She folded her hands together before her abdomen as she turned to face Pamela, announcing, "Well, my girl! I certainly hope Lawlton did not notice I quite forgot to put on any kind of a bonnet! When I was startled from my bed by that odious loose-screw, Marchmont, I only had the sense to pull my sleeping cap from my head, not to replace it with something more seemly. You will now, of course, tell me exactly what occurred."

Pamela sank into a chair. "In a sentence: I behaved as a very great paperskull, Grandmama."

"That is quite evident. What I wish to know is

how the man pulled you from this house without any of us knowing about it.''

"He did not pull me; I went willingly.''

A terrible scowl crossed Grandmama's face, and she moved to sit in a chair, her fingers gripping the arms tightly. ''Tell me all, girl.''

Pamela did so, leaving nothing out—nothing, that is, except for her feelings during the unplanned late night rendezvous. She explained how she had wished to make her memories, how she had allowed Marchmont to kiss her, how he had been taking her to Gretna Green. Grandmama's anger subsided as she listened, horrified consternation taking its place.

Pamela fell silent, staring toward the flickering candles.

"I do not understand,'' her grandmother said at length.

Pamela looked away from the candles, for the question mirrored the confusion in her own soul.

"I do not understand why he brought you back,'' Grandmama said in a faint voice. ''He held every trump! He could easily have made you travel on with him—after a night together, that would have forced you to accept his offer. There would be no question but that you were compromised. Instead he brought you back, came up to my balcony in that loose-screw fashion, and made it possible for you to return, your reputation intact! Why did he throw his opportunity away? It makes absolutely no sense!''

Pamela's eyes swung back toward the candles, as though to stare at their glow would explain away the tears that sprang to her eyes. ''It makes perfect sense to me. In the end he had to admit, even to himself, that he never loved me in truth.'' She lifted her chin, a crooked, bitter smile crossing her lips as she gazed at her grandparent. ''Your plan worked to a nicety, Grandmama: we almost turned him into a husband, and so now he has fled. He never cared for me one whit, only for the game he played.''

Grandmama stared at her. ''Good gad, Pamela, I should think quite the opposite!''

''What?''

''An uncaring man would have turned events far more to his own advantage, never minding what became of you. For some unfathomable reason, the man just surrendered an easy chance at padding his pocket and marrying higher than himself. No one would sniff at his breeding once he was married to an Earl's daughter. I tell you, it makes no sense, not unless we are to come to the unlikely conclusion that Marchmont has some shred of decency in him.''

Pamela stared back, astonished. Grandmama was right. Why had he given so much away? Of course it was possible that in the end he had found her person or her nature too repulsive to contemplate being bound to her for life, but then he would have to be far finer an actor than even Garrick had ever been, for she had kissed him and believed—then and even now—that her kiss had been returned, relished, desired. She had seen a sadness in his eyes when he had left the coach, a sadness that had made her weep. Had he seen, at last, that she was intended for another, and decided he would not stand in the way? Did he then care enough for her that if *he* could not have her regard, he would then leave her to a future that did not include him? Oh, yes, Grandmama's plan had worked to perfection, only not in any way they had foreseen.

"I feel as though I have betrayed my best friend," she whispered.

Grandmama did not hear, or ignored the comment, saying, "We must wait and see what the gossipmongers make of this, for I fear we may not rely upon the man's discretion." She rapped her knuckles against the chair arm to emphasize her point, and then both ladies startled as a knock came at the door. At Grandmama's call, Lawlton entered, leaving the requested pot of tea.

When he was gone, Grandmama poured them each a cup, and then spoke again. "Perhaps he means to trap you that way, by the spread of tittle-tattle. I could conceive that such a one as he would have no real liking for an enforced Gretna wedding, for you had said you would not agree of your own free will, and force is the only other way."

"He would not force me to anything," Pamela said, and was sure of it. Perhaps that was why he had looked sad: because he had still believed at some level, up to the last words they exchanged, that she would choose him. He had built a fantasy in his mind, not so very different from the dream she had of a happy, carefree future with a safe man, a good man. She had forced Theo to understand he was not that man, and—rake or no—the knowledge had wounded him.

Grandmama sniffed, but conceded, "So it would appear. Or perhaps he did not want his newly elevated status to be sullied by the aspect of a Scottish wedding. It is not done, you know. He would have a care for that.''

Pamela nodded mutely, for that made as much sense as anything, for nothing made any true sense to her anymore. It was late. She was heartsore. She just wanted today to be over.

"I let him know tonight that he is not welcome here anymore," Grandmama said firmly.

"As did Mama earlier today." She remembered the quick look of pain that had crossed his features—had it been regret that their mornings together were then lost to him? Had she set them both up for a sad parting when she had invited him to be her friend?

"I see! All the better! Pamela, we must avoid the man entirely. You will not receive him if he comes to call. You will not drive out with him. You will not accept any letters from him. We shall not deign even to deny any prattle that comes as a result of this. No one knows a thing but he, you, I, and Lawlton, who only knows what we allowed him to think. No one would take Marchmont's word over ours. This is a storm we can ride out, emerging victorious on the other side. All shall be well, my dear, you shall see.''

"Yes," Pamela said, exhaustion making the words mushy.

"To bed with you now!"

"Yes, Grandmama," she mumbled, automatically giving the woman a kiss on the cheek before leaving the room.

She found her own room without benefit of a candle. She welcomed the dark, but its shelter, even

279

combined with the physical and mental exhaustion that had made her feet almost too heavy to lift, was not deep enough to keep her from replaying every moment of this day. Over and over played each word, each glance, each inflection, becoming hopelessly muddled in her mind. She understood nothing but the fact that she was utterly miserable. Yet, despite her exhaustion, it was hours before she found succor in sleep.

Chapter 20

Two evenings later brought the first hint of prattle from the gossipmongers, but not as Pamela expected.

She did not wait to see if Marchmont tried to come to her home (surely he knew they must abandon the thought of going to Vauxhall Gardens!), and instead went to a card party at the home of Mama's friend, Lady St. Clair. There were not many young people present, but the ones that were there gave her curious glances, as did some few of the older company as well. As she became aware of the attention, Pamela's heart sank. If Marchmont had spoken, it would not be so simple as Grandmama believed to face down the viciousness of gossip.

Lady St. Clair circulated among her guests, coming to the table where Pamela and her mother played against an elderly brother and sister pair, the Fredericks. Lady St. Clair inquired after their comfort and, receiving the information that their beverages were not in need of replenishment, turned to Pamela.

"Lady Pamela, how surprised I am to have you

join us tonight," she said. "I thought that you would be in the company of a certain gentleman instead of coming to such a tame thing as a card party."

Pamela paled, and Mama frowned. "Whatever are you nattering on about?" Mama demanded of her hostess.

Lady St. Clair beamed at her friend. "Why, 'the kiss' of course! Everyone saw Captain Penford kiss Lady Pamela at the theatre."

Pamela gave a sigh of relief, quite out of keeping with the appalled glare she was receiving from her mother. "Oh. Yes," she said, because her hostess seemed to expect her to say something.

"I daresay we all look forward to learning of an announcement in that direction. Is there perhaps some little hint as to the future that you would care to share with us tonight, Lady Pamela? I mean to say, we all discounted it when your name was linked with that of Marchmont, rascal that he is, but this is a trifle different, eh? Kissing in the theatre, and all, I mean to say."

Pamela felt her ears go crimson, aware that all eyes were on her. She would have to say something, for to say nothing would be to only increase the rumors. "There is no reason to disturb your party, Lady St. Clair. What shall be, shall be, and that is all I have to say to the matter."

"Sly minx!" Lady St. Clair trilled. "You refuse to tell, but you know what they say: the singing bird has caught no worm, but the silent bird has his—or hers—already."

Pamela knew no such saying, but offered a noncommittal smile. Lady St. Clair's comment, however, seemed to set just the right tone, for it was clear from the nods and whispered conferences around them that others thought this silence an exercise in maidenly discretion. Soon enough to announce wedding plans when the couple was together, or the banns had been posted, their nods and smiles seemed to say.

Lady Premington stared at her daughter, her eyes quite wide but her mouth firmly pressed closed for once, much to Pamela's relief.

That was not the case on the way home, when she had to confess to her mother that not only had there been a kiss, but there had been no offer forthcoming. As her mother rang a peal over her head, Pamela watched out the window, seeing nothing but vague darkened shapes, only really hearing half the condemnation, at most. It had been a mistake to allow that kiss, she realized in retrospect, but then the last few days had been so full of mistakes such a little one hardly seemed to matter.

"Mama, I believe the captain may be very close to offering," she said when that lady paused to take a breath.

Somewhat mollified, Mama continued her lecture on propriety only until the carriage stopped before their home, allowing Pamela to escape into her rooms without further disparagement.

The next two days brought much of the same. Even Lord Gilbury, when he came to take her up for another drive, brought up the subject.

"I say . . . that is . . . Lady Pamela, have you heard aught about . . . well, about a kiss?"

"Yes, my lord. It is true. Captain Penford kissed me at Covent Garden," she said rather wearily.

"Well then . . . that is to say, I wish you . . . and . . . er . . . the captain well," he said, turning his remarkable shade of crimson in his disappointment, blithely assuming the same outcome that all society had assumed must come from such an act.

Despite being the subject of the latest *on dit,* there was no hint of scandal that linked her name with that of Marchmont. It seemed he had said nothing concerning the attempted elopement, and that she had indeed survived the events of the last few days with her reputation only slightly tarnished. And whatever luster had been lost, it had not been brought about by Theo, but her own actions with the captain.

The next day was Sunday, but her time in morning services gave her no sense of peace. When she returned from chapel to the parlor, she found no company but Phyllis, who applied herself to the basket of endless items that required stitching. Pamela sat alone and lonely, listlessly reading the newspaper, until she set it aside, finding it extremely dull without anyone with whom to share it. Finally Sir Eugene and Mister Appleton came to call. She brightened briefly at the sight of them but the curious thing was that as soon as they had worn out the standard social comments, she wished nothing so much as that they would take their silly random prattle and be gone. The next day she did not even bother to come down and see who her mother's morning callers might be.

Late that afternoon the captain came as promised. "What say you to an evening water party upon the

Thames? General Holbank has arranged it, and I have been invited to bring a guest. Or two,'' he said, standing as Pamela came into the parlor where he waited with Mama.

She saw that Mama was in her pelisse and bonnet, ready to go out. It was abundantly clear that there would be no more occasions alone, or even with a mere maid as chaperone, between herself and Captain Penford. ''How delightful,'' she said to his suggestion, taking his offered arm.

''Then we should leave at once.''

''Of course.''

Mama rose as well, and they went straight away to his carriage.

As they left the carriage on the Strand, Pamela saw that there were four boats readied and waiting. Each of them might hold fifteen, and had elaborately painted scrollwork interiors that gave them a fairytale atmosphere. The deck was carpeted, and the permanent seats were plushly padded in deep red velvet. There were torches mounted at bow and stern, already lighted even though the sun had not yet quite sunk below the horizon. Three of the boats held passengers, plus a crew of three, including a servant, while the fourth held an orchestra. The orchestra played a fanfare as they were launched upon the river, and the servants poured champagne around for all.

Toasts were offered, the ladies squealed as they became used to the rocking motion of the boats, and some of the gentlemen had a minor splashing contest that was quickly frowned down by their host, the general. Dusk came over the river as they floated along, calling comments from one boat to the other. Gaiety rose to match the occasion, the laughter echoing around them as it bounced off the surface of the river and back to their ears. Pamela listened to the clever conversation and the laughter, but felt no compunction to join in.

"You are thoughtful today," the captain said at her side.

"Yes."

"Am I correct in assuming you have been exposed to a great deal of scandal-broth regarding the . . . er, moment at the theatre?" he said, lifting one corner of his mouth in a smile that invited her confidences.

She lowered her eyes. "Yes."

"I am sorry for that."

"Do not think overmuch on it."

"But I have. I wish to set things right." He lowered his voice as well as he might to a kind of rusty grating, but she was grateful for the boat's creaking and the conversation that buzzed around them, for even his quiet tones were nowhere near a whisper. "I know you must have expected an offer following that . . . moment, but I will confess that I was considering . . . things. A soldier must be particular about his family, you see. After our first kiss, I feared that perhaps your . . . well, spontaneous nature might mean you are not well-suited to be a captain's wife, where diplomacy is everything. I mean to say, we scarce knew one another, and there we were kissing in the moonlight. That is hardly seemly! Kisses, toys, the fact that your enthusiasm may make you laugh a little too much at times—all these things made me doubt.

But, Pamela, in the last few days you have shown me that you may be all that is seemly, even in the face of the tattlemongers. Any difficulties are merely a lack of maturity, which is"—he smiled—"a fault that is easily corrected with the passage of time."

How his words mirrored thoughts she'd had herself! As much as they stung, they must be right. Despite the fact that it felt quite the opposite, he was actually paying her compliments.

"So, although I fear this is neither the time nor the proper place," he went on, "for I may not go down upon one knee, dearest Pamela, do say you will marry me."

He had asked. The very thing for which she had longed had happened. He had asked. Well, not really, for he had not so much asked as ordered. "Do say you will marry me." Curious that she did not leap upon the words as once she would have thought she might.

"Why?" She heard the whispered word come from her lips, or perhaps it came from her heart.

"Why?" he repeated, startled.

Mama turned to look at her, frowning, but then she turned back to her conversation with the general's wife.

Pamela turned to the captain. "Do you love me?"

"Ah, yes, I take the meaning behind your question! Indeed I do. Do you love me?"

She paused just a moment. "I have thought so."

"What say you then?"

"I say. . . ." She looked away, over the waves, toward the near bank where some children were being called from their play by their nanny. They laughed and cried to one another, trying their best to ignore the nanny's mandate that they must come along.

She knew that children of proper families were raised primarily by their nannies; fathers had very little to do with the raising of children; the male parent knew very little about their offspring until they achieved adulthood. Fathers were not to waste their time amusing children, but rather to concern themselves with the adult tasks that made a comfortable, safe, happy life possible for those children. A man did not need to appreciate the structure of a toy. He was not to behave as a child, laughing too much, too easily. A man could not be carefree, not if he was going to provide for his family.

"Pamela?"

She looked away from the children. "I need some time . . . to think. I am very flattered. It was all I ever dreamed," she said numbly. Oh, how Marchmont would taunt her if she spoke such words to him! He would demand an answer, yes or no.

"Of course. Very well. Let us say nothing more to the matter now," the captain said.

"Yes."

"These things must be done properly. Announcements to the family, and such."

"Even so. Yes. Of course."

"I shall call in the morning, and then, I think, perhaps it would be pleasant to ride?"

"Pleasant," she echoed.

After the carriage ride home, Mama stopped her

before she could hurry up the stairs. "You two had your heads together for some while, whispering."

"If you could call it a whisper." Pamela actually smiled, recalling the captain's raspy attempt at muting his voice.

"What was said?"

"Nothing, Mama. Nothing of import tonight," she said.

She went up to her room to change for dinner, passing the stair railing where, as a seven-year-old, she had carved the shape of a crucifix in a bout of religious fervor. Her attempt at pious art had earned her an early bedtime with no supper, a punishment she had half a mind to emulate this evening, only it would mean that Mama would come up to see why she refused her dinner and no doubt decide she was worsening for something. Better to sit at the table and avoid unnecessary and unwanted bedside care.

When Phyllis stopped in to inform her that dinner had been put back half an hour, to accommodate a late arrival by Owen, she moved to her special wardrobe and got out the dissected map puzzle Marchmont had bought her the day of the fair. She idled away the time, putting the puzzle together and taking it apart again many times, trying not to think. She had yet to unlock her diary from the escritoire, and tonight the thought of attempting to write out the confused muddle that was her thoughts was the last thing she wished to do. Instead she played with the puzzle and refused to diagnose the heavy lump that sat in the center of her chest.

Chapter 21

Pamela spent her morning meal being admonished for her peevish tongue. Even in the midst of her mother's various denouncements on her behavior, she had to admit to herself she deserved these reproofs. She was edgy. Uncertain. Very near combative. She could not seem to keep herself from snapping at any little thing, so that in the end Mama became so annoyed with her daughter's petulant tongue that she had sent Pamela back to her room to finish her meal there.

Things did not improve in the parlor, especially when it was announced that Captain Penford had come to call and was in the library with Papa. Pamela sat stunned, realizing such an action's portent. She could not imagine why it had not occurred to her last night that the captain might come today and formally address her father, asking for her hand. Her heart began to pound, making her temples hurt, and her already uncertain temperament slipped into true testiness. Mama even called her from the room for a scolding when she made a face behind Owen's back.

"Gracious, Pamela, but you are in a pet today! What if Reverend Harker had seen that face?"

"Owen deserved it. He can be quite odious. It was clear as day that Reverend Harker did not wish any more of that lemon tea, and Owen would press it upon him. I swear he does it to torture the man," she said warmly. "Not everyone has a care for lemon tea, Mama. You ought to be aware of that."

"Pamela! You must be in a nervous state to make you speak so sharply, my dear! But that is not to be wondered at, with the captain locked in the library with your father. Oh, is it not exciting? To think that one day my daughter will be a Marchioness!"

"Please, Mama, we do not know that he is requesting my hand . . . ," she said, ashamed of her own lie even as she spoke it, "and that thought makes me feel like a positive ghoul, waiting for the captain's own brother to expire."

"You would not be waiting for it, my dear, but there are some things in life one cannot ignore. The only thing that worries me is the knowledge that Captain Penford is soon returning to the war. I would abhor unseemly haste, but do you think it might be best to marry before he returns to duty?"

"In the next three days!" Pamela cried. "Oh, Mama! And you the one always lecturing me on propriety!"

"Well, of course you are right. 'Twould never do, not even by special license."

Pamela picked up her skirts and flounced away, going to change into her bottle green riding habit, for the captain had said they would go riding this morning . . . after his meeting her Papa, she now realized.

She wished she could let her horse have his head, for a gallop might clear her own. Instead she rode docilely at the captain's side, greeting people as they made their way around Hyde Park. Mama was driven by a groom in a low phaeton behind them. As they rode, Pamela could not help but note the captain's boot, for his foot was sufficiently healed that he now could war both Hessians. The sight of the boot that replaced the bandages was just another reminder that he would soon be gone.

Although time was no longer an obstacle, for an offer had been made.

She had not been below stairs to see the captain come from Papa's library, had not witnessed her mother's demand to be told the news. She had learned of it not long after, however, for Mama had stormed into her room, hands clasped in joy, and announced, "He has asked for your hand. Oh, Pamela!"

She had submitted to a tight hug, hoping to steal some of her mother's joy. This betrothal was just as she had hoped and dreamed these past weeks, but now that Papa had given his consent she was overcome, numb, blocked off from her feelings.

Now she rode, scarcely speaking to the captain, wondering when he would take her aside and again ask her to marry him. And what would her answer be? Yes. Of course it would be yes.

She rode with her chin down, seeing only the path

in front of her that she might guide the horse's progress.

Laughter caused her to raise her eyes, and then she gasped. She had not seen Marchmont in three days, and seeing him now made her heart lurch painfully. He was not mounted, instead sitting on a bench next to Lady Austin. They were feeding nuts to the park's squirrels, with a bevy of children surrounding them. The nannies stood by, gossiping among themselves, evidently having received permission for their charges to assist in the feeding. A little dark-haired girl approached Theo, hand outstretched to receive some more nuts from the paper bag open on his palm; Pamela saw in a moment that it was Liza.

Liza turned, scattering the nuts from her little hand, she and another little girl squealing with delight when a squirrel hopped near to retrieve some of the bounty. The squirrel ran off at the sound, and Liza was back at the bag, getting another handful. Theo ceased talking to Lady Austin long enough to smile at the little girl and check the level of nuts still left in the bag, handing a few more to a tow-headed boy, then turned back to the beautiful woman.

She would ride on by. She would not stop, Pamela told herself. Their friendship was ended.

"Pamewa!" a shriek of delight split the air, and then there was no chance to ride quietly by. Pamela's horse tossed his head. She reined in, making the animal dance sideways. The little girl was dashing toward her, and her mount was snorting his disapproval of the charge. If Liza did not stop, or if the horse decided to rear, Liza would quite probably be hurt.

Pamela opened her mouth to call to the girl, but suddenly Liza was caught up in a pair of soberly dressed arms. Theo had come from the bench before Pamela could even cry out her alarm.

Liza wrapped her arms around his neck and demanded, "Take me to Cousin Pamewa!" blithely unaware she had just been rescued.

Theo propped the girl on his hip, looking from her to where Pamela was still seated, the horse now snorting to reflect his recent spooking, but otherwise now standing quietly.

"So this is your cousin?" Theo asked the little girl, who nodded. "Well, little miss, it seems your cousin is riding today. We must allow her to go on her way, and not keep her."

Pamela's heart sank at the dismissal. It was clear he had nothing to say to her, but that did not negate her own good manners. "Thank you," she said, "for saving Liza."

He inclined his head. "Of course." He hesitated, then added, "So, this is Liza, is it?"

Captain Penford directed his horse next to Pamela's as Liza proudly recited her entire name. Mama was several yards back, calling a greeting.

When Theo looked away from the chattering child in his arms, Penford nodded coolly at him. "Marchmont."

"Penford."

There was a tense, silent moment, but then the captain resettled on his saddle, leaning forward, a slight smile forming under his mustache. "My lord, you must be the first to congratulate us. The Lady Pamela and I are to be married.''

Pamela looked sharply toward the captain, but just as quickly her gaze returned to Theo. It seemed he blanched, as though he had just been struck, although a moment later she could not even be sure she had seen the flinch, for then his features hardened, becoming coolly and lifelessly polite. ''Ah. Is that so?'' he asked softly.

''Yes, the lady has accepted me only just—''

''But I did not,'' Pamela said. Her horse's ears flicked back again at the sharp sound of her voice.

The captain turned to her. ''What!''

''I said I needed time to think.''

''You said you were flattered, and it was all you had ever dreamed. I took that as acceptance, my dear.''

Now she could no longer look toward the stony-faced Theo, although she was keenly aware he was staring up at her. ''My father has consented, but I have not. Not yet.'' Her voice rose, taking on an edge of hysteria. ''You would have to ask me, myself, again. I do not think that is too much to ask.''

''But, our ride today . . . following my time with your father? I presumed—'' the captain began.

''It was exactly that: a presumption, Captain.''

The captain stared at her, his lips thinning. He took a deep breath, and said, ''Pamela, I believe we are in no position to discuss this now. It is something we should discuss in private.''

''Why? Why can you not ask me, now, here?''

she cried, and her horse began to snort again, tossing his head at the distress in his rider's voice.

"It is not seemly—"

"Oh, but I am weary unto death of all that is 'seemly!' " Pamela wailed.

Theo looked up at her, his gaze steady, the coolness receding from his face. His left hand supported the child, but the other rose as though he might reach out and take the reins of her horse. There was an indentation at the base of his fourth finger, the mark where recently a ring had resided.

She shook her head, then tossed it back to stare at the sky, thinking for a moment she might actually howl from the confusion and strain of this day. As she struggled to suppress either the howl, or now something that was too close to a sob, she loosened the reins in her hands. She lowered her eyes again, glancing from one man to the other. Suddenly she dug her heel into the horse's side, causing the animal to leap into action. Half-blinded by tears, she let him have his head, galloping from the park, ignoring her mother's startled cry as she rode past, uncaring of the spectacle she was creating.

Pamela, grimacing to herself in the dark, listened to her mama's excuses.

"She is very young. I believe you may realize she is feeling a trifle overwhelmed by your most gracious offer, Captain. Do come back tomorrow, and I know she shall be all that is joyful. Sometimes for a young lady, her happiness makes her behave like nothing so much as a peagoose, you must know!''

"Tomorrow! I should care to have this matter settled today. Do you not know that I return to my regiment in but three days? There are things to be done yet, to prepare, important things.''

"My dear Captain, tomorrow is soon enough. I swear it. Do say you will return tomorrow, when everyone is rested. You shall ask Pamela for her decision, and she shall give it, mark my word!''

There were more words to urge his return, but eventually he agreed to come tomorrow, rather to Pamela's surprise. She had treated him very poorly.

She knew that when she faced her parent at last, Mama would be furious, and not just because of the scene in the park that had without doubt brought her perilously near to losing a most advantageous offer. No, Mama would be doubly infuriated, because Pamela had taken it into her head to hide.

When Mama escorted the captain to his horse, and Pamela was certain the room was unoccupied, she climbed from her old hiding spot in the linen wardrobe. She had overheard many a titillating conversation while concealed therein, but today's secretly overheard discourse had brought her no smiles. It was only right that the captain was upset. Although, a stubborn little voice within argued, was it not also true that he should have received her agreement before he spoke?

She made her way up to her grandmother's room, knowing she would be found there sooner than later; but now the captain was gone, so she could stand to face her mother's outraged censure. As unpleasant as that would be, it would still be better than facing the captain in the morning, for she had no idea what answer she would give him.

Chapter 22

"Pamela," her mother said sharply as she set aside her serviette, "how is it that you have come downstairs in your peignoir and your hair still in a braid? Please note that it is after eleven, and I, myself, am already dressed and on my way to buy some ribbons. We have never been a household to keep town hours, and I cannot allow you to begin such habits today! You must hurry if you are to be dressed and ready to receive *visitors*—" she stressed the word, making it clear she meant the captain, and that she would brook no nonsense today following her lengthy and justified lecture the night before—"by noon."

"I could not find it in myself to get dressed yet," Pamela said truthfully.

Her mother frowned. "Well, how nonsensical! All one must do is ring for a servant. But you shall have to hurry to it if you have any desire to appear well. I wish you to look exceptionally fine today, for after all the captain will be requesting your hand in marriage!

You will not want to look back on this day with regret.''

Pamela sat at the table, tilting her head to one side, a rather philosophical expression crossing her face. ''That is true enough.''

''Why, I cannot say what you mean by that tone, young lady, but I am telling you now that you will hurry through your breakfast and go straight away up to Phyllis to be dressed.''

Pamela did not respond, looking at her reflection in the Sheffield plate before her. A pretty girl looked back at her, a quizzical look written in her eyes.

Mama left, scolding even as she exited the room.

Owen, coming in to the breakfast parlor just long enough to snatch some triangles of toast, merely lifted his eyebrows at the sight of his sister in her sleepwear and wrap, and made a point of closing the door behind him as he left. When Papa made his appearance, he startled at the sight of his daughter, turned, and stated he would take his breakfast at his club.

Pamela did not mind that she was left in solitude. She did not want company. She did not want breakfast on a tray in her room. She did not feel like dressing before breakfast.

''In fact,'' she said to no one, ''I do not know if I wish to get dressed ever today.'' Maybe she would just stay in her room. Maybe she would claim to be ill, even though she did not feel in truth at all unwell. She supposed she was deadened to feeling much of anything, after all that had happened last night. Even Mama's voluble denunciation had left her strangely unaffected.

She filled her plate from the sideboard, settled at the table once more, and decided that since she was alone, she would play the hoyden by reading the newspaper at table. She spread the pages and skimmed the news. She even looked at articles of which she knew Papa would never approve, just because there was no one to catch her in the act.

She turned to the society page, reading the various announcements as she spread marmalade on her toast. Suddenly the knife fell from her hand, clattering against her plate, and she cried, "Oh!" She threw down the toast, thrust aside her plate, and pulled the paper closer, her hands pressed flat on either side of the announcement that had pinned her attention.

It read:

Lady Marchmont is pleased to announce the betrothal of her son, Theopholus Dunmire, Baron Marchmont, to Lady Pamela Thorpe, daughter of Lord and Lady Premington. Wedding plans to be forthcoming.

Pamela stared at the paper, checking it over and again to see if she was misreading the names. A hand rose to cover her mouth, which had rounded to an "O" of surprise.

She had to give Marchmont his due, for only he had been able to crack the shell of numbness that had surrounded her, for now she was tingling from head to toe.

Belatedly she became aware of the sound of raised voices before the house. She rose, with unsteady legs, and moved to the window in time to see Theo and Captain Penford striding toward the door, yelling at one another as they walked. The captain had a paper under his arm and a terrible scowl on his face. Theo's expression was unreadable.

Pamela flew to the door of the morning parlor, coming from the room as the two men came to a halt in the entry, voices rising again. Lawlton stood back, visibly unsure what to do now that two gentlemen had charged noisily into the house.

"I shall know the meaning of this!" Penford shouted, waving the folded paper at Theo.

"What? That flapping? Looks as though you are attempting to fly if you ask me," Theo responded, a speculative hand raised to his chin.

"This announcement!" the captain roared, tapping the paper with the back of his fingers.

Pamela hurried forward. "Captain . . . Roger, please!"

He spun to face her, thrusting the paper toward her. "Have you seen this . . . this outrage? This lie! How could such a thing happen?"

"I just saw it myself. I do not know how it came to be in the paper," she said in a voice meant to soothe.

He seemed to respond to her effort, reaching to tug his red-breasted coat once more into place following his exertions, breathing deeply to steady himself before he went on. "Of course I know, my dear, that you are not responsible for this pack of lies. I know it was Marchmont." He spun to face the other man.

302

"Sirrah, I demand a retraction! And a public notice of apology."

"Do you indeed? And where, pray tell, is your name in this announcement that I must make any sort of apology to you?" Theo replied, crossing his arms.

"Do not mock me, sirrah, or I shall strike you down!" the captain roared.

"And I shall call you before the magistrate for assault," Theo said calmly. He turned to Pamela, saying pleasantly, "Good morning, Pamela. My, but you appear most fetching this morning."

Even though she knew it would enrage the captain, and even though this man had concocted yet another elaborate game at her expense, she smiled at the compliment. Oh, it was so good to see him again, here in her home! She had not known how much she missed his early hour presence. It seemed he had forgiven her for choosing someone else, that they could somehow remain friends after all. He would have his little joke, but in the end it would be harmless. She was not quite sure how that end was to be achieved, but she had no doubt he had something in mind. He always did. She was actually anxious to discover what scheme he had planned now.

"Good morning, Theo. Now, everyone shall sit down and we shall take chocolate. Lawlton, do have a tray brought in to the front parlor."

"Begging your pardon, Lady Pamela, but I was instructed not to allow this . . . er, gentleman into the house," Lawlton said, pointing at Marchmont.

"It seems to me he is already in," Pamela said. "Now, will you please see to that tray?" She turned back to the callers, and said, "Gentlemen?" She led the way into the parlor as Lawlton retreated to the kitchens.

"Pamela, I must tell you your attitude strikes me as decidedly odd," Penford said as he limped into the room. As Pamela settled on a settee, he took a chair before the morning fire, his voice reflecting the stiffness of his posture. "Do you not realize what the man has done? He has bandied your name in the papers." Then he frowned terribly, for Theo sat down next to her.

A pot of chocolate was carried in by a maid, who informed them that a tray would be along shortly. Mama always had cups at the ready on a sofa table, so Pamela poured for them all as she responded, "I admit it was not well done of him."

"To say the very least!" Penford boomed, lowering his voice a little to add in what was supposed to be a hiss, "And for heaven's sake, woman, go and put on some clothing!"

"I care for this look, myself," Marchmont said, setting aside the chocolate she had just handed him, looking her up and down. "Although, given a choice, I would have your hair free of its braid."

"You scoundrel—!"

Marchmont waved away the insult, saying, "Penford, you have had your chance to speak, or perhaps I should say 'bellow.' Now you shall give me mine." He turned to Pamela, catching up her hands.

The captain's eyes bulged, but a shake of the head from Pamela kept him in his seat as Theo spoke on.

"It is hardly a disaster, this newspaper campaign

of mine. I *can* have them run a retraction, of course. I shall probably need to leave London then, or else be the laughingstock of the city, but I should want to go anyway, at least for awhile, until I missed you too much to stay away any longer. You would not be ruined, for the retraction would state that you have accepted an offer from Penford rather than myself. People would believe the *Gazette* made an idiotic error. But that is not to the point: the point being that I have read your diary and I know that you . . . care for me. I know that you have felt something of what I have felt. That is why I took you with me that night. But . . . you denied me. I had to assume—despite the diary—that I knew nothing, that I was mistaken. I am not so much a cad that I wish my wife to weep in sorrow on our wedding day. You made your choice, and I was to live with that decision, no matter how dreadfully wrong-headed it was.

"But, then, in the park yesterday, when you refused to be bullied into a betrothal, I saw that what I had read in your diary might be true after all. Hope sprung anew. The thing of it is, Pamela, I have come to ask if you will choose security, or if you are willing to gamble just a little and choose me."

The door opened, admitting Grandmama. She came slowly, cautiously into the room, accompanied by Lawlton with the tray. The servant had obviously described the scene to Grandmama, who surveyed the room's occupants with a wary eye. She did not speak, and her clasped hands were held at her heart.

Pamela glanced at her grandparent ever so briefly, but then she looked once more into Theo's green eyes.

It was too bad of him that he had broken the ice around her heart, for now her lower lip trembled and tears pooled. "A curious choice of words to come from a reformed gambler," she said. She hoped that maybe she managed to smile teasingly at him despite the tears.

He held up his right hand, wiggling the fingers, showing the absence of the ring. His expression was gentle. "No longer reformed, or at least no longer in need of reminders, Pamela. Lady—that is to say, my lady friend was delighted when I asked if she might take back the ring, for she knew it meant I needed it no longer."

He drew a breath, which she could tell was a little shaky, and looked directly into her eyes to say, "You must know, Pamela, that sometimes you have to gamble. You can never lose your heart to someone unless you first experience the joy of giving it. You can never fulfill a dream unless you dare to chase it."

Tears tumbled down her cheeks, and now she did smile, a watery smile that was as shaky as his breath had been. "You would lead me a merry dance, would you not, dear Theo? Even now, when I know you so well. You have proved to me over and again that you are the most charming will-o'-the-wisp, an idler, a ne'er-do-well, and a liar, and yet you bid me ignore that knowledge."

"I own I am all those things but for the last."

"I have heard you lie with my own ears," she said, but there was nothing harsh or condemning in her voice. She pulled free a hand, reaching up to run her thumb along his jawline.

"When?"

"When?" she half laughed, reaching up her other hand to dash away some of the tears that rolled freely down her cheeks.

"When have I ever lied to you?"

She lowered her hands, her bittersweet smile falling away, even as her tears ceased to form. "Well . . . when you told Mama you liked lemon tea."

Grandmama made a noise of disgust.

"I never told her that. I drank it, but I never claimed to like it. And that was not my question: I asked when I had ever lied to *you*. When?"

"I . . ." She stared at him. Several heartbeats later, she slid a glance at the captain, but if he was ever to be her husband, he had the right to know everything. "The night you tried to elope with me. You tricked me into the carriage."

Penford rose to his feet. Grandmama hurried forward, taking his arm, forcing him to take his seat once more, speaking low, rapid words in his ear.

"But did I lie?" Theo pressed. "No. I said we were going on an adventure, and you have to admit an elopement is an adventure."

"Then when you said there was a way to return me to the house late at night."

"I told you getting back into the house would not be a problem, which was only the truth, for I never intended to bring you back. When it happened that I did, did I not keep my promise? Did I not return you to the safety of your grandmother's bosom, with none the wiser?"

307

"By all that's holy, I shall call you out for this!" Penford said from between gritted teeth.

Theo twisted toward him to sharply order, "Be silent! You are not her father or her brother, or even her betrothed."

The captain's mustache twitched and his face turned red, and he turned to Pamela, his every motion, from the fisted hands to the twitch in his jaw, seeking her condemnation of this man.

She stared back at him, but in truth scarcely saw him, for she was searching her memories. Try as she might, she could not think of one, not one single time Theo had ever lied to her. He had manipulated her. He had persuaded her. He had used her own inclinations against her—but he had never lied. He had not even hidden the fact that he had taken her diary.

What could it mean? If he only spoke the truth to her, then how could his protestations of love be false? Could he truly wish her for his wife?

Emotion swelled inside her, blocking her throat for a moment, leaving her breathless. She gave a squeaky little noise, and then breathed again, and wondered if it could possibly be true that Theo loved her, truly loved her. Despite her nature. Or perhaps because it was so like his own.

But if that was so, then why had he suggested she become his mistress when she had told him she hoped to marry another?

"Theo," she said slowly. "How can it be possible that you love me enough to ask me to be your wife, but then say you would settle for making me your mistress?"

Penford flew to his feet, advancing on Theo. "I shall pummel you for that, sirrah!" he roared, lifting his fists. Grandmama hung on one of his arms, attempting to hold him back.

Pamela looked up at him, startled to find she had forgotten for a moment that he was still in the room. "No," she said calmly. "No, Captain, sit down. Sit down, or else leave. I wish to hear the answer to my question."

The captain sat, his jaw working.

Theo gave the sheepish grin she was coming to cherish, and perhaps he even blushed a little. "Because I knew I had to be with you, one way or another. At first it did not matter to me in what way, or for how long. And, too, my dear, it was a way to fix your attention on me. Were I as polite and indirect as every other man you were to meet this Season, you would not have remembered me two moments after I first proposed. Your mama certainly dismissed me easily enough! I know I am not a fresh young buck, full of titles and promise and endless blunt. I am a rake. A man of experience, the very kind of man of which every young woman is warned. A man whose wife shall live comfortably, but shall not live in such splendor that she may have a new dress for every meal. I am a mere Baron who stinks still of trade, beneath your notice. How well I know it! I was—am—too full of faults to do anything but attempt to make my faults my strengths, you see."

Oh, how easy it would be to believe in such pretty words, such implied devotion! She shook her head, hair falling from her braid. "At first, you said."

"Ah, you merciless baggage! You would have it all, then? Very well, I lay my heart before you. 'Tis yours forever anyway, so you may do as you please to it." He ducked his head, perhaps embarrassed—or undone—by the confession, and went on. "I decided it would not serve not nearly well enough, to have you merely as my mistress. You had to be my wife. No one else's, for every other man would expect you to be quiet in chapel, to give up your papercuttings, and to never, ever speak naughtily, which is something you could excel at, my dear. I could not bear the thought of you thusly squandered. Even were you my mistress, eventually the playful side of you would have been smothered into nonexistence by the kind of man—" he glanced ever so briefly toward Penford— "the kind of man you sought, and that was unthinkable.

"I have never wished for a wife of my own before; but it became clear, when I read your diary, that you had a real care for me, and suddenly nothing else would do but that we should marry and be entirely blissful together in a ridiculous homelife of our own making. I concocted notions about sunny days and oh-so-warm nights; and screaming, paint-covered, scissor-wielding, laughing children; and arguments over duns from dressmakers that end in a whirlwind of passionate lovemaking; and found—quite absurdly, I must say—that I desire to know such an existence for the rest of my days. I went so far as to attempt to whisk you away to Scotland, to compromise you and force you to take me that way."

The captain's face had turned purple-red over the

collar of his military coat. He was so stiff with anger, he made no sound nor did he move.

"And how is that different from now? Do you not force me anew by this announcement in the *Gazette?*" Pamela asked logically.

"No, for as I said, I can renounce it if that is your wish. Although, 'twould be very cruel of you, for you would be condemning me to a horrific scolding from my mama. She shall be exceedingly incensed when she finds I have placed an announcement in her name, and all the more so if I must tell her it was a false announcement. I would far rather not have to explain my misdeed to her. I would far rather it have the end I desire, bringing you to see where it would be best to give your heart, and wed."

A silence fell, as she attempted to take in all he had said.

"Pamela," Grandmama said, her voice trembling. Pamela turned to her, alarmed by the quaver in that voice. She held out her hands, and Grandmama rushed to her side, taking up those hands. "Oh, Pamela. Now I understand why he brought you back! He brought you back, because you said you would not have him. Can you not see it, my girl? I questioned his decency, and now I have to wonder if perhaps it is possible he, in truth, has a care for you? And then he did not tell what he had done, that he had attempted to take you to Gretna Green; he protected you from ruin. He did not just want your person, but your respect as well!"

Theo looked down at the carpet. It was so strange to see him thus at odds, Pamela thought.

"What utter nonsense," said the captain in a tight voice.

A troubled frown settled between Pamela's brows as she looked at him and then back to her grandmother, speaking her worst fear, the fear the captain had voiced. "But can you have been beguiled yet again, Grandmama? Was not Grandfather much the same as this man? Did he not woo you with the sweetest words? Did he not fool you into believing in his love?"

"He did. Oh, he did, and more the fool me for telling you those tales! Pamela, perhaps there is a difference here: your grandfather never would have brought me back. He never would have offered to retract a public notice. He cared too much for himself to risk any such humiliation for my sake."

"Ah," Pamela said, looking beyond her grandmother to where the captain sat, tense and rigid, scowling terribly. It was as though the two parts of her mind were manifested in the room: the captain as the part of her that saw through pretty words to a future that threatened every kind of hurt; and Grandmama, the part that looked past the discernible to a golden dream of what could be. The fear or the dream. The known or the possible. The assurance or the blind trust.

The adult she had become hesitated, but the child she had once been would never have thought twice.

"Ah," she said again, the fretful frown smoothing from her forehead, her mouth relaxing.

Marchmont stood, putting out his hand. She saw that it trembled.

"Come, love, say you will go with me to the church today, that we may arrange to have our banns read for the next three Sundays, to marry on the fourth."

She sighed, but not unhappily, for confusion had fallen away, leaving her eyes clear at last. Without hesitation she took his hand. His fingers closed around hers, and for a moment he stared down at her, uncertainty flickering in his eyes.

He helped her to her feet. She shook her head at his confusion, amused to see it. "Oh, Theo. You have ever manipulated me terribly! I should feel badly, but it is past time you had some of your own sauce served in return."

The captain stood as well, one shoulder forward as though he was prepared to throw himself into whatever fray might erupt.

"I have never pretended it is not my nature to be manipulative," Theo said, his chin rising slowly, as though he readied himself to accept a blow.

"No," she said. "No, you never have. Now, I would have you tell me that you will love me forever."

He became very still, and his voice dropped very low. "Oh, sweet Pamela, how you torture a man. I have but to speak a lie, and you are mine. But I cannot say it. Do you know that it is the very difference between the captain and myself: he would make you such a promise, and you would trust him, when it is possible that he may not love you forever. I can only promise that I shall love you today and tomorrow, and that it is my greatest desire and intention to love you for all time, but to swear it shall ever be: that I cannot say.''

Pamela looked up at him, her face serene. She even smiled slightly. She cocked her head to one side, asking, ''What think you, Grandmama? Is it possible that the great rake has fallen? Is it possible to bind such a man to one's heart?''

''Oh, my dear, I have to think. . . .'' Grandmama hesitated, biting her lip, remembered pain warring with hope on her face.

''Think, Grandmama?'' Pamela asked. ''But perhaps you may be more sure of his character when I tell you that he detests lemon tea, even as you do.''

Grandmama gave a bark of laughter quite in contrast to the anxiety in her eyes. ''Oh, well then,'' she said, her voice unsteady, ''to be sure, I must believe it is possible he loves you, Pamela, for why else would he consider marrying a woman whose mama will constantly attempt to serve him the vile brew?''

Pamela tilted her head the other way, absorbing this logic.

Theo remained still, returning her gaze as he had the day she had so openly examined him at the fair, waiting for the evaluation she would offer this day.

She knew she would be a fool to ever quite trust him, for he would ever play his games. It was his way to exploit every opportunity, to twist every event the way he wished it to go. If she were willing to risk being a fool by marrying him, her life would be one long, topsy-turvy tumble. They would make, no doubt, a thoroughly disreputable couple. They would romp and play with their children in the most ill-bred fashion. She would probably be known as a far less respectable person than she had aspired to become.

"Captain," she said, her fingers leaving Theo's as she moved to the captain's side. He caught up her hands, his blue eyes taking on a triumphant sheen that she had come to him. "I thank you for your offer, and I regret the scene yesterday," she said softly. "It was very poor of me. I hope you will accept my apology—"

"Of course, my dear, we shall put such moments behind us—"

She went on, disregarding his interruption, "And I hope you will be able to understand when I say I cannot accept your offer. I have discovered I do not love you."

"Oh," he said, the light in his eyes fading.

"I am a ridiculous creature, I know, but I find I cannot marry without love."

He sputtered, "It happens all the time. We shall learn—"

"No, dear Captain. You deserve someone far less unpredictable than myself. I hope one day you shall forgive me for ever letting you believe otherwise."

She withdrew her hands, stepping away from him to turn to Theo.

He regarded her through slitted eyes, the hope in their green depths guarded by lowered lids. "You do not love the one, but will you have the other?" he asked bluntly.

"But, dear Theo," she said, smiling up at him through misty eyes. "I find I have the same problem with you that I had with Captain Penford. You have asked me to go to the church with you, but you have not asked me if I wish to marry you.''

For an instant a wave of relief was visible across his face, and perhaps his knees threatened, for a moment, not to support his weight; but then his mouth twitched, and his usual teasing expression was back as a spark lit deep in his eyes. ''Must I ask every time we meet? Recall I have done so any number of times, including during our first waltz together.''

''So you did. You claimed even then that you loved me.''

''I have known since we met that we were common souls. If only you had known it, too.'' He took both her hands, pulling her toward him.

She went to him, into the circle of his arms. ''I know it now,'' she said as she laid her head against his chest, her arms wrapping around his torso.

''Marry me, Pamela?'' his voice was a whisper.

''Yes,'' she answered simply. Then she raised her face, that he might kiss her and thereby seal their bargain. She did not care that she was in her peignoir, or that the captain and Grandmama looked on. She knew little but the welcome joy of Theo's mouth on her own—just as she wanted it to be, dared to hope it could be, for all her life.

Grandmother gave a funny, happy sound that was almost a hiccup, and it caused a bubble of gladness inside Pamela to swell and burst forth in a laugh against Theo's mouth. A moment later he was laughing with her, hugging her close, and then Grandmama joined them, hiccuping even more as she sobbed happily.

The captain did not join their merriment. He pulled his shoulders back and gave them a clipped bow, and then he strode from the room without another word.

Theo watched the man leave, and said with feeling, "I am, at this moment, feeling quite sorry for that incredibly stuffy gentleman."

"I meant to marry him."

"It would have been a disaster."

"I know. But you would have remained my friend through it all," she stated.

"That horrid word again: 'friend.' But yes, after a spell of drunken revelry somewhere in, oh, the Americas, I could not have helped but return to you." He smiled down at her, then hugged her to him. "Ah, Pamela, now that you have said you will have me, should I tell you there will be a price for agreeing to marry me, love?"

"Tell me." She doubted there was much of anything that could be too much to ask, not if it meant she could go on loving him as much as she did today.

"I meant it when I said I needed a wife to help me with my estate. Your first duty will be to assist me in finding exactly the right woman for Robbie, for now that my every wish is coming true, I can see how sadly he is in need of something like the happiness you and I shall share. No, come to think on it—" he smiled, his eyes flashing with deviltry—"that shall have to come second, for I have another duty in mind that must come first."

She laughed, blushing. "I think I should meet

Robbie before I begin to plan his life. And your mother, for that matter.'' She smiled up at him.

He made a face. ''I suppose you shall have to meet them before we ever get around to that first duty, eh?''

''I am afraid so, unless we go to Gretna Green.''

He laughed and shook his head, then put a finger on her chin, pulling her face back up to his for another kiss.

''That is quite enough of that!'' Grandmama pretended to scold, happy tears marking her face as she put her hands on Pamela's arm and pulled her away. ''Get yourself above stairs, sweeting, and get dressed. You've a curate to see this day, and you cannot go as you are.''

''Yes, Grandmama,'' Pamela said, blushing again even as she smiled widely.

Theo reached out, pulling her back to his side long enough to whisper in her ear, ''Can I come up and watch?''

''No,'' she told him with a smile of reluctance, but even as she spoke she knew it would be the last time she would ever deny him anything.

Taylor—made Romance From Zebra Books

WHISPERED KISSES (3830, $4.99/$5.99)
Beautiful Texas heiress Laura Leigh Webster never imagined that her biggest worry on her African safari would be the handsome Jace Elliot, her tour guide. Laura's guardian, Lord Chadwick Hamilton, warns her of Jace's dangerous past; she simply cannot resist the lure of his strong arms and the passion of his *Whispered Kisses*.

KISS OF THE NIGHT WIND (3831, $4.99/$5.99)
Carrie Sue Strover thought she was leaving trouble behind her when she deserted her brother's outlaw gang to live her life as schoolmarm Carolyn Starns. On her journey, her stagecoach was attacked and she was rescued by handsome T.J. Rogue. T.J. plots to have Carrie lead him to her brother's cohorts who murdered his family. T.J., however, soon succumbs to the beautiful runaway's charms and loving caresses.

FORTUNE'S FLAMES (3825, $4.99/$5.99)
Impatient to begin her journey back home to New Orleans, beautiful Maren James was furious when Captain Hawk delayed the voyage by searching for stowaways. Impatience gave way to uncontrollable desire once the handsome captain searched *her* cabin. He was looking for illegal passengers; what he found was wild passion with a woman he knew was unlike all those he had known before!

PASSIONS WILD AND FREE (3828, $4.99/$5.99)
After seeing her family and home destroyed by the cruel and hateful Epson gang, Randee Hollis swore revenge. She knew she found the perfect man to help her—gunslinger Marsh Logan. Not only strong and brave, Marsh had the ebony hair and light blue eyes to make Randee forget her hate and seek the love and passion that only he could give her.

Available wherever paperbacks are sold, or order direct from the Publisher. Send cover price plus 50¢ per copy for mailing and handling to Penguin USA, P.O. Box 999, c/o Dept. 17109, Bergenfield, NJ 07621. Residents of New York and Tennessee must include sales tax. DO NOT SEND CASH.

MAKE THE
ROMANCE CONNECTION

Come talk to your favorite authors and get the inside scoop on everything that's going on in the world of romance publishing, from the only online service that's designed exclusively for the publishing industry.

With Z-Talk Online Information Service, the most innovative and exciting computer bulletin board around, you can:

- ♥ CHAT "LIVE" WITH AUTHORS, FELLOW ROMANCE READERS, AND OTHER MEMBERS OF THE ROMANCE PUBLISHING COMMUNITY.

- ♥ FIND OUT ABOUT UPCOMING TITLES BEFORE THEY'RE RELEASED.

- ♥ DOWNLOAD THOUSANDS OF FILES AND GAMES.

- ♥ READ REVIEWS OF ROMANCE TITLES.

- ♥ HAVE UNLIMITED USE OF E-MAIL.

- ♥ POST MESSAGES ON OUR DOZENS OF TOPIC BOARDS.

All it takes is a computer and a modem to get online with Z-Talk. Set your modem to 8/N/1, and dial 212-545-1120. If you need help, call the System Operator, at 212-889-2299, ext. 260. There's a two week free trial period. After that, annual membership is only $ 60.00.

See you online!

KENSINGTON PUBLISHING CORP.